RUTHLESS RIVAL

CRYSTAL KASWELL

Copyright

This is a work of fiction. Similarities to real people, places, or events are entirely coincidental.

Also by Crystal Kaswell

Pierce Family

Broken Beast - Adam

Playboy Prince - Liam

Ruthless Rival - Simon

Tempting Teacher - Max

Dirty Rich

Dirty Deal - Blake

Dirty Boss - Nick

Dirty Husband - Shep

Dirty Desires - Ian

Dirty Wedding - Ty

Dirty Secret - Cam

Inked Hearts

Tempting - Brendon

Hooking Up - Walker

Pretend You're Mine - Ryan

Hating You, Loving You - Dean

Breaking the Rules - Hunter

Losing It - Wes

Accidental Husband - Griffin

The Baby Bargain - Chase

Inked Love

Sinful Serenade

Dangerous Noise

Standalones

Come Undone Trilogy

Sign up for the Crystal Kaswell mailing list

Chapter One

VANESSA

Most days, I'm good at resisting temptation.

But tonight?

Tonight, my gaze keeps flitting to the one man I shouldn't want: Simon Pierce.

The most powerful man in Manhattan.

The sexiest man in any room.

The man I've wanted and hated since the ninth grade.

Between handshakes and small talk, I watch his deep blue eyes scan the room. I study his soft lips. I imagine his strong hands on my skin.

For two hours, I mingle.

For two hours, I ignore the dirty thoughts circling my mind.

Finally, after my last *thanks for considering a donation* handshake, I slip out of the hotel ballroom, find the bar, order an Aviation.

One drink to celebrate the victories of the day.

Only I'm not drinking alone.

He's here.

"On me." Simon drops his credit card on the bar.

I swallow the *fuck off* that rises in my throat. The *fuck me* too. "Thanks." I'm well-mannered.

The same as him.

No, that's another way he bests me.

Since the first day of high school, Simon and I have competed.

Top grades?

Simon wins.

Better manners at a bar?

Simon wins.

Intense, panty-melting, desire-inspiring stare?

Simon definitely wins.

"My pleasure." He half-smiles. The Simon Pierce signature. Amused, above it all, hot as hell.

"For you?" the bartender asks.

"Whiskey, neat," he says.

"Coming right up," the bartender says.

"Whiskey, really? Are you going to smoke a cigar too?" I ask.

"If you have one."

"Smoked my last cigar on the balcony."

"Next time."

The bartender drops off our drinks.

Simon wraps his fingers around his short. Raises his glass. "Cheers."

I copy the gesture. "Cheers."

He watches as I bring the cocktail glass to my lips.

Mmm. Gin, lemon, floral liqueur. The perfect mix of sweet and tart.

"And you?" he says. "Ordering an Aviation?"

"I like purple."

His eyes flit to my wine lips. "I've never seen you in purple."

"You keep track?"

"A color-coded diary."

Is that a joke? I'm too surprised to laugh. "The color of my outfit?"

"What else?"

2

Another joke. What the fuck? I actually smile.

We've known each other for a long time. More than fifteen years now. We're not just old classmates.

Our families are friends.

Our companies—I run a nonprofit, he runs a cybersecurity corporation—attend the same events.

We see each other once or twice a month. We make polite conversation. We ignore our past rivalry and current sexual tension.

Occasionally, he teases me about trying to save the world.

And I tease him about having all the money in the world.

No jokes.

Never jokes.

Lingering stares, yes—I can't help it, he *wears* his designer suits—but never jokes.

"Do you really drink it because it's purple?" he asks.

"I drink it because I like it."

"You drank gin in high school," he says.

"You brought five-hundred-dollar bottles of whiskey to parties in high school."

"You noticed."

His eyes fix on me.

They're dark and intense, like the deepest parts of the ocean.

He watches as I take a sip. Watches my lipstick mark the glass. "What was it you called me then? The Prince of Darkness."

I did.

"Do you still see me that way?"

"By now, you're the king."

He smiles. "Is that a compliment or an insult?"

"An observation."

"You don't like me?"

"Do you care?"

"Yes."

It hangs in the air. He cares what I think of him. He's sitting here, intense and unreadable, and interested in my opinion of him.

"But you're right. I'm not here for polite conversation."

Right about what?

Wait.

He's not here to talk.

Then—

Fuck.

"I want to fuck you." His voice is matter-of-fact and sure, like he's complimenting my dress, not professing his desire to see me out of it.

"You want to fuck me?"

"Yes. I have a room upstairs. A suite. We can stay here, talk about the gala, or your sister's wedding, or my resemblance to Beelzebub. Or we can go upstairs." Intent drops into his voice.

He turns to me. Brings every bit of his attention to me.

My stomach flutters. My thighs shake.

My brain tries to cut in. To remind me, Simon Pierce is a spoiled rich boy turned stuck-up suit.

But I'm too lost in his blue eyes.

He's too handsome.

He's way too handsome.

"It's up to you, Vanessa," he says. "Do you want to stay? Or do you want to go?"

Chapter Two

VANESSA

"*I*t's up to you, Vanessa. Do you want to stay? Or do you want to go?"

My fingers curl into the cool glass.

My thighs shake.

My legs struggle to stay upright.

Simon Pierce is inviting me upstairs.

A million high school fantasies delivered.

And adult ones too.

How many winter breaks did I spend wondering if we'd sneak upstairs at Mom's New Year's party?

How many galas have I spent watching him from across the room, wanting to slap him and kiss him in equal measure?

He's my rival.

And he's besting me again.

Better at broaching the subject of our immense sexual tension.

Better at solving the problem.

Better at fucking probably too.

But then I can't exactly complain about that possibility.

"You can say no." He finishes his whiskey. "I won't be offended."

"You won't?"

"No. I know you want me." His eyes stay fixed on me. "You might hate me, but you want me. You've wanted me since ninth grade."

"I—"

"I want you too."

"You've never said anything."

"You either."

That's true. But I'm not the one making the offer. "Why now?"

He hails the bartender. "You want the truth?"

"As opposed to what?"

"A lie."

"Has anyone ever said, yes, I want a lie?"

"No. But they did."

"And you're kind enough to give it to them?"

"Yes." He holds strong and sure.

I don't agree with him, but I can't argue with his conviction. "What's the lie?"

"You don't get both."

"Why not?"

He chuckles. "You're a demanding woman."

"Thank you."

He nods to the bartender, orders another round, closes his tab.

He's leaving after this. With or without me, I guess.

My heart thuds against my chest. I'm a thirty-one-year-old woman—almost thirty-two.

How am I this nervous around a boy? A man, a man with all the power in the world, yes.

But it's not about that. It's not about Simon's money or status or company.

It's about how much I want his hands on my skin.

How terrified I am to feel his hands on my skin.

How terrified I am I'll miss the feel.

Or miss out on the feel.

I finish my drink. The bartender takes my glass. Drops off another round.

Simon motions to the balcony. "It's more private outside."

The view is better outside. All steel and glass. The blue of the Manhattan sky against the pockets of yellow light.

With the breeze, the August heat feels temperate.

Warm enough to undress.

Cool enough to soak up the heat of his skin.

We find a couch around the corner. A leather loveseat far from prying eyes.

He sits across from me.

I focus on my drink.

"I made someone a promise," he says.

"You promised them you'd fuck me?"

"Ask you."

"For sex?" I ask.

"Yes."

"Really?"

"Really." He looks to his drink. "My brother saw us together. Saw the way I looked at you." He takes a long sip. "He made me promise I'd seize the day."

"Those were his exact words?"

"In Latin." His smile is sad. "Carpe diem."

Simon Pierce saying carpe diem. It's absurd. Beyond absurd.

He's calculating, patient, still.

He seizes opportunities, yes.

But he's not living in the moment. He's not living life to its fullest.

Not that I can talk.

I love my job. I don't mind the way it consumes me, but it does.

That's why it's been a year.

That and my complete inability to let go of control.

But I won't let him best me there.

"When did you promise?" I ask.

"A while ago."

"Then why now?"

"I had a deadline. Midnight."

"It's ten thirty."

He nods.

"Cutting it close."

"I know."

"Will you tell him?"

"No." Something slips into his voice. Something I can't place. Then he shakes it off. "But I'm a man of my word."

He's hurt. It's there for a second; then it's gone.

It's strange on him.

I know he's human. I know he's subject to normal human frailties. I even know he's suffered horrible loss.

But he just—

He never shows it.

Even when we were kids, even when his father died—

He's always that same aloof, above it all guy.

"Is that all it is? A promise," I say.

"No. That's why I asked today." He turns toward me. "I asked because I want to fuck you. I've wanted to fuck you for a long, long time."

"I hate you."

"I know."

"You don't mind?"

"I do." He brings his hand to my cheek. "But I still want to fuck you."

"Oh."

"We don't have to go upstairs." He runs his thumb over my temple. "We can stay here."

"Fuck, here, on the balcony?"

"Talk."

No. I don't want to talk. I want to mount him.

"Or fuck, here, on the balcony." He brings his lips to my ear. "Is that what you want?"

Yes. Here. Now. Everywhere. Why are you still wearing pants?

"Upstairs."

"Now?"

"Not yet." I reach for my drink. Bring it to my lips. Try to find some sort of conscious thought.

The gin isn't helpful.

It's a sledgehammer to my inhibitions. That voice, the one whispering *how will you feel in the morning*, is long gone. Replaced with a neon light flashing *Fuck. Simon. Now.*

He's sure and steady as he sips his bourbon. Settles into his seat. Watches me down half my drink. "You're nervous."

"You're unnerving."

"Why?"

"You're always in control."

"I like it that way."

"I do too."

He raises a brow.

"I do. Like staying in control. But I didn't mean—" With sex, too, but not in the issuing orders way. "I don't mean sex. I mean everything. It's your demeanor. Nothing affects you."

"It does. I just don't show it." He peels my fingers from my glass. Sets my drink on the table.

He brings his hand to my cheek. Runs his thumb over my temple.

His other hand curls around my neck.

He pulls me into a soft, slow kiss.

A light brush of his lips. The taste of whiskey. And, under that, something all him. Something equally masculine.

He pulls back with a sigh.

"You taste good." He runs his thumb over my temple again. "I've wondered for a long time."

He pulls me into another kiss.

His lips close around my bottom lip. He sucks softly. Then harder.

The light scrape of his teeth.

My fingers curl into my thighs. The smooth silk of my dress.

It's too much fabric.

I need it gone.

I need his hands on my skin.

I don't care what happens tomorrow as long as I fuck him tonight.

He releases me. Brings his eyes to mine. "Better than I imagined."

He pulls me into another slow, deep kiss. He keeps one hand curled around my neck. Brings the other to my skirt. The slit of my dress.

He slips his hand under the silk fabric.

His fingers brush my skin.

The top of my thigh.

The inside.

Higher and higher.

"Spread your legs." His voice is heavy. Breathy.

In any other circumstance, I'd curse his bossiness, but the way he purrs is intoxicating.

I part my knees.

He slips his hand higher, higher, higher.

Until his fingers brush the silk fabric of my panties.

A groan falls from my lips.

He runs his first two fingers over the fabric, pressing the silk against my clit.

The friction is intense. So much I have to close my eyes.

Too much.

And not enough.

Not his hands.

He runs his fingers over me again and again.

Winding me tighter and tighter.

Giving me so much, but not enough.

Again and again, tighter and tighter, until I'm sure I'm going to break.

"Simon." It falls off my lips. "Touch me."

He pulls me into another slow deep kiss, then he brings his lips to my ear. "Come on my hand."

He pushes my panties aside. Runs his thumb over my clit as he brings his lips to my neck.

Soft kisses.

Soft brushes of his thumb.

Then harder.

The scrape of his teeth.

The perfect amount of pressure.

Again and again.

My hand finds his skin. The back of his neck. Soft, exposed, vulnerable.

Mine.

Only for tonight.

But mine.

I dig my nails into his skin.

With the next brush of his thumb, I come. The tension in my sex winds so tight I can't take it.

Then it unravels.

My sex pulses.

Pleasure spills through my pelvis.

Every part of me feels awake and alive and perfectly in bliss.

And every part wants the same thing.

More of him.

He rubs me through my orgasm, then he pulls his hand from my thighs, rights my dress, returns to the version of Simon Pierce I know well.

In control, intense, impossible to ruffle.

Only there's something in his eyes, something I recognize —desire.

He finishes his drink. Stands. Offers his hand.

I take it. Ignore the rest of my drink. Follow him through the bar, the lobby, up the elevator.

All the way to the presidential suite.

This is it.

One night with Simon Picrce.

I'm going to use it wisely.

Chapter Three

SIMON

I'm out of my fucking mind.

Honoring a promise to my dead brother.

He was a hopeless romantic. Big-hearted, open, in love with the concept of love.

This isn't the promise he meant—he had no concept of no strings attached sex—but the promise I made.

He saw the way I looked at Vanessa. The way she stared back, with desire and frustration in her dark eyes.

He knew I wanted her. Wanted more with her.

So I promised I'd try.

If he were here, he'd call bullshit. Tell me I need to do more, try harder, open myself to the beauty and majesty of love.

You fuck, Simon. You have time. You like women. You need more. Everyone needs more. Not that soulless, joyless, mechanical bullshit you do.

You need to make love.

Yeah, it's cheesy. I don't fucking care.

You need sex, at the very least.

An actual connection between you and someone else.

You're capable.

You want her.

You like her.

She hates you. Which makes you like her more.

I see the way you look at her. It's not just fucking. It's more. So go, ask for more. Get more. You owe me.

I do.

This is how'd he want me to repay him. Not the twisted path I'm walking. Something beautiful, happy, joyful.

But I'm not Bash.

I'm not a beautiful soul. I'm not jubilant or romantic or capable of loving with every ounce of my heart.

And I'm not nervous around women.

Not even Vanessa Moyer, the one woman I've wanted since the ninth fucking grade.

Fuck. He's in my head.

It's 'cause you actually like her, Simon. Because it's more than f-u-c-k-i-n-g and that terrifies you.

I roll my shoulders. Fix my tie. Smooth my jacket.

She's in the main room, making herself comfortable, like a scene in an old movie.

And I'm here, impossibly uncomfortable, completely out of my depth.

It's sex.

It's not my final promise to my late brother.

It's sex.

That's all.

I step out of the bathroom.

Vanessa is sitting on a leather armchair, poised, confident, commanding the entire room.

A queen, ready to control her kingdom.

She demands respect. She has to work twice as hard as I do to claim it and it shows in her posture.

She doesn't see it.

She doesn't see how much I admire her.

But I do. I always have.

"This room is ridiculous." She runs her fingers over the supple leather, equal parts amused, appalled, astounded. "How much does it run, a night?"

"It's a company room."

"Of course."

"Of course?" I motion to the minibar.

She points to the glass next to the sink. "It suits you. Suits Pierce Industries."

I fill two glasses. Bring one to her. "You don't romance clients?"

Her fingers brush mine as she takes it. "I don't use that word."

"Clients?"

"Romance." She brings her lips to the glass. Takes a long sip. "I don't mind asking for money. It's part of the job. But I don't appreciate the expectations." She motions to the high slit of her wine-red dress.

My eyes flit to her dark skin. She looks gorgeous in the moonlight. Luminous.

"Men want to fuck me."

"As a quid pro quo?"

"Sometimes."

My veins surge with protective energy. It's a familiar sensation, but not in this context. Not with her. "They ask?"

"Imply."

"I'm not."

"I know." She finishes her glass. Sets it on the table. "You wouldn't pay for sex."

"I wouldn't?"

"It's not a compliment." This time, she offers her hand.

I take it. Pull her to her feet. "What is it?"

"An observation."

I raise a brow.

"You want to prove something with the notches on your bedpost," she says.

"And that is?"

"That women don't want you because of money, or status, or looks even."

"They don't?"

"But because you have a big dick."

Fuck. A laugh spills from my lips.

"Am I wrong?"

I set my glass on the counter. Pull her closer. "Yes."

"It's small?"

"No."

Her hand goes to my chest. Her dark eyes fix on me. "No?"

"Are you that impatient to find out?"

Her lips press together. She is.

I don't call her on it. "I don't have anything to prove."

Not the way she means.

I'm not trying to prove skill. Or desirability.

It's something else.

Something deeper.

Some ability Bash challenged. Some emptiness he claimed I was capable of filling.

No, it was worse. He called me a coward. Said I was afraid to try.

"I want something real." I wrap my arm around her waist. Try to ignore the memories of my brother's voice. *Deep down, you're desperate, Simon. Desperate to love someone. When you admit that to yourself, you'll be a lot less miserable.*

She undoes the button of my suit jacket. The other. "Is that what this is?"

"Yes." It's terrifying. But I keep my promises. And I—

I'm going to unravel if I keep thinking about my late brother.

I don't fuck for connection or love or physical release.

I fuck because it makes sense.

Making Vanessa come, watching pleasure fill her expression, feeling her nails on my back—

That makes all the sense in the fucking world.

I need to step into my role. To take control of something. "Turn around."

"You didn't say please."

"I don't say please."

She freezes. "I don't like rough."

I'm not usually rough, but I am who I am here too: demanding and determined. Determined to hear my name on her lips. "What do you like?"

She sucks in a sharp breath. "Teasing."

"And?"

"Mirrors."

Fuck. Teasing Vanessa until she watches herself come.

How the hell did I get so lucky?

"Firm requests?" I ask.

She nods.

"Turn around." My voice drops to something deeper. Not the tone I use at work. Not even the one I use with other women.

Some tone I've never heard before.

Some tone that exists exclusively for her.

I'm out of my fucking mind. I am.

But I'm done thinking.

Tonight has gone too long. There's been too much in my head. I need the world to make sense.

I need this to make sense.

Vanessa turns. Her eyes flit to the mirror in front of us. She watches as I bring my lips to the soft skin of her neck.

I find the zipper of her dress. Pull it down slowly, an inch at a time.

I trace the line of her spine with my index finger.

Up.

Down.

Up.

Down.

Her breath hitches in her throat. She waits patiently, trying to outlast me.

A battle of will.

Of course.

People are who they are. They do what they do.

Even when she's standing here, watching me undress her, Vanessa is a queen commanding her kingdom.

Steady.

Sure she'll win.

And she will. But not the way she thinks.

I peel her dress down her torso. Over her chest, waist, hips.

All the way to her toes.

She stands there, in only her thong and heels, poised and patient.

I hook my thumbs on the straps. Pull the slick fabric over her ass, down her legs, all the way to her ankles.

She steps out of the underwear. Stands tall and proud and gorgeous.

I study every inch of her. Tight curls, pulled back in a loose knot. Dark eyes, staring back at me through the mirror.

Round hips. Thick thighs. Lush tits.

The pert brown nipples that beg for my lips.

"Beautiful." I press my lips to the small of her back. Stand.

She gasps as I pull her body against mine. "Simon."

"Yes."

"Fuck me."

I bring my hands to her hips. Pull her closer, so her ass is against my hard-on.

A groan falls from her lips.

I rock my hips against her.

"Now."

"Now?"

"Yes, now." She breaks my touch. Turns to face me. "Do you have a condom?"

"In the dresser."

She leans in to press her lips to mine.

It's a hard, deep kiss. Patient and unyielding. Claiming me. Claiming some part of me I'm incapable of reaching.

Does she want more?

Or am I the egomaniac everyone assumes I am?

Vanessa is a smart, capable woman. If she wants a relationship, she'll find one. If she wants sex—

She's gorgeous.

Maybe too successful or strong or powerful for men who are easily intimidated. But there's no shortage of shallow members of my gender.

What sane man would turn her down?

Vanessa pulls back with a sigh. She stares into my eyes, asking for something. No, demanding it.

But what?

I don't have a fucking clue.

She runs her thumb and forefinger over my tie, tugs gently, moves into the bedroom.

Straight to the dresser. She finds the box of condoms. Tosses one on the bed.

No fuss, no muss, no romantic interludes.

She crosses the space to me. Hooks her arm around my neck. Brings her lips to my lips.

She kisses me hard.

With intention.

I wrap my hand around her wrist. Bring her hand to my cock.

She cups me over my slacks. Groans against my mouth as she rubs me with her palm.

Again and again.

Then she brings her hand to my belt. Undoes the buckle. The button of my slacks. The zipper.

She pulls me back toward the bed.

The backs of her thighs hit the comforter.

I bring my hands to her hips. Lift her into my arms. Onto the bed.

She groans as I push her up the comforter and climb on top of her. "Fuck."

I slip my hand between her legs.

She's still wet, but I warm her up anyway. Run my thumb over her clit until her eyes flutter closed.

Again and again, until she's groaning my name like a curse.

I should make her come here again, I know, but I'm a greedy motherfucker. I need to feel her pulsing around me.

I need to feel her.

I find the condom on the mattress, tear the package, slide the rubber over my cock. "Spread your legs."

She looks up at me as she pushes her thighs apart.

I bring our bodies closer.

Closer.

There.

My tip strains against her.

Then it's one sweet inch at a time.

She feels so fucking good. Warm and soft and safe.

She curls her hand around the back of my neck and pulls me into a slow, deep kiss.

Asking for something I can't explain.

Finding it.

Vanessa wraps her legs around my hips.

I drive into her again.

Again.

Slow to start.

Then faster.

Harder.

Deeper.

She groans against my lips, rising to meet me, pulling me deeper.

Again and again.

Until she's there, pulsing around me, digging her nails into my skin.

She pulls back with a sigh.

Her eyes fall closed. Her lips press together. Her entire body tenses and relaxes.

Her bliss is the most beautiful thing I've ever seen.

It pulls me over the edge.

My thoughts dissolve.

The rest of the world disappears.

It's only Vanessa.

Her low groan. Her soft lips. Her sharp nails.

Her pulsing, pulling me closer, deeper.

With my next thrust, I come.

Pleasure fills my senses.

All ecstasy and Vanessa Moyer.

She rocks through my orgasm. Pulls back. Looks up at me with hazy eyes.

All softness.

No guard.

One more moment without defenses.

Then she blinks, and the softness is gone.

I'm not hers.

She's not mine.

Neither of us expects anything from the other.

I untangle our bodies. Take care of the condom. Clean up in the bathroom.

She waits her turn. Runs the shower. Emerges from the bathroom in a terry cloth robe. "It's your room." She watches me fix my tie and jacket. "You don't have to leave."

"I know."

"You can ask me to go."

"No. Stay." Usually, I stay. Usually, I'm a gentleman. But not tonight. Not with her. I don't trust myself. "I have to check on Opal."

She nods, accepting my answer. "Good night, Simon."

"Good night."

"Take care."

"Take care," I repeat her words. As if they're some kind of conclusion. The fulfillment of my promise. The end of the chapter. The resolution of the magnetic attraction between us.

But they aren't.

She occupies my mind every fucking second of the drive home. As I take the elevator to my apartment, check on my kid sister, shower, slip into my pajamas, fail to find sleep.

I'm not satisfied.

I only want her more.

Chapter Four

VANESSA

I 'll say this for Simon Pierce; the man knows how to handle the morning after.

He's waking up at home, in his bed, feet from his clothes and his coffee maker.

Whereas I'm here, in the too soft hotel bed, with only last night's dress and a machine incapable of making a decent cup of tea.

Not the ideal Sunday morning.

But the best possible end to our night together.

The smell of his soap—sandalwood and lemon—is sending my thoughts to dangerous places.

If he was actually here, tempting me with soft kisses and dirty demands?

That's not good for me.

This is just sex.

And this is it. Fourteen years of sexual tension resolved. No more imagining the taste of his lips or the feel of his skin or the sound of his groan in my ears.

Now I know.

Sure, I keep replaying the feel of his body against mine, but that's just an aftershock.

I repeat the mantra as I climb out of bed and shower, slip into last night's dress.

It's not the ideal outfit to wear home, but then I'm not worried about comments from the doorman.

I just—

I don't want to tell my sister.

She has questions. Especially since I left my fiancé.

No one understood it. He was a sweet guy. Loving, supportive, generous.

But every time I closed my eyes, I saw my mom hiding a bruise.

Huddled in the corner.

Begging my biological father to stop.

Not in front of Vanessa.

Not *don't hurt me.*

Not *pack your shit, we're leaving.*

Only *not in front of Vanessa.*

She knew he would hurt her. She accepted that.

She only wanted to protect me.

And she did.

Eventually.

Eventually, she left, met Daddy, married him, made us a real family.

But no matter how hard I try to see them—happy, smiling, madly in love—when I envision marriage, I don't.

I see the rage in my biological father's eyes.

The fear in my mother's.

The empty silence and dread that filled our apartment.

I ended things with my fiancé.

I didn't trust him. I don't trust love.

People who love you are the ones who hurt you. They take that love and wrap it around you like a leash.

Or a noose.

So, no, I'm not going to keep replaying last night. I'm not going to ask for seconds. I'm not going to fuck Simon again and again and put myself in a situation where I can't help but fall for him.

It's biology.

Oxytocin.

Released when you orgasm, when you cuddle, when you stare into your partner's eyes.

I don't care what Lee thinks. I don't care how much she wants to push me into Simon's arms.

She doesn't get it.

She's ruthless. It's one of my favorite things about her. I never worry someone is going to take advantage of her.

But she'll never understand how that feels.

The fear of harm coming to the person you love most.

The fear of harm coming from the person you love most.

I'm glad she's never been through that. I'm glad Daddy is a good man, a man she can trust, a man who taught her to trust.

It's just—

It means I can't explain this to her.

I slip into my gown, collect my things, double-check the room.

It's still beautiful, barely touched luxury.

It still screams of Simon Pierce.

Gold drapes. Cream walls. Wide windows.

Tall buildings stretching into the bright blue sky.

The perfect mix of old and new money.

And I'm late for brunch with Lee.

I text my sister an apology and call a rideshare, but, for some reason, it doesn't feel right leaving the room like this.

So I leave my thong and a note.

Thanks for the hospitality.

— *V*

It's not a lot, but it's something. My claim on the room, the night, the memory of Simon Pierce.

———

So much for discretion.

My kid sister (stepsister, technically) is in my living room, flush with a post-workout glow, sipping decaf in yoga pants and a crop top.

"Holy shit, Vanessa." She sets her glass on the coffee table. "This is why you're late."

I shrug like I have no idea what she's talking about.

"Sell that story to someone who buys it."

"I didn't say anything."

"You didn't have to say anything." She stands. Runs her fingers through her long, blond hair. Checks a French manicured nail. "You're wearing a gown at nine a.m."

"This is the new look."

"Please, I know the new looks. None are that."

"Hey."

"You look gorgeous, babe. It's not that."

I raise a brow.

"Don't even, Vanessa. I was here, last night, helping you into that dress, oohing and ahhing."

That is true.

"And I stand by it. You look like a Greek goddess. You're welcome, by the way."

"You have such a charitable mind."

"I know. We're in sync that way. Your charity work. My charity of—"

"Bossiness?"

"Support for my sister."

"Where's Harrison?"

"Nice try."

Damn. She's laser focused. If the subject of her husband—
and their enthusiastic attempts to make a baby—don't distract
her, nothing will.

"My husband is sleeping. I wore him out. Now, you ruined
my line," she says.

"What line?"

"I was going to say now, who helped you out of that dress."

"Not bad."

"I know. But since you fucked it up—"

"Gee, I'm awful."

She nods *I know*. "Who wore you out?"

"No one."

"Uh-huh."

"Aren't we going out?"

"No. Change. I'll make breakfast."

"You'll make breakfast?"

"I'm not bad," she says.

I raise a brow.

She laughs. "Okay. Maybe I'm not good, but I know how to
toast bread. Now, go. Change."

It is a reprieve from questions.

Even if she absolutely will burn that toast.

I move into my bedroom. Listen to Lee sing as she cracks
eggs and fixes tea. She really is the picture of newlywed bliss.
It's strange, especially on her. She's not usually the happy-go-
lucky type. More *I will destroy you if you stand in my way, hell yes, let
me savor my victory* type.

I'm happy for her. Really, Harrison is her perfect comple-
ment. Book smart, practical, kind.

A man who cherishes her.

A man who will never, ever hurt her.

But even though I know him, know her, know they're
okay—

I worry.

Sometimes, the monster is hiding in plain sight.

Sometimes, the man who looks like Prince Charming is actually the Big, Bad Wolf.

Maybe it's nothing serious. I'm her older sister, after all. It's my job to protect her. And that means worrying about her boyfriend. Even if he is her husband. Even if he's the sweetest guy I've ever met.

I want to trust it.

I just don't.

I ditch the gown. Slip it into a dry-cleaning bag, find a comfortable sundress.

A deep blue maxi that hugs my chest and flares over my hips. Easy enough for brunch with my sister. Cute enough, I don't mind if her husband has a friend in the den when she convinces me to walk her home.

Not that he usually has friends hanging around.

More that his oldest friend is Simon Pierce's kid brother.

I take a deep breath. Let out a steady exhale. Try to center myself.

This is my apartment. Maybe it's small. Maybe it's lacking luxury.

But it's mine.

My ecru walls, my abstract art, my bookshelf lined with non-fiction texts and under-appreciated classics.

"Vanessa." Lee's voice is singsong. "I may not know much about cooking, but I know you fucked someone last night."

"What does that have to do with breakfast?"

"Uh… something about eggs?"

"What about eggs?"

"Just get out here and tell me who you fucked." She knocks on my bedroom door. "Is it too hard getting out of your dress on your own?"

"Maybe I've been wearing it all night."

"And maybe I'm going to win Miss Congeniality."

"It's not that unlikely."

"Mm-hmm." Her footsteps move from the door. "Did you send me the guest list? Or do I need to ask your assistant?"

If she sees Simon's name on there—

She knows I had a crush on him in high school. She knows I cried when I caught him kissing another girl one Christmas—seriously, it's so annoying I'm family friends with my rival. And she knows I accidentally overheard him fucking himself one summer.

And, uh—

Well, I didn't mean to hear him, honestly. But once I realized what was happening, I didn't exactly make an effort to listen to something else.

I need to prepare a fake answer. An excuse. Any excuse, really.

Anyone is better than Simon.

I try to recall the guests in attendance. The man who introduced me to his wife. The professor who invited me to speak at his class. The young guy who asked if I had a boyfriend.

He was cute.

He was probably twenty-two, but he was cute. A charming smile and all that youthful energy. Like he knew his whole life was ahead of him.

But what the hell was his name?

"English breakfast?" Lee asks.

"With milk."

"Extra milk. You think I just met you?"

No. She knows me well. Too well. She knows my tells.

I practice my story in my head—the young guy with light hair, and it was great, energetic—and step into the main room.

She sees it the second she looks at me.

How the hell does she do that?

"No," she says.

"No what?"

"You did. Holy shit, Vanessa! You fucked Simon and you didn't tell me."

I say nothing.

"I just asked Harrison. And he said that Liam said that Opal said that Simon rolled home in the middle of the night with lipstick on his collar."

"Is she his sister or his wife?"

"A very dark shade of red. One much too light for most complexions."

"Doesn't Liam's girlfriend wear that shade?"

"Really? Liam's girlfriend was running her lips over Simon's neck?"

Ahem.

"You didn't even deny it." She jumps from her seat and claps her hands together. "You always deny it."

I do.

"Was it good?"

My cheeks flush.

"Oh my god. That good? Seriously, Vee! I'm a married lady now. I need to get my fix somewhere else."

"You've been married for two months."

"And we have sex every night. True."

This is why people don't like Lee. The way she shares her joy sounds like bragging. But it's not. It's just her way. "Maybe the sad single lady needs a fix."

"No. You had your fix last night. I demand details."

"What details?"

"You know what details, Vanessa Moyer."

"We had a few drinks in the bar. Whiskey for him. The brand he bought Harrison last Christmas. I had an Aviation—"

"You know those aren't the details—"

"Do you want the story or not?"

She pouts, falls into her chair, folds her arms. "Fine."

"He asked about his nickname, if I still called him the Prince of Darkness."

"And?"

"I said by now he's the king."

She nods *fair*.

"He asked if I wanted to sleep with him. I said yes. We went to his hotel room. The end."

"The. Beginning."

I shrug like it was no big deal.

She doesn't buy it. "And then, once you were in his hotel room…"

"We had sex."

She shoots me a death glare. "That's it? You had sex."

"We did."

"Did he make you come?"

"Yes."

"Did he have a big dick?"

"Lee."

"Oh my god, that's so annoying. He's such a smug prick, *and* he has a big dick to back it up. Tell me he was selfish or clumsy or something."

I wish I could. I wish I could say *it was nothing special really, I've already forgotten*, but it's not true.

It was better than I ever imagined.

I'm already picturing round two.

His long, hard body over mine, his hands on my hips, his cock driving into me again and again.

Ahem. "You won't say anything to Harrison?"

She shoots me a death glare. "Are you really asking that?"

"He's your husband now."

She swoons for a second. Then she course corrects. "Never,

Vee. Never. You're my sister. That comes before anything else. Always."

"You promise?"

"I promise." She offers her pinkie. The way we swore when we were kids.

I hook my finger around hers.

We pinkie swear.

And, all of a sudden, I'm a nervous teenager again.

Hungry for her approval.

Desperate to fit into my new family. The kingdom of the rich and powerful. The old money elite at our school.

But I didn't. I never did. I wasn't the only black girl, but I was the only one with an asterisk next to my name.

Not the daughter of New York's biggest defense attorney or the sister of the cute blonde ballerina.

The stepdaughter.

The stepsister.

The girl who didn't earn her spot.

Even now, people add *adopted* when they ask about my family.

Especially now, I stand out.

Lee never treats me less-than. She's seen me as a sister since the day we met.

But at school, parties, work—

It's my issue. Not hers.

And I want to tell her, I do.

But some part of me refuses. Some part of me wants to hold this close.

I tell her a few details. I sip milky English breakfast and eat overcooked eggs and ask about her and Harrison.

Eventually, she relents, starts talking about her husband, asks me to walk her to a family event.

Even though I stay busy—post gala calls and emails, a run

around the reservoir, a few episodes of *The Americans*—I keep thinking of Simon.

The sound of his groan in my ears.

The taste of his skin.

The feel of his cock driving into me again and again.

I need him again.

I don't want to need him again, but I do.

Chapter Five

SIMON

All night, my thoughts drift to Vanessa.

During every break in my day.

In the middle of meetings.

On the ride home.

When my kid sister, Opal, greets me with her usual fanfare. "Oh my god, Simon, finally! I'm starving."

"Then why did you wait?"

"Because I want to hear the beginning of your love story."

Opal is my half-sister, but she's a Pierce through and through—determined, focused, high-achieving.

She's also an eighteen-year-old girl.

Romantic, stylish, obsessed with the secrets of her inner circle.

There's only one way to deal with her interest—ignoring it.

I move into the kitchen. Pull our dinners from the fridge.

Before Opal lived here, I used a meal delivery service so bland it "made her tastebuds cry." I didn't mind the lack of flavor.

I treated food the way I treated sex: a need to be filled.

The meals nourished. What did it matter they were plain?

I don't have the time to prepare dinner. According to Opal, I don't have the skill either.

She's an excellent cook. Heavy on the cayenne. But I wasn't about to dump this responsibility on my teenage sister.

I'm her older brother, her surrogate father even. It's my job to take care of her. To make sure she's clothed, has a bed, is safe.

So I found a new service, one with more flavorful meals and dairy-free options—she's allergic. She hates how much I fuss, but I don't let that stop me.

Now that I sit down to dinner with her every night, I actually taste my food. I look forward to the ritual.

Family dinner.

It's everything.

"Simon." She tries to push past me. When that fails—I'm twice her size—she ducks, moves around me. "Why don't you admit to your love?"

"Cashew chicken or sesame?"

She makes a show of pouting.

"I can eat both."

"Cashew."

I heat the food on the stove.

She stands at the kitchen island, waiting extremely impatiently. "So…"

"Did you finish your homework?"

"It's summer." And she's taking an art class.

"Did you?"

"Simon."

"Yes or no?"

"Yes, Mr. Grumpy Pants." She taps the tile. "You were totally swooning when you came in."

I don't reply.

"Thinking of your new love?"

The stir-fry sizzles. Warm enough. I turn off the stove,

scoop our dinner onto ceramic plates, bring both to the island. "Chopsticks or fork?"

"Details."

I grab her a fork.

She pouts.

So I grab chopsticks too.

"Simon!"

"Opal."

"Do we really need to do the coy thing? It's so played."

"It's played?"

"Yes. How many times have I caught you staring at Vanessa? A hundred? A thousand?"

She hasn't seen Vanessa and me together a hundred times, much less a thousand. "She's a beautiful woman."

"Strange how you don't stare longingly at any other beautiful woman."

"I do. You don't notice."

"Really? Who?"

I hand her the hot sauce.

She covers her food in it. And I mean covers. Opal has an absurdly high spice tolerance.

We used to fight about it. I was worried she'd wear a hole in her stomach. She told me I was ridiculous but agreed to see a GI doctor if it would end my complaints.

She knows exactly what buttons to push.

With everyone else, I'm a brick wall.

With my kid sister, I'm a sucker.

I see the lost girl, crying over her mother's death, demanding a place in my life.

Opal was my father's dirty secret. An actual secret love child. Like something in a bad movie.

Opal never believed it. She thought her mom was telling her a fairy tale to make her feel better. That there was no way she really had a rich, powerful father who couldn't claim her.

Then her mom died, and she found out it was true. She discovered every secret. Ran into the light.

That's the only way she's not a Pierce. She embraces the truth.

Everything else—

The demanding demeanor, the charming smile, the intense blue eyes—

She looks so much like our father. It still surprises me.

She has my ability to ask for what I want and Liam's ability to make it sound like a favor.

She has Adam's eye for art and Bash's flair for the romantic.

She annoys me, sometimes, the way Liam does.

But, mostly, I adore her. I want to protect her. See her soar.

She's been here since she was fifteen. She's practically my adopted daughter.

I never thought about kids. Not the way people talk about it. I never asked myself if I wanted to be a father.

It was an inevitability. My duty, to carry on the family line.

After three years as Opal's guardian—

I want it so badly I can taste it.

I'm thirty-two. I'm supposed to be married, with a kid, by now. But then, Dad wasn't supposed to die when I was eighteen.

An accident wasn't supposed to kill Bash and leave Adam in critical condition.

I wasn't supposed to discover an ugly truth.

Shit happens.

I don't make excuses.

This is my choice; to put my siblings first, to put our business second, to put everything else far away.

I know Bash would want something else, want me to forget the strings I'm pulling, take a year off work, fall in love, name my kid after him.

But that was Bash.

I'm no good at love.

These thoughts of Vanessa—

They're ridiculous.

"Oh my god, Simon! Are you still trying to think of a single other woman you want?" Opal shakes her head. "You're usually a better liar."

"I don't lie to you."

"Uh-huh."

I try not to lie to her. Whenever possible.

"Why don't you admit it? You stared at Vanessa all night at the rehearsal dinner. Then at the wedding. At the reception after."

At the gala last night.

Every event between the two.

The lunch meetings, business dinners, corporate parties.

The wedding changed something.

Before that weekend, I thought of Vanessa on occasion. When I saw her at events or recalled our high school competitions (she took top spots in English and History and won every writing contest the school hosted, and she was fast, the best runner on the girl's cross country team).

Late nights, alone.

The memories of her plaid skirt hiked up her thighs.

Her low-cut homecoming dress.

The time I saw her skinny dipping on a shared family vacation.

I wanted her then. I wanted her every time I saw her.

But it was a passing thought, not something I considered.

After all, she saw me as a spoiled rich boy with the world at his fingertips. And I—

Yes, I thought she was stuck-up and self-righteous when we were kids. I hated that she bested me in half our classes.

But I loved that she challenged me, made me better.

I respected her. Admired her. Wanted her.

Knew I could never have her.

Then I made that promise to Bash, and he died and—

That's the last year. Investigating the mysterious circumstances of his death, finding ugly truths, trying to find a balance between revenge and letting go.

The wedding underlined everything.

Life is short.

I owe my brother this promise.

But I did it. I asked her; I kissed her; I fucked her.

That's supposed to be the end.

I'm not supposed to fall asleep imagining her body melting into mine.

"Already?" Opal laughs. "You're already thinking about her. Simon and Vanessa, sitting in a tree, k-i-s-s-i-n-g."

"I didn't say it was Vanessa."

"You didn't say it was someone else."

"It's none of your business."

"Maybe."

"Maybe it's your business?"

She tastes her food. Makes a *hmm* face. Pours even more hot sauce. "I'm a concerned sister."

"What's your concern?"

"Your denial. Of your deep and pure love."

"I have deep and pure love?"

"Don't you?"

I almost believe her. Even though I'm incapable of all matters love and affection. All matters beyond a physical arrangement.

Opal is that confident. And that sure of the power of love.

She sounds exactly like Bash.

"She was staring too," Opal says. "Of course, you are very conventionally attractive. It could be that. But I think it was more."

I don't answer. "What do you want to watch tonight?"

She looks at me carefully, deciding if she wants to take the bait. Then she smiles, sure, inspired.

Strange.

Concerning.

She's as stubborn as the rest of us.

She mentions her current teen soap. Swoons over the broken bad boy. Shoots me an *I know you're thinking about Vanessa, you're not fooling anyone look*.

We finish our stir-fry. I give her my dessert, the way I always do.

For three episodes, Opal watches teenagers scheme and sleep around.

For three episodes, I think of Vanessa's smile, laugh, groan.

When we're finished, Opal rises, shakes her head. "You didn't even stop to lecture me about the girl flirting with her friend's dad. That's prime lecture material."

It is. These shows are all horrifying. Students sleeping with teachers, keeping secrets from their guardians, scheming to destroy each other's lives.

Was TV this fucked up when I was younger?

Has the world always been this hostile to teenage girls?

Probably.

We didn't have a television when I was a kid. I grew up with three brothers. I had no reason to wonder what life was like for the fairer sex.

Now that I have a surrogate daughter?

I have no idea how to make the world into a place that's safe for her.

She's not considering it. She's still focused on her mission to get me to admit I want Vanessa. "How about I do the lecture this time?"

"You've earned it."

"It's classic Simon." She drops her voice an octave to imitate me. "Opal, you should be comfortable with your sexual partners. If you're embarrassed with someone, they aren't right for you." She returns to her normal voice. "I know, I know. None of my business. Whatever. We both know you're thinking about Vanessa." She hugs me good night. "Good night, Simon."

"Good night."

"Are you going to dream about her?"

"Good night."

"Okay, okay. But ask yourself, can you name one reason why you shouldn't give it a chance? Besides the usual 'I'm too busy' bullshit. Can you give me one single reason why you shouldn't see Vanessa again?"

Chapter Six

SIMON

T he next morning, it's the same. Thoughts of Vanessa creep into every nook and cranny of my day.

I replay her groan during the ride to a meeting.

I recall the taste of her lips in the elevator.

I imagine her naked, spread wide in the conference room.

All night.

All week.

All weekend.

I'm distracted, unfocused, completely consumed with thoughts of Vanessa.

Monday, I wake early, spend an extra hour at the gym, commit to my most intense work.

Finally, I fall into the zone. Spend the afternoon approving and rejecting pitches. Think only of bottom lines and potential businesses.

Until Opal knocks on my office door at six on the dot.

Immediately, my thoughts go to Vanessa.

Her French-manicured nails on the door, her pumps tapping the hardwood floor, her dark eyes fixed on me.

But she isn't here.

Opal is, and she's impatient.

She doesn't wait for a reply. She pulls the door open. Steps inside. Smooths her long, dark hair. "We're going to the park."

"We?"

"Me and Liam." She looks to the corner office on the other side of the room—Liam's office. He's standing in front of the door, in a grey suit and a bright blue tie, not bothering to hide his stare.

"You finished your homework?"

"It's August."

"Yes or no?"

"It's an art class. For fun."

I raise a brow.

She pouts *god, you're difficult.* "No. The homework is to draw my favorite brother."

"It is?"

"Yes. And I want to go to the park with my sketchpad while there's still light. Unless you want me to draw Liam. And turn in a lie." She presses her hands together and shoots me a *please* expression.

She plays me like a fucking fiddle. She always does.

"Simon?" Opal taps her sketchpad. "Really? If you want me to lie… or maybe, you want me to change my mind, decide Liam is my favorite brother."

"Do you think that's going to work?"

She smiles, equal parts *whatever do you mean* and, *of course, it is.*

It is. "Twenty minutes."

She pouts.

"Or you can wait until I'm home tonight." She lets out a schoolgirl giggle. "Can we order Thai?"

"Are you going to draw me eating take out?"

"Between bites."

"Opal."

"Aren't you hungry? I'm starving."

"We can order on our way out. Take it uptown."

"Fine." She makes a show of pouting, pulls the door closed, practically skips to Liam's office.

We've worked together since he graduated from school. We built Pierce Industries together. Adam did the technical work, Liam ran the numbers, I led the charge.

And Bash—

He was the glue that held us together. He charmed investors, encouraged colleagues, inspired everyone with his romantic visions.

It's not the same running Pierce without Bash. The sense of loss creeps up on me. Hits me when I least expect it.

Every time, I push it aside. I focus on concrete steps I need to take to conquer the challenges of the day.

Work is what makes sense to me. It fills me. Fuels me.

The more challenging, the better. I accomplish, I learn the rules, I play by them. Do better than everyone else.

I work.

I protect my family.

I fuck.

Those three things make sense.

They did.

Until I failed at one.

Now?

It's not the same. The sense of loss returns. The order in the world turns to chaos.

Watching Vanessa come?

That makes sense.

Everything around it is a complicated mess.

But my thoughts of her groan, her lips, her thighs?

I don't fall for women. I don't count the notches on my bedposts. I don't savor conquests.

I fuck, I fill my needs, I move on.

Why am I picturing Vanessa in my bed?

In one of those sexy sheath dresses, surveying the room with wide eyes and a *Simon Pierce, you truly live up to the image I have of you* smile.

Studying my book collection and telling me it's too full of dead white men.

Asking why I don't have any pictures.

Looking at me funny, like she can't believe I'm human, when I tell her I took them down after Bash died.

I close my eyes. Try to conjure something else.

Instead, I see her here, on my desk, picking up the paperweight my mentor gave me, asking how much it cost, if the guy could have spent his money elsewhere.

Pulling her dress up her thigh as she crosses her legs.

Whispering, *are you always goal-oriented?*

Dammit.

I need to get out of here. Go somewhere else, somewhere I won't think of her.

I power down my computer, put my work away, meet Opal at Liam's office.

She looks at me funny. "Are you wearing that? To the park?"

"What else would I wear?" I ask.

"You basically live in your office. Don't tell me you don't keep a change of clothes here." She eyes my suit jacket. "It's eight-five and humid. I know, summer wool, but still…"

Liam practically jumps out of his office. "That's his skin suit. He has to wear it or we'll see his true form."

"Yes, yes, we've heard that one." She rolls her eyes. "Simon is an alien. Blah blah."

"Brutal," he says.

"Get new material if you want new feedback." She turns to him, suddenly disinterested in my wardrobe. "Can Briar come?"

Briar is Liam's assistant turned fiancé. She's perfect for him. Smart, creative, tough. They banter like characters in a screwball comedy (our father only approved of black-and-white movies and theater). The spoiled playboy and the smart-mouthed artist.

Opal adores her.

She's a good influence, ambitious and honest, so I like her too.

"Did you ask her?" he asks.

"Can't you?" she asks.

"If I ask her to come, it's going to sound different."

"Oh my god, Liam! Gross." She holds her hands over her ears. "Not listening. Come on. Let's go."

He mouths *what did you say?*

She rolls her eyes and turns to me. "Okay. I'm walking to the park with my favorite brother. You can come too, Liam."

"You do realize—"

"Of course I realize." She shoots him the same death glare she shot me. "And I also realize we're running late. So come on." She motions *let's go.*

They banter all the way to the elevator.

She and Liam have the same mix of charm and skill at pushing people's buttons. But he's ten years older. He's had ten years to practice.

Opal puts up a fight, but she always ends up on defense.

I tune out their teasing as we step onto the street, walk to Battery Park.

It's a hot night, and the Financial District is bustling. Business people heading to meetings. Vendors selling dinner. Tourists staring at skyscrapers.

Then we step onto the green, and I see her.

Vanessa, in black shorts and a loose tank top, stretching next to her sister.

Staring at me with equal parts desire and frustration.

It's not a coincidence.

It's the two of them meddling.

Vanessa is as surprised I am.

But she swallows, shoots me a *look at you, in a suit at the park* stare, shrugs like she doesn't care I exist.

I know it's bullshit.

But it still tugs at something deep inside me.

Chapter Seven

SIMON

"Do you want to sit on a bench?" Opal adjusts her sketchpad. "Or stand for this? Maybe in front of the water." She motions to the sidewalk, where Vanessa and her sister Lee are standing. The railing behind it. The deep blue of the Hudson.

I raise a brow.

She plays dumb. "The lighting is better on this side. You can hold still, right? It will only take twenty minutes."

I can play dumb too. I nod *sure* and follow my sister to the railing.

Vanessa ignores me. Bends to stretch her hamstrings. Shows off her lush ass.

Immediately, my thoughts go to the gutter.

Those shorts around her knees, her hands around her ankles, my name falling off her lips as she comes on my cock.

This is not the time.

Or the place.

Or the audience.

I can't react. That's what Liam and Opal want.

They want a reaction.

They want to whisper about my history with Vanessa—the time she backed out of a dare to kiss me, the way she stared when I brought a date to her mom's New Year's party, the look on my face when she announced her acceptance to the Sorbonne.

The time I saw her kissing the lead in the school play.

He was everything I wasn't.

Open, creative, kind.

It lasted a few weeks, like most high school relationships, but I was still jealous.

I wanted her.

I hated that someone else had her.

Opal watches as I take my place at the railing.

She sets her backpack by her feet. Pulls out her sketchpad, a collection of pencils, a rubber eraser.

She looks behind her, notes Vanessa and Lee, both pretending not to notice us, and turns to me. "You ready?"

I turn my gaze away from my sister and the women behind her. Look out at the river.

I don't linger in the beauty of the natural world. That was Bash's domain. He saw wonder in everything. The deep azure water, the warm the sun, the bright blue sky.

The tall buildings, steel and glass, pockets of light and life, thousands of people in one structure, with their unique goals and desires.

I can repeat him. When I remember his voice, his expression, the way he talked with his entire body—

I almost understand what he meant.

But I don't.

Fuck, how is a dead man influencing me?

I'm lost in thought when Opal tells me I can move.

She puts her sketchpad away and announces herself to Vanessa and Lee as if she can't believe they all happen to be here.

Lee is already chatting with Liam.

Strange. Liam hates her. She's always putting his girlfriend down in not all that subtle ways.

Liam is good at pretending, but he's not usually this good.

"Simon Pierce, in the flesh." Lee waves me over. "It's been a minute."

Since her wedding, but I'm not untangling that mess. "How's Harrison?"

"Good." She smiles and glances at her watch. "I have to head back soon."

"To ride him bareback," Liam says.

"Oh my god, Liam! Why are you such a frat boy? They're trying to have a baby," Opal says.

"Yes. I'm surprised I'm the first." She places her hand on her flat stomach. "I thought you'd be married with kids by now, Simon."

Vanessa shoots her a *what the fuck* look.

She shrugs *the truth hurts*. "I promised Vanessa I'd take her to dinner, but Harrison's work ran late."

"We're going to get Thai food," Opal says. "You should join us."

"It was supposed to be a quick dinner. I have an early meeting," Vanessa says.

"Simon lives around the corner," Lee says.

"Four blocks," Vanessa says. "And an avenue."

"But you are heading home, yeah? You can ride together," Lee says.

"You and Vanessa," Opal says. "I'll crash with Liam and Briar tonight."

They might as well sing *we want the two of you to fuck* in unison.

I almost admire the effort.

And the sheer transparency. They're not hiding their intentions. Or their meddling.

They push because they care, yes.

And I can't object when I do the same—

But it's none of their damn business.

Vanessa shoots me a *do you believe this* look.

Unfortunately, I do. "You want to stay at Liam's tonight?"

Opal nods enthusiastically. "Briar agreed to watch *Gossip Girl* with me."

"Is Liam watching too?" Lee laughs.

"Hell yeah," Liam says. "Have to figure out who the most annoying character is. Learn from their wisdom."

Lee whispers something in Vanessa's ear.

Vanessa shakes her head *fine* and turns to me. "Shall we?"

Reward them for their meddling? No.

She shoots her sister a *we'll talk about this later* look and turns to me. "It will go faster this way."

True. Pragmatic.

I don't want to give them what they want.

But I can't admit I'm letting pride trump practicality.

"Text me before you go to bed," I say to Opal. "No sneaking out. Briar will tell me."

Liam nods. "She's a terrible liar."

"Why would I sneak away from my favorite future sister-in-law?" She looks at Vanessa, considering her position on the list.

I almost see her checking boxes.

Gorgeous.

Successful.

Passionate.

Caring—Vanessa runs a charity for domestic violence survivors.

Well-dressed—most days, Vanessa wears a tailored sheath. Most nights, she wears a gown fit for a goddess. Even now, in her snug running shorts, she looks put together and sexy.

Opal cares about style. She admires stylish people, especially women who could serve as role models.

I wonder sometimes if she's going to keep pursuing art or learn business or run a charity.

She's young. Her entire life ahead of her. She can become anything she wants.

Even a fucking matchmaker.

Opal smiles with victory. And pure excitement. "Good night. Have fun!" She waves goodbye.

Vanessa takes my hand. "The subway is around the corner."

"I can call a car," I say.

"The train stops three blocks from your apartment." She leads me away from the park. Keeps her eyes in front of her. Not giving her sister, or my siblings, the satisfaction of attention.

"The train is crowded."

She shakes her head *of course*. "You have a driver?"

"I go to meetings all over the city."

"A personal driver?"

"The family does."

She chuckles *of course*.

"He stays with Adam now." My brother Adam, the second oldest after me, was in the car accident that killed Bash. He barely survived. After months in critical condition, he recovered, regained full use of his body. As good as new, except for the scars, both physical and emotional. He rarely leaves the house, though he tries more now that he's seeing someone.

But that's a long story.

A long, messy story.

Vanessa doesn't know the ugly details. Only the public ones. He was in an accident that killed Bash and nearly killed him.

And Adam was closer to Bash than anyone.

"Oh. Fuck." Her expression drops. "I didn't mean—"

"I know."

"Adam is a good guy. I'm sorry about the accident. Is he doing okay?"

"He is." Better, now that he's with someone. That's a fucked-up mess, but I'm happy he's happy.

I drop Vanessa's hand. Try to take the lead as we round the corner.

She keeps pace with me. Walks faster.

She's in athletic sneakers. I'm in dress shoes.

And she's a former track star. If we race, she's going to win.

I need to play to my strengths. "Pierce has a service on retainer. For employees who work late."

"Generous."

"What do you suggest?"

"Reasonable hours."

"How late do you work most nights?"

"It depends on the night." She looks to the subway stop. "But point taken."

"A car is more comfortable." And private. A place to touch her, tease her, kiss her.

A bad idea.

But a tempting one.

I pull out my cell.

She nods. "Go ahead."

Because she wants to get away from me as quickly as possible?

Or because she wants to get to her apartment, where we can fuck, as quickly as possible?

I push the thought aside. Call the service.

Five minutes.

I slip my cell into my pocket. Relay the information.

"You sound different on the phone," she says.

"How is that?"

"More demanding." Her eyes flit to my tie. My waist. My pockets. "Is that… most men, executives, they're tired of taking control all day. They want to release after work."

"Have you done a survey?"

"I hear things. From escorts," she says. "A friend runs a charity."

"Free escorts for CEOs?"

"Is that a joke?"

"I hope so."

She smiles, and her eyes light up.

My heart thuds against my chest.

"Yes, the poor CEOs can't afford rising escort prices."

"Tragic."

Her smile widens. "Thousands a night. It's too much."

"They'll have to pass the cost of living increase onto their customers."

She shakes her head *you're ridiculous, and I like it.* "No, she helps women get out of the industry. Teaches them new skills. Offers support. We use some of the same services."

Of course.

"You'd think it's easier for women who are charging five hundred dollars an hour to leave. They can save, they have nice things, they know people in power. But many are addicted to the money. Or the thrill. Or drugs. Even when they start having issues. Threats. Clients who are too interested. Clients who don't want people to know about their taste for bondage or humiliation."

"What do you do?"

"It's not my organization. But my friend… she moves them to a new city, changes their hair. Usually, that's enough. The men don't know their real names. They don't want to look into things enough to risk their wives discovering their infidelity." Her eyes meet mine. "I've heard a lot, through her. She's not supposed to gossip, but when she drinks…"

"Anyone I know?"

"Yes. But that's all I can say."

"Is this what you meant by teasing?"

Her chest heaves. "That seems fair."

"It does."

"You're good at it."

"Teasing?"

"Yes."

Let's do it again. Now. Tonight. What are you wearing under those shorts? How many times can you come in one night?

"But I shouldn't say anything. It will go to your head."

"It will."

"Inflate your already massive ego."

"I always take feedback."

"Bad feedback?"

"Do you have some?"

"No."

Tell me everything. What else do you like? What can I do, right now, to drive you out of your fucking mind?

"The stories about executives…" She takes a deep breath. "Do you think it's true?"

"It makes sense."

"For you?"

"Am I submissive?"

"Yes."

"No," I say.

"Have you ever tried?"

"No. It's never interested me."

"Would you?"

"Are you asking to tie me up?"

"Would you say yes? If I was?"

"Yes."

She bites her lip. "Really?"

Not for anyone else. But for Vanessa? I want to give her everything she craves. I want to conquer every challenge she issues. "Are you asking?"

She sucks in a shallow breath. "No. Well, maybe. If I can cover your mouth. Keep you from issuing orders."

"You're a CEO."

"I am."

"Is it true for female CEOs too?"

"Probably." Her eyes flit to her shoes. "But I'm not interested."

"You prefer to issue orders?"

"No. Well, probably. But I'd rather no one issue orders."

"Only firm requests?"

"Especially if they end with please." Her chest heaves. She's surprised by how dirty her words sound.

"When you make requests?"

"Why should I say please if you don't?"

"I don't need a please."

She swallows hard. "You can follow orders?"

"Depends on the orders." My voice drops. "Touch me. Kiss me. Fuck me."

"Oh. Right. You did. Last time."

Last time.

There might be a next time.

"I can follow closely," I say. "If you want."

"Have you done that?"

"No. But I'd try." For her.

"Would you really?"

With anyone else? No. With her? "Yes."

A sound interrupts me. The driver, calling for us.

I open the door for her.

She looks up at me, equal parts nervous and intrigued. "You're bluffing."

"Call me on it."

Chapter Eight

VANESSA

Simon Pierce is flirting with me.

Fourteen years of sexual tension underlined and bolded.

I know the taste of his lips.

The feel of his hands on my skin.

The sound he makes when he comes.

But my curiosity isn't sated. My desire isn't filled.

I want him more. Here. Now. Tonight. Tomorrow.

Again and again.

It's a bad idea. I want him too badly. I hate him too much.

No, it's not hate. It's something else. A frustration. With his above-it-all attitude. The silver spoon in his mouth. The way he runs his company, his life, his family.

The man pursues profits. I can't fault him for existing within the system of capitalism. I ask men like him for money every day.

But is he driven by anything other than cold, hard cash?

Does he want to make the world a better place?

Does he give a fuck about anything except his bottom line?

Two weeks ago, I was sure I had the answer. I was sure

Simon Pierce was a stuck-up suit. Successful, yes. Handsome, hell yes. Skilled, absolutely.

And heartless.

But he's not.

He's not cold.

Or arrogant.

He's loving. Sweet even.

I was right about one thing: Simon is a control freak. Maybe worse than I am.

I took off my dress.

I stayed.

He kept his suit on. He left the second he cleaned up. He kept his heart far, far away.

But it was there. The glimpses of the hurt boy under the steely exterior.

I want to see more. To peel back his defenses. Know where he hurts.

That's dangerous.

Way too dangerous.

Wanting him is one thing. Hating him is another.

This desire to know him?

That's the first step on the path to affection, love, heartbreak.

Or worse.

I suck a breath through my nose. Smooth my spandex shorts. Adjust my seat belt.

This is a normal town car. I'm on the passenger side. He's on the driver's side. There's a middle seat between us.

Two feet. Maybe three or four.

But it feels like two inches.

He's close. I can smell his soap. His shampoo.

I have to press my palms into my thighs, so I don't touch him.

I need to touch him.

I absolutely, positively can't touch him.

One night.

One time.

That's all.

My body whines in protest. *Why not him? Why not another time? Tonight.*

It's just sex.

I can handle just sex.

If he can handle just sex, I can handle just sex.

He's not besting me here too.

But that's my pride. It's not true.

Maybe Simon can handle just sex. Maybe he has arrangements with a dozen women across the city.

It doesn't matter.

We're different people.

He's a man.

A tall, muscular, powerful man.

Simon has no reason to fear his sexual partners. Or his lovers.

He didn't grow up watching his father beat his brother.

He might be afraid of love or intimacy or connection, but he's not afraid of falling in love with a monster.

Is he afraid of something else? An inability to trust or connect or let go?

He's a control freak too. As bad as I am.

But he was gentle with me.

He gave me what I wanted.

Maybe the stereotypes aren't true.

Maybe the rumors are wrong. Though there are enough, one must be true. I hear a lot of "Simon is as much of a control freak in the bedroom as he is in the boardroom."

And I hear tales of interns asking to tie him up. A secret taste for older women. A vow of celibacy.

Anything and everything.

The last I heard, he ended things with a fuck buddy who called him a heartless bastard but praised his massive, ahem, ego.

She also said—

Well, we're already talking about sex. What's another drop in the ocean?

"The car is fast." I smooth my seat belt again. "Private."

He looks to the driver, a professional in a suit and cap. A rarity in the world of Lyft and Uber.

"Compared to the subway."

"Is that an offer?"

"No. Still too public," I say.

"Is it?"

The driver's eyes flit to the mirror. He looks back to us, but he doesn't say anything.

So he is listening.

Watching.

What does he think is happening here?

What the hell is happening here?

"You like mirrors," he says.

I do.

"The balcony?"

"I did."

I smooth my shorts. Suck a breath through my nose. Try to ignore the smell of his soap. Lemon and sandalwood. Why does it smell so fucking good? "Did you?"

"Yes."

Yes, let's do it again. Go straight to the hotel bar. Fuck right on the balcony. Here, now. I'm already sweaty and spent. Why not? "Have you done that before?"

"No."

"That's not what I've heard."

"What have you heard?"

"About you, specifically?"

"Unless you have more stereotypes about executives."

"I guess I should know them," I say. "Since I am one."

"What would you guess?"

"We work too hard. Spend all day in control. Don't know how to relax or let go."

He nods. "Which means?"

"We're all freaks."

He laughs, actually laughs. "Probably."

"That's what I hear about you. The romance novel story."

"The romance novel story?"

"The stuck-up billionaire who likes to take off his tie and wrap it around an ingenue's wrist."

"An ingenue?"

"A sweet young woman."

"A virgin too?"

"And a mention of your girth."

He chuckles. "You're making this up."

"Exaggerating for effect."

"What's the truth?"

"You're rough. Bossy."

"When I fuck? Or normally?"

"Both."

"Sometimes," he says. "It depends who I'm fucking. What she likes."

"What's your preference?"

He turns to me. "You're right. I'm usually bossy. I'm usually with someone who expects me to step into that role."

"Wrap your tie around her wrists?"

"It's happened."

"Do you like it?"

"It fucks with the tie."

A laugh spills from my lips. "Really?"

"Creases in the wrong places. But I can't complain. I enjoy filling fantasies."

"Is that your fantasy?"

"No."

"Do you have one?"

"Only one?"

Fuck. What am I doing? I'm not trying to fuck him. Or go for round two. Or start some sort of enemies with benefits arrangement.

I'm surviving the drive.

And we're almost there.

I need to lower the temperature. Think of something incredibly unsexy. Like Lee's meddling. Or the accident that killed one brother and maimed the other?

Which brother did he promise?

The one who's gone?

That's sweet. Almost romantic. Completely unlike the Simon Pierce I know.

I unfold and refold my hands. Try to find some other topic. Something unappealing.

But my thoughts stay in the gutter.

The smell of his soap.

The taste of his lips.

The sound of his groan.

What if I unzipped him here, in the back seat of the car, with the driver watching?

I've never wanted that before.

Anything close to that.

But the image refuses to leave my mind. My clothes on the floor. His hands on my chest. My lips wrapped around his cock.

His eyes flit to my thighs, waist, chest, lips.

Meet mine.

It's like he knows exactly what I'm thinking.

Like he's thinking exactly the same thing.

I need to say something. Anything as long as it's not *take off your pants* or *do you want to come upstairs?* "I didn't tell Lee. But she guessed."

"Opal too."

"Are we obvious?"

"Apparently."

"I did show up in a gown at nine a.m.," I say. "Not discrete."

His eyes flit to my bare thighs.

"And Lee said you had lipstick on your collar."

"I did."

"I'm not going to apologize."

"I wasn't going to ask."

My chest flushes.

"How did she know?"

"I guess Opal told Liam and Liam told Harrison."

"Harrison is gossiping?" he asks.

"It's that or Lee and Opal are friends."

"Hell has frozen," he says.

"You would know."

He lets out a low, deep laugh. "It's been a few days since I've checked in, but it wouldn't be unusual."

"It wouldn't?"

"Eternal flames don't scare everyone. We need icy landscapes for that."

"Hell for people who hate winter."

He nods.

"Is that the part you oversee?"

"How'd you know?"

"It suits you. The cold demeanor. The clear blue eyes. Simon the Ice King."

"Not the King of Darkness?"

"Dark ice. The days are short in the winter."

He smiles. A full smile. A panty-melting smile.

Why am I still wearing panties?

Why am I wearing any clothes?

I could take off his pants and mount him.

And—

Fuck. "I tried to tell Lee it was none of her business, but she doesn't take no for an answer."

"You don't either."

Not usually. But—"She knows how to work me."

"A younger sibling gift."

"It must be." Did he tell someone?

Did he want to brag to friends? Or hold the memory close and replay it again and again?

The image fills my head. Simon, in some massive masculine bedroom, in a king bed, wrapped in silk sheets, his hand around his cock, his thoughts tuned to me.

The car stops.

Fuck.

We're already here.

I grab my bag, unhook my seat belt, reach for the car door.

But the driver is too fast. He opens for me.

Simon gets out, helps me onto the sidewalk. Stands tall and broad and proud.

I'm not used to seeing him in running shoes. I only have an inch of lift in these. Not the four inches of my heels. Or the two and a half of my sensible pumps.

I want to rise to my tiptoes and kiss him.

I want to demand he come upstairs. Then make me come upstairs.

"I'll walk you up," he says.

I expect a no to fall from my lips. Or some other sensible excuse. *I'm sorry. I can't trust myself alone with you for another second.* Instead, I say, "Thanks," and lead him into my building.

Past the doorman and the security guard at the desk—a little security is necessary in my line of work, but this is nothing compared to the office.

Into the tiny elevator.

He carries my bag. He punches my floor. I'm not sure how he knows it. A party or another night he walked me home.

Some gentleman power, maybe.

Chivalry is in his bones.

I focus on my inhale, my exhale, anything other than my desire to pin him to the wall.

Finally, the car arrives, the doors slide open.

He waits and follows me around the corner to the front door.

"I'll ask my siblings to drop it," he says. "But the more I say, the more they'll push."

"Better not to mention it."

He nods. "Let them think we talked about something boring."

"Taxes?"

"Zoning laws."

"Zoning laws," I say. "What's your stance?"

"I want to see you again."

Fuck.

He takes a half-step toward me. "I know, I only asked for one night, but I can't stop thinking about you. Replaying the sound of your groan. Imagining you, in my apartment, coming on my hand."

That's a brilliant idea.

"If you say you aren't interested, I'll accept it. I won't like it, but I'll accept it."

"See me…"

"I want to fuck you again."

I swallow hard. "Why?"

"Because you're gorgeous. And smart. And principled. Because you're trying to save the world."

"It's not a whim."

"I don't think that." His hand curls around my waist. "I'm sorry if it sounds that way."

My stomach flutters.

"I admire you."

"Since when?"

"As long as I've wanted you." He leans closer. "Always."

His lips brush mine.

Softly at first.

Then harder.

My lips part.

His tongue slips into my mouth.

His fingers dig into my skin.

My body responds to his. My hips buck, my knees knock, my chest melts.

I want him.

I want him so fucking badly.

"Take the night. Think it over. Remind yourself I'm the King of Darkness. Realize you want me anyway."

Chapter Nine

VANESSA

Most days, work occupies every inch of my mind.

Today, my thoughts wander.

The columns of my spreadsheets blur together. I barely catch a word at a donor lunch. And the afternoon meeting with a sister organization—

I agree to a joint effort. A gala.

But I don't remember when or where.

I need focus for my job. I need to make every decision, and every dollar, count.

Nonprofits are businesses like any other. Only, instead of selling a product or service, we ask for donations.

Every penny I spend is a penny I need to raise.

I try to get my head back in the game. I push thoughts of Simon aside. I fix another cup of tea. Then a second.

But the tea sends my temperature to triple digits.

Even when I call the day early, change into leggings and a sports bra, run five miles at the gym in the building—

Even when I shower in the too-cold water, smell the lavender body wash I use after every workout here—

I think of my night with Simon. The Aviation on my lips. The taste of whiskey on his.

The sound of his groan in my ear.

The offer echoing through my mind.

I want to see you again.

I want to fuck you.

I slip into a cocktail dress. Dinner with a donor. Though I can't remember who or where at the moment?

The wool sheath is the exact right mix of professional and sexy. So I don't look like a slut or a stuck-up bitch.

Not my words.

Words that have been used against me too many times to count.

It's impossible, sometimes, but I know how to maneuver this world now. Know the appropriate hem, necklines, fabrics.

Different in the summer and winter.

Different at lunch and dinner.

Different at cocktail parties, galas, business meals.

I slip into my work pumps, fix my makeup, let down my hair.

But my thoughts don't go to my dinner companion.

They go to Simon.

I've never seen you in purple.

I want to see you again.

I want to fuck you.

My cheeks flush. My chest too. I'm dark enough no one can tell, but I add an extra coat of blush anyway. For cover.

Then I grab my stuff from the office. Take the elevator to the lobby.

Besides the gym, the building is low-frill, but we have plenty of space and amazing security.

That's what I need.

Xavier, the guard who works the evening shift most weekdays, is an ace. He's gentle with survivors and rough with people who issue threats.

He nods from his spot behind the desk. "Hot date tonight?" Xavier is a quiet, no-nonsense guy. But I've known him long enough we chat.

"Dinner with a donor," I say.

"Somewhere nice." He gives me a quick once-over. Not the ogle of a man who expects something. The observant gaze of a man trained to keep an eye on everyone and everything. "New dress?"

No. But I haven't worn it in years. And now, after Simon mentions my lack of purple attire, I'm wearing the color. "A few years old."

"Looks great."

"Thanks. What are your plans tonight?"

"Here until two a.m."

"Then a rave in Brooklyn?"

"How'd you know?" His smile lights up his dark eyes. It's a rare sight. Only appears as a response to teasing. "How's Lee?"

"Still married."

"Not my type."

"You don't like gorgeous blondes?"

"Prefer brunettes."

Is he flirting? No. He's teasing. That's all. I've got sex on the brain. I'm seeing things that aren't there.

"I'm happy she's happy."

"She's very happy."

"Still trying?"

"How do you know that?"

"It's my job to know everything."

I nod. "She was here, talking about it?"

"Maybe. Maybe not."

"She can't stop talking about it."

"I'm sure her husband isn't complaining."

No. He's not.

"Most men wouldn't."

"You?"

"Maybe if I was married to a Moyer."

That's flirting. That's absolutely flirting.

Xavier is handsome. As handsome as Simon. They're both tall and broad with masculine features.

But Xavier has soulful brown eyes, short, dark hair, light brown skin.

He looks fantastic in a suit, but he doesn't look like a CEO. He looks like a detective or a bodyguard. Someone capable of neutralizing a threat.

He's not violent. At least, I've never seen him violent. But he's clearly capable.

Simon is good at everything. He might be capable too. I don't know.

But it's hard to imagine him settling his problems with his fists.

It really is.

And usually—

Usually, it's not hard for me to imagine that. Especially not with men. Especially not with men I've kissed.

There's always something. A love of boxing. An obsession with vigilante super-heroes. A desire for rough sex.

These men, with their perfectly normal, socially acceptable interests, scare me.

As soon as I feel that fear, I see signs everywhere. I can't unsee them. I can't trust someone enough to talk to them. I don't even talk to the people I do trust.

And since I can't admit to the fucked-up state of my brain—

Still not over my fucked-up childhood.

Still holding on to my teenage coping mechanisms.

I try to get over my fear. I try to unsee the signs.

When I can't, I end things.

"Ms. Moyer." Xavier slips into serious, security mode. "You all right?"

"Yeah. Sorry."

"Busy day?"

"Always."

He nods *of course.*

"Is everything okay here?"

"A woman came by. She looked like Lee, actually. Lee in fifteen years. She said she wanted to talk to you personally. I told her you were out, asked if she wanted to leave a message, but she said no. Said a friend referred her and she could only trust you."

"How did she seem?" I know a lot of people. A lot of people know me. It's not usual for someone to offer my name, especially if they suspect violence. Especially to women like Lee—

Upper West Side wives in designer sunglasses, who spend their free time on charity boards. After all, they can claim they're volunteering, not looking for help.

It saves face.

Sometimes, it even keeps them safe.

"Scared," he says. "But holding it together. I asked her to leave a note, but she declined."

That's a red flag, but there's nothing I can do. It's true in every field; people won't accept help until they're ready.

I can't force her to accept.

Hell, I'm the worst person to ask her to accept help. I'm not good with survivors. I see my mother in them. See the rage in my father's eyes. See all the fucked-up shit piling in my head.

Some survivors cope enough they're able to work victims, but it's rarer than TV and movies make it seem. For most people, it's too much to take, being surrounded by reminders of their trauma.

But now I'm late for dinner, with—

Fuck, I need to check my phone.

"There was something about her," he says. "I'm worried."

He has good instincts. "If she comes back, call me."

"Anytime?"

"Anytime."

"Might interrupt your date."

"It's not a date."

"You sure?"

"I'd be wearing something shorter on a date."

"Haven't seen you in anything shorter."

"And when was your last date?"

He nods *fair enough*. "Have a good night, Ms. Moyer."

"You too, Xavier." I hold my purse close and make a mental note to keep an eye out for his call.

My head stays in work mode as I step outside. August in New York. Hot and humid, but not unbearably so.

My dress is a summer wool. That's why I picked it.

Not because Simon teased me about wearing purple.

Not because I thought of him all weekend. Or all day.

I check my plans again—a lawyer who worked with my father, at a hotel restaurant a few blocks away—and try to push my thoughts to work.

It's a comfortable place for me. I'm in control.

I like control.

I don't like losing control.

It's been a problem before. A big one, when I was younger. Then recently.

It was easier then, even though it was worse. People expect teenage girls to try to control their bodies. They expect a "normal concern" to occasionally turn to obsession.

They watch for signs.

Teachers, counselors, parents, coaches.

Sure, I didn't fit the pale blond part of the stereotype, but I aced the other criteria.

Perfectionist, family trouble, high achieving sport.

I got help.

I was better.

It was miserable, but it was understandable.

A thirty-one-year-old woman restricting her food intake to cope with her mom's illness?

It's common. That's what statistics say. But no one looks out for it. No one understands it. No one sees it as a problem.

Maybe Mom would have if she was all there.

But she wasn't. And Daddy was focused on her. We were all focused on her.

I'm an adult now.

A grown-up.

I watch over myself.

I tend to myself.

I keep myself in check.

That's how it is.

And that's how I like it.

It's just sometimes…

Sometimes, it's too much. Sometimes, I'm tired of holding up the world, and I want to crumble into a million pieces and know someone else will pick them up.

I want to fall apart in someone's arms.

Feel safe.

Understood.

Loved.

But it's not in the cards. Not anytime soon. My ex-fiancé, Sol, loved me. He did. I saw it. I heard it. But I didn't feel it.

And I couldn't trust him.

And now he's married and happy, and I'm here, trying not to think about how much I want Simon.

Trying to imagine anything other than the taste of his lips.

I slip into the hotel, find the table in the pack, thank the donor for his generosity.

For thirty entire minutes, I stay focused. I order a sparkling water and a steamed fish entree. I gush about my father and my father's adoration for him.

He returns all my gushing times ten. Adds *adopted* to every mention of Father. Looks at me like he's in awe of how I ever managed to accomplish anything, what with being so *unusual* in this world.

Slowly, my thoughts return to Simon.

But I keep the dirty images at bay until I'm accepting a too-close good night hug, taking the subway home, changing into my pajamas.

Until I'm in bed, at home, alone.

Unable to think about anything except Simon.

I need the shiny distraction.

The healthy coping mechanism.

Exercise. Only with orgasms.

No emptiness or self-loathing or obsession.

I can do that.

Can't I?

I close my eyes. Let my thoughts drift to him. Come so hard I see stars.

For the first time in forever, I sleep easy.

But I wake flushed.

Think of him all morning.

For another day.

Another night.

It's no good. I can't deal with this level of distraction.

This is the sensible decision.

Fuck him until I've had my fill.

I can handle that.

I can absolutely handle that.

After my next meeting, I find my cell, and I text him.

Vanessa: How does this go?

Chapter Ten

SIMON

Before Opal showed up at my door, I lived and died by routine.

Six a.m. alarm. An hour at the gym. Coffee at the office. Work until the morning meeting.

A simple lunch.

Coffee with afternoon meetings.

Then work.

I run a tight ship, but I can't escape the laws of time and space. Meetings are inefficient.

I minimize them as much as possible. But that isn't much. Not with my job.

I don't mind the burden, the extra hours.

Or I didn't. Until Opal arrived.

I no longer work until eight.

Or spend free nights with fuck-buddies.

Or even with friends.

Now, I live with a teenage girl. She's not particularly difficult, but she's still a whirlwind of chaos.

I can't control it or organize it or turn it into something that makes sense.

I have to live with it.

I'm not good at it.

But I'm better than I used to be.

So when my phone buzzes in the middle of a meeting, I don't do what I would have done three years ago and wait until I'm finished to take it.

I excuse myself. Find privacy in my office.

I'm not a worrier. It's not in my blood.

I focus on the things within my control. Or I find a way to control them.

But after Bash—

My heartbeat picks up.

For a split second, I think the worst.

Another accident.

An attack.

A sudden illness.

I sit. Pull my cell from my pocket.

Vanessa.

I expect my heart to slow. I expect my breath to steady.

Instead, I'm in knots.

I need to see her.

Touch her, taste her, fuck her.

I need it more than I've ever needed anything.

Vanessa: How does this go?

Simon: What do you want?

Vanessa: I love my job, but it wears on me sometimes. I need a break. Something fun and easy.

Simon: Stress relief?

Vanessa: Exercise with orgasms.

My laugh breaks the tension in my shoulders.

Simon: I'll suggest athletic positions.

Vanessa: You have one in mind?

Simon: A few.

Vanessa: And after we've… exercised, we say good work, kiss goodbye, go back to our lives?

Simon: We could.

Vanessa: One more time?

Simon: As often as we like.

Vanessa: A regular thing?

Simon: Friends with benefits.

Vanessa: Rivals with benefits.

Rivals. It suits us.

Vanessa: Is that how you usually do things?

Simon: I don't usually fuck people who call me the King of Darkness.

Vanessa: You have arrangements?

Simon: Yes.

I do this all the time. My heart never races.

My skin never flushes.

My thoughts never refuse to focus.

I'm not cool or collected.

I'm desperate to have her here. Touch her, kiss her, fuck her, hold her.

Vanessa: When was the last?

Simon: A few months ago.

Vanessa: What ended things?

Simon: She met someone.

Vanessa: She left you?

Simon: We weren't committed to each other.

Vanessa: You weren't monogamous?

Simon: Monogamous, yes, but not committed. An easy out. No questions asked.

Vanessa: Did that bother you?

Simon: No.

She's quiet for a moment.

Is she cursing me for not caring?

Or calling me pragmatic?

I don't know. Maybe I'm a monster. Maybe there's something broken about me.

I don't care.

I want her.

I protect my family.

What else matters?

Vanessa: Are you safe?

Simon: I have a recent test. I'll send it when I get home.

Vanessa: I have one from my last yearly. It was a few months ago, but I haven't been with anyone else since.

Simon: No arrangements?

Vanessa: I've had them before.

My stomach churns. An unfamiliar sensation. Jealousy.

Vanessa: One when my mom was sick. I needed an outlet for a while.

Simon: Then?

Vanessa: I found a different outlet. We said goodbye. No hard feelings.

Simon: Do you think about him?

Vanessa: Only when I see him on social media. He's married now. A kid on the way. Your ex-fuck buddies?

Simon: They invite me to their weddings.

Vanessa: Really?

Simon: They want to thank me.

Vanessa: For the orgasms?

Simon: For showing them they didn't want someone like me.

Vanessa: What do they say?

Simon: I work too hard. I'm not emotionally available. I remind them of their fathers.

Vanessa: Really? They admit that?

Simon: Usually.

Vanessa: What do you say?

Simon: What's there to say? I don't know their fathers. I do work hard. I'm not looking to fall in love. They're right. I'm happy they found what they wanted.

Vanessa: Really? You never feel a pang of regret? You sit there, watch them say I do, and you don't think once, that could have been us?

Simon: Us? Never.

Vanessa: You and someone else?

Simon: That was the life I imagined. When I was younger.

Vanessa: Marriage to a Park Avenue Princess? Cute blond kids?

Simon: Blonds again?

Vanessa: What can I say? I see you with a blond.

Simon: I don't.

Vanessa: You imagine your wife?

Simon: I used to?

Vanessa: And?

I'm not answering that. It's not a good idea.

For either of us.

Simon: I don't have a type.

Vanessa: As long as she's hot?

Simon: My exact words, yes.

Vanessa: I got it from Liam.

Simon: You talk to Liam?

Vanessa: No. But it's not for lack of trying on his part.

Simon: He likes to fuck with me.

Vanessa: Younger siblings.

Simon: Try having four.

Shit.

Vanessa: I'm sorry about Bash.

Simon: Don't.

Vanessa: Okay. I won't. I just wanted you to know. Even though you're my ruthless rival, I want your family to be okay.

Simon: My family? Not me.

Vanessa: They're great. You're an asshole.

Simon: I'm not going to argue.

Vanessa: I didn't know him well, but he went out of his way to make me feel comfortable.

Simon: He liked you.

Vanessa: Really?

Simon: He loved beautiful women.

Vanessa: Was that all it was?

No. But it was part of it.

Simon: He was a romantic.

Vanessa: And we're two overly pragmatic realists?

Simon: That's how I saw it.

Vanessa: He saw otherwise?

Simon: He thought I was a cynic. Lying to myself about my true desire for love and connection.

Vanessa: He's the one you promised?

Simon: Yes.

Vanessa: Is that what this is? More of that promise?

Maybe. But not the way she means.

I'm not doing this out of blind obligation.

Simon: No. This is because I want you to come on my face.

Vanessa: Fuck. You unnerve me.

Simon: I know.

Vanessa: You do it on purpose.

Simon: I do.

Vanessa: Why?

Simon: You're a queen. Strong. Regal. Poised. I want to affect you. To see your composure fall.

Vanessa. You can't tell you do?

Simon: Only at certain times.

Vanessa: The times we're discussing.

Simon: Yes.

She's quiet for a minute.

Vanessa: Is it like your other arrangements?

Simon: I don't have a rulebook.

Vanessa: I don't believe that.

Simon: Nothing in writing.

Vanessa: I barely believe that.

Simon: Do you want something in writing?

Vanessa: Maybe. I, Simon Pierce, promise not to lie to or manipulate one, Vanessa Moyer.

Simon: I promise.

Vanessa: The rest?

Simon: Tell me what you want. I'll make it happen.

Vanessa: I want to be monogamous.

Simon: Done.

Vanessa: I want to be honest. No excuses, no lies, no bullshit. I spend all day listening to bullshit.

Simon: The truth is ugly sometimes.

Vanessa: Even so.

Simon: If it's too ugly?

Vanessa: Say that. Say, 'I can't talk about this.' The way you did just now. About your brother. You're Simon Pierce. You know how to say no.

Simon: My favorite word.

Vanessa: Is it really?

Simon: It's up there.

Vanessa: With?

Simon: Fuck.

Vanessa: Fuck. Really?

Simon: Of course. It's efficient, adaptable, powerful.

Vanessa: It reminds you of you.

Simon: It reminds me of you.

Vanessa: Really?

Simon: Yes. Elegant. Dirty. Strong. All at once.

Vanessa: That sounds like a compliment.

Simon: It is.

Vanessa: You're unnerving me again.

Simon: Because I admire you?

Vanessa: Because you say it.

Simon: I do admire you. But that's not why I want to fuck you.

Vanessa: This is not how I thought this conversation would go.

Simon: Me either.

Vanessa: I like no too. It's authoritative.

Simon: Like you.

Vanessa: Compared to anyone else.

Simon: Even compared to me.

Vanessa: We're both in the 99th percentile.

A laugh spills from my lips. She's calling me a bossy bastard. With statistics.

Simon: Is that it? No one else and no bullshit?

Vanessa: No feelings. We can be friends. We can talk. We can eat dinner first. Or eat breakfast in the morning. But it doesn't mean anything.

Simon: You want me to spend the night?

Vanessa: Not necessarily. But I don't want you to leave the moment you're done. There's no shame in paying for it, or taking payment for it, but I'm not a whore, and I don't want to feel like one.

Simon: Did you?

Vanessa: Not exactly.

Simon: That wasn't my intention.

Vanessa: I know.

Simon: I can't stay often. I have to keep an eye on Opal.

Vanessa: She's an adult.

Simon: Even so.

Vanessa: Will you tell her?

Simon: No. She already assumes. And Lee?

Vanessa: She knows.

Simon: Then she knows.

Vanessa: You don't mind?

Simon: It depends what you're saying about me.

Vanessa: It's dick size again.

Simon: It is?

Vanessa: That girl in high school, the one who said you two hooked up, but it didn't fit. You paid her to say that, didn't you?

Simon: How did you know?

Vanessa: Ruthless. Efficient. Exactly like you.

A laugh spills from my lips.

She's teasing me because she's nervous.

But I'm nervous too.

I can't remember the last time I was this nervous.

Simon: You liked the balcony.

Vanessa: I did.

She's an exhibitionist.

Simon: Let's meet there. Tomorrow.

Vanessa: Tomorrow?

Simon: On the balcony. We can stay there. Take things to the hotel room. Go back to your place.

Vanessa: Yours?

Simon: Opal has a friend staying over. She asked me to clear the apartment.

Vanessa: And you said yes?

Simon: No. But I can.

Vanessa: You'll leave her home alone, really?

Simon: Of course not.

Vanessa: She is an adult.

Simon: Do you want to fuck me after breakfast, or do you want to argue about my sister?

Vanessa: Both.

Fuck, I like her.

I like her too much.

Vanessa: But I have to get back to work. Tomorrow.

Simon: Eight. On the balcony. Wear a dress. Nothing under it.

Chapter Eleven

VANESSA

For a few hours, my thoughts quiet. I run, I work, I lead meetings.

The second I finish, say good night to my assistant, find myself in my office, alone?

I think of him.

After an hour, I give up on work. I change in my office, fix my hair, apply an extra coat of lipstick.

I look good.

No, I look sexy.

This dress is all play, no work. Black silk, low neckline, high hem.

Revealing.

Sensual.

Perfect for this.

I grab my purse, walk the five blocks to the hotel, lose my panties in the bathroom.

Then I check my makeup one more time.

One more coat of lipstick.

There.

I'm ready.

And I can handle it.

I step into the lobby. Walk past the bar.

To Simon, sitting on the balcony in his suit, prepared with a glass of bourbon and an Aviation.

His eyes light up when he spots me.

He stands. Pulls me into a tight embrace. Wraps his strong arms around me.

This time, my thoughts really do disappear.

No work.

No issues.

No family troubles.

Only the hard, safe feeling of his body against mine.

What the fuck have I gotten myself into?

Chapter Twelve

VANESSA

"**I** appreciated the favor." Simon brings his lips to my ear. "Even if it was sarcastic."

The favor.

My thong on the table.

The thank you note with it.

I teased him.

He's teasing back.

And tonight—

He's really teasing back.

"Was it?" I'm not ready for the other tease. I need to banter. To stay in control.

For a little longer.

I know I need to release my vice-grip on control. At least a little.

But I did take off my underwear. As he asked.

That's something. A lot.

"You appreciate the hospitality?" His fingers curl into my skin. "Really?"

It's strange being here. Déjà vu.

Because we were here before.

Because I've been here before, with other people, when I was another person.

No one since my relapse.

Only him.

"When did you find it?" I ask.

"I didn't."

"Oh?"

"My assistant."

A laugh spills from my lips. "Really?"

He nods. "I sent him to check the room before a client meeting."

"Housekeeping didn't move it?"

"No."

"Nice hotel. I should refer donors."

"I have a discount." He pulls back with a smile. "If you need it."

"Generous."

"It's not lingerie." His fingers brush the thick straps of my dress. Intent drops into his voice. "Do you always wear silk?"

"For formal events."

"It suits you." He traces the strap over my shoulder. Down my back.

"I'm expensive?"

He doesn't come back with his own banter. He traces the line up my back, over my shoulder, down my chest. "You're nervous."

I swallow hard.

"It barely shows." He presses his other hand into the small of my back.

I am nervous. But I hate admitting it to him. He's always the picture of cool. "You're never nervous."

"I am."

"Now?"

"Yes."

"Because of your brother?"

He brings his hand to my cheek. Runs his thumb over my temple. "Because I like you."

My heart thuds. It should set me at ease, this proclamation. Simon Pierce likes me. He *likes me* likes me.

But it only makes my stomach flutter.

He's still calm and in control, even when he admits affection.

"Did I offend you?" he asks. "Leaving quickly?"

"Yes."

"I'm sorry."

The words feel strange in my ears. Simon Pierce apologizing.

But he seems sincere.

"I'll stay tonight," he says. "But I'll have to leave early in the morning. Early enough to check on Opal before work."

"I get up at seven most days."

"To run?"

My stomach flutters. He remembers. "Yes."

He steps back enough to take my hand. Helps me to the couch.

I sit. Fold one leg over another. Smooth my skirt.

His eyes go to my exposed thighs. The hem of my black dress.

The short skirt demands every ounce of his attention.

It's intoxicating, affecting this calm, in control man. Having his deep blue eyes on me. Controlling my ruthless rival.

No, not control.

Something else.

Something symbiotic.

Leading him.

This is a dance. Only there isn't one lead and one follow.

We're both vying for position.

"What did he say?" My hands go to the edge of my dress reflexively. "Your assistant?"

"He played dumb."

"He didn't call you a stud? Ask who you'd fucked?"

He looks at me funny. "A stud?"

"People say that."

"Older people."

"We're older."

"You're thirty-one."

"You're thirty-two."

"Our parents' generation." His eyes lock with mine. "Or Liam."

"What would Liam say if he saw it?"

Simon chuckles. "I never know what's going to come out of his mouth."

"But…"

"He's like you. He thinks I'm an asshole."

"You object?"

"No." That same cool confidence. Only it's tinged with something. A disappointment. "Liam was a teenager when our father died. He didn't want to take orders from me. But he didn't have a choice. Neither of us did."

"I'm sorry."

"Don't—"

"That's the second time you've refused sympathy."

"Only the second?"

"In twenty-four hours." I reach for my drink. The glass is cool, but it doesn't steady me. It only knocks me more off-kilter. "Is it that uncomfortable?"

"Yes."

"Why?"

His blue eyes fill with surprise. Not the question he expected, I guess. "It feels like weakness."

"Grief?"

"Any sign of emotion." He wraps his hand around his glass. Brings it to his lips. "That was my father's way. He held his cards close. He loved us. And he showed us, in his way, but only in his way."

"What was that?"

"He pushed us to be better. To thrive in a cold, hard world."

Is that really how Mr. Pierce felt? He was rich and powerful, controlling an empire from a mansion worth millions.

They had everything. The world on a silver platter.

And their father believed they needed a stiff upper lip to survive in the cold, hard world.

It's strange, but I understand it.

There's a power to stillness. To silence.

I know that power.

I revel in it too often.

Simon takes a long sip. Lets out a soft sigh. "I know. We had everything. He grew up with everything too. His father was the same. Always firm. Unyielding."

"Your mom?" She died when he was a kid. I remember that from school. "Do you remember her?"

"Bits and pieces."

"Was she cold?"

"No. She was luminous. Like Bash." His eyes go to the amber liquid. "I take after my father."

"All orders. No smiles."

He half-smiles.

"You're soft, with your sister."

"I love her."

"You don't love Liam?"

He chuckles. "He'd kill to have this on tape. Proof I'm an asshole."

Does Liam really think of Simon that way? I don't know the trouble-making younger brother well. There's hostility there, yes, but there's a begrudging admiration too.

Or maybe that's my older sibling bias talking.

Of course, Simon has to be harsh sometimes.

Of course, he makes sacrifices for his family.

But he doesn't have to be tough all the time.

"I did my best," he says. "To keep everything in order. But I was young. I wasn't ready. I didn't get through to Liam."

"He's functional."

"He's happy." He finishes his drink. "But he still resents my attempts to protect him."

"There's something in your voice."

He looks at me funny.

"You agree with him?"

"Not usually."

"But sometimes?"

"I haven't decided."

"That sounds like a story."

"A few months ago, he found out I knew something, but not what it was." He sets his glass on the table. "It was ugly. I tried to shield him."

"He didn't appreciate it?"

He nods. "No. He called me an asshole for trying to protect him."

"That's how you see it?"

"I don't want to burden him."

"What if he wants that? To support you, as your brother?"

Again, he looks at me funny. "If it was you and Lee? If you knew something awful, something that would hurt her."

"It depends."

"Something in the past. Something she couldn't change?"

Like my biological father hurting my mother. "It might help her. To understand."

"Understand what?"

"You." Does she know? Did Mom tell her? Did Daddy? I

was young when they met. When they married. With the work I do now—

It's hard to believe it escaped her.

We never talk about it.

And my relapse—

Fuck. I'm a hypocrite. "You're right. I do the same thing with Lee. Keep things from her to protect her."

His eyes flit to my glass. "Do you want something else?"

"No. I'm just…" Nervous. Even more, now that we're talking. It's easier touching him. I understand the appeal of his body. I accept the appeal of his body.

His mind? His heart?

Not as much.

"You talk to your sister about sex," I say.

"Yes."

"Is it awkward for you?"

He nods.

"But you do it anyway. You push past the discomfort. I do that too, sometimes. But, sometimes… sometimes I keep something from Lee to protect her. And because it's easier for me. More comfortable."

"More comfortable carrying it on your own?"

"Isn't it?"

"Yes," he admits.

"People say it's easier, in the long run, to share."

"You don't believe it?"

"Do you?" I ask.

His eyes flit to my glass. "You're not drinking."

Right. I'm not. But I want to finish this first. "We do it for ourselves too. Because we don't want the discomfort of the truth."

"You must keep secrets. With your job."

"It *is* your job to keep secrets." I take a long sip. Let the delicate mix of gin, liqueur, and lemon dissolve on my tongue. "That should be a red flag."

"No bullshit. We agreed."

"You meant it?"

"I only say things I mean." He watches me bring the glass to my lips. Watches me taste the purple cocktail.

"Do you want to try this?" I offer him the drink.

His fingers brush mine as he takes it. He moves the way he does everything, with power and finesse.

He sips. Swallows. Returns the glass to me.

Fuck, he's unnerving.

So much for it being easier to touch him. I take the last sip. Let the drink warm my tongue and dissolve my inhibitions.

It's slow. A hint.

Then Simon's hand is on my cheek. And his lips are on my lips. And the glass is on the ground.

Not broken, somehow.

Not a concern.

He pulls back with a sigh. "It tastes better on your lips."

"The mix of bourbon."

"No. You." He bends. Picks the glass from the ground and places on the table. "Do you want another?"

"Only one."

"Give me a minute." He stands. Moves around the corner. Inside, to the bar.

I take a deep breath. Let out a steady exhale. Try to find the thread of my thoughts.

Some semblance of calm.

I'm out here, on the balcony, without a single scrap under my dress, waiting for Simon Pierce to bring out our next round.

The air is warm. Almost sticky. But I still crave the heat of his body. The pressure of his touch. That hint of bourbon on his lips.

Simon returns quickly. With that same firm, in control posture.

Again, his fingers brush mine.

Again, he watches me bring the glass to my lips.

"I looked it up," he says. "The Aviation. It was forgotten for ages, because it was impossible to find Creme de Violette or maraschino liqueur. It built a reputation. A mystique. When the liqueurs finally became available in the US, everyone wanted it. For a few years, it was all the rage."

"Then?"

"It fell out of favor. There was no more mystery. People didn't care."

And I'm drinking it, because I tried it at one of my mom's parties and loved it. Because I don't need the mystery. I appreciate the truth.

Or because I like the mix of tart and herbaceous.

It's not too sweet, but it's not as biting as straight gin either.

But that isn't what Simon means.

What the fuck does he mean?

"What does that make me?" I ask.

"Loyal."

"To a cocktail?"

"People are who they are," he says. "When they run, when they eat, when they fuck."

"I'm loyal. And you're… old-fashioned?"

"I've heard worse."

"It could be worse. You could drink old-fashioneds."

"Do you like them?"

"I don't like whiskey. Any kind of whiskey."

He pulls me into a quick kiss.

"But it's not terrible. In this context."

"High marks."

"I try."

He smiles, actually smiles, then he peels my fingers from the drink, sets the glass on the table, pulls my body into his.

This time, his kiss is slow.

My lips part.

His tongue slips into my mouth.

He explores my mouth with steady swirls of his tongue. It's not rushed. It's not slow.

It's Simon Pierce.

Steady and sure.

I'm not sure if people are who they are all the time.

But he is who he is.

A man who knows what's expected of him.

Who follows duty. Honors tradition. Favors simplicity.

Straight whiskey. Silk lingerie. Soft kisses.

His hand goes to the strap of my dress. He traces the neckline, from the tip of my shoulder, over my chest, to the v between my breasts.

Then back up.

Down.

Up.

His thumb against the edge.

His fingers on the silk, brushing the fabric over my nipple, the perfect hint of pressure.

Soft strokes.

Teasing. Again and again.

And again.

Until I pull back with a sigh.

He brings his lips to my ear as he slips his hand between my thighs. "Are you wearing anything under this?"

"If I am?"

He nips at my ear as drags his hand higher, higher, higher.

There.

His fingers brush my sex.

"It will be harder to make you come." He rubs my clit with his first two fingers. "But not impossible."

Fuck. That feels good. My eyes flutter closed.

He pushes my dress aside, exposing my breast. The right side. Then the left. "You're fucking gorgeous."

My eyes flutter open. Find his. "Thank you."

His eyes rake over me slowly.

My wine lips.

My exposed chest.

The silk fabric clinging to my stomach and hips.

My thighs just barely parted for him.

I'm on display.

On the balcony, where anyone could see me.

There's a window behind us. We're barely covered by the couch.

This is dangerous.

Illicit.

Potentially disastrous to our reputations.

Mine especially.

The thought makes my sex clench.

Am I reckless? Or am I finally listening to my body?

I don't know.

At the moment, I don't care.

I don't care about anything except the desire in his eyes.

Simon gives me another long, slow once-over, then he pulls me into his lap.

I place my knees around his thighs to straddle him.

He pulls my body into his, so my sex is against his cock.

His slacks are in the way, but I can feel him, hard against the soft wool.

Ready for me.

It feels good. It feels really fucking good.

A simple pleasure. Familiar. Like a memory. Or a dream.

I was here with him a few nights ago, but that was different. Tangled.

This is easy.

Easier than it should be.

The thought dissipates as he brings his hands to my hips, rolls my body against his.

Again and again, the soft wool, straining to cover him, rolling against my tender flesh.

He pulls me into a deep kiss. Cups my breasts with his palms. Runs his thumbs over my nipples.

Slow circles, again and again.

The perfect friction, again and again.

Winding me tighter and tighter.

Almost too much to take.

I sigh when he releases me.

This is heaven.

This is torture.

The sweetest fucking torture.

His lips find my neck. He kisses a line down my skin. Wraps his lips around my nipple. Sucks softly.

A moan falls from my lips.

"Fuck." My nails dig into his skin. His bare neck. The only part of him I have. But I like it this way.

Like being undressed for him.

He toys with my nipple. That soft suction, again and again.

Then he moves to the other and teases it just as mercilessly.

I rock against him, feeling as much as I can, again and again.

So close to what I want.

But not close enough.

I shift back. Bring my hands to his belt. "Here?"

"Here." He presses his lips to my neck as he pulls something from his pocket. A condom.

We're going to fuck right here, on the balcony.

What he asked.

What I want.

"We could get caught." I undo his belt buckle. Unbutton his slacks.

"We could." He looks up at me, soft and giving. A Simon I don't know. A chance to back out. Say no. Insist on privacy.

I don't. I kiss him hard as I unzip his slacks. Rub him over his boxers.

Fuck, he feels good. Hard and thick.

It's been a long time since I've felt someone. Since I've wanted to feel someone. I'm not sure I've ever wanted to feel someone like this.

With other guys, I was curious.

With Simon, I'm insatiable.

One fucking time and I'm already insatiable.

I run my palm over him one last time, then I shift my hips, so he has room to slide his boxers out of the way.

He rolls the condom over his cock.

Then he brings his hands to my hips. Brings our bodies together.

His tip strains against me.

I dig my nails into his skin, savoring the feel, soaking in every sweet inch.

I lower my body onto his slowly, taking him deeper and deeper.

He looks up at me like I'm heaven-sent.

Then he brings his lips to my chest. He sucks on my nipple as I take him again and again.

He feels good. Too fucking good.

I have to put my hand over my mouth to stifle my groans.

He moans against my chest as he rocks with me.

We stay like that, locked together, moving in time.

Again and again.

Every rock of my hips winds me tighter.

Tighter.

But it's not enough.

I take his wrist. Guide his hand under my dress, so his thumb is against my clit.

And I rock against him.

A little left.

A little up.

There.

The perfect pressure.

My eyes close.

My nails dig into his skin.

My body fills with pleasure.

More and more and more.

Tighter and tighter.

With the next rock of my hips, I come. I groan his name, rocking through my orgasm, one hand tugging at his skin, the other digging into his hair.

I'm too loud.

But he doesn't do anything to muffle me.

We're outside, in the summer air, fucking in front of the entire city.

And every part of me feels so fucking good.

I work through my orgasm, then I bring my hands to his shoulders, use them for leverage.

He keeps his hands on my hips, guiding my body over his.

Again and again.

His groans blur together. A perfect friction against my skin.

Again and again.

Louder and deeper.

Until he's there.

He guides me faster, harder, scraping his teeth against my nipple as he pulses inside me.

It doesn't pull me over the edge.

But it still feels so fucking good.

I work him through his orgasm, then I shift back, off him, into my dress.

He takes care of the condom. Slips into his clothes. Adjusts his belt, tie, watch.

The Simon Pierce I know.

Smooth composure.

Except for the lipstick on his collar.

The satisfaction in his eyes.

The claw marks on his neck.

He catches me staring. "Don't apologize."

"I wasn't going to."

"Good." He motions to our still full drinks *shall we?* "I want more upstairs."

My nails, marking his chest, thighs, back.

The two of us, fucking again upstairs.

Spending the entire night in his hotel room.

How the fuck am I going to survive that?

Chapter Thirteen

VANESSA

Simon Pierce is sitting at the tiny dining table; sleeves rolled to his elbows.

And he's eating Thai food.

Greasy Thai food.

Not a fancy, modern restaurant.

A hole in the wall.

He scoops noodles from a takeout container. Sips his orange-red Thai iced tea.

Sure, it's not the usual beverage—he ordered an off menu version with coconut milk—but it's still as bright as a neon sign.

Surreal.

Almost impossible to believe.

He catches me staring—not that I'm trying to hide it—and looks me over. Studies my barely touched sparkling water and basil eggplant and chicken. Raises a brow.

I'm sitting and staring.

He's eating and drinking, like a normal person.

Only that's abnormal. Because he's Simon Pierce.

"It's strange, seeing you eat," I say.

"Strange how?"

"Spicy noodles and Thai iced tea. That's not what I expect."

"Should I order steak and whiskey instead?"

"No."

"But that's what you imagine?" he asks.

Do I imagine him eating? "No, I imagine you gaining nutrients though victory."

"Photosynthesis by domination?"

I nod.

He laughs, actually laughs. "How would that work?"

"I don't know. It would be a scientific miracle. Doctors would study you."

"And that's why I never let on?"

"Exactly."

"It could still be the case. I could be hiding it." He scoops noodles with his fork. Offers me a bite.

I take the fork—a disposable utensil, but a nice one, made of bamboo—and bring it to my lips. The spice hits my tongue first. Then a mix of heat and sweetness.

Basil. Garlic. Ginger.

Soft noodles. Crisp vegetables. Tender beef.

It's fucking amazing.

The best thing I've tasted in days. Months. Years even.

When was the last time I sat and savored a meal?

I stopped tasting food when mom got sick. Then I started restricting, and I turned off my senses completely.

It wasn't severe the way it was when I was a teenager. I didn't lose too much weight or eat so little I passed out. I stayed reasonable. Enough to help me cope. Not so much I drew attention.

People noticed I lost weight, but most paid me compliments. Even in my field, with people who should know better.

The people who showed a shred of concern nodded when I mentioned my mother.

Of course, I wasn't eating much.

Of course, I was losing weight.

It happens to so many people. They stress eat. Or stress not-eat.

It was the same for me.

Just more intentional.

"You're hard to read," Simon says.

I return the fork. "You too."

"But I'm learning."

"Oh." I find my fork. Stab an eggplant.

"You're off somewhere."

"That's how I am." I bring the bite to my lips. Fuck, it's amazing. Oil and basil and spice. The perfect mix of rich, savory, herbaceous. And just a little sweet. I let out a soft groan.

"I like your thoughtfulness." His voice is sure. Steady. "I like having you here, with me. I understand you're not always in the moment."

"You aren't either."

He nods. "Where do you go?"

I can't tell him this. I can't admit I'm a thirty-one-year-old wrestling with her teenage eating disorder.

Not to Simon.

He's always in control.

Maybe he'd understand that impulse, but the rest?

Even if he would—

It's mine.

He's still sitting there, watching, waiting.

Endlessly patient.

I have to say something.

I want to say something. To tell someone. To not be alone with everything all the time.

"My mom," I say. "When she was sick last year, I… lost my appetite."

He nods with understanding.

"This is the first time in a while I've really tasted. It's delicious. But overwhelming."

"I was the same, after Bash. I've never lingered on sensory pleasures."

"No?"

"No."

"Your reputation…"

"I know my reputation."

"All rumors?"

"Some. I fuck, yes. It feels good, yes. But that isn't why I do it."

"Why do you do it?"

"Because it makes sense."

That's not what I expected him to say.

But I guess it tracks. He's like me. In control. Precise. Goal-oriented.

"After he died, I lost interest," he says.

"When did you find it?"

"I'm not sure I did. Until the other night."

Fuck.

"No. Before, it was a need I filled. I enjoyed it, but I didn't savor it. I didn't replay the sound of someone's groan. Or picture her in my bedroom naked."

It's hot in here.

I need to say something to keep my composure.

Or I need to tear off his clothes immediately.

One of the two.

"I don't usually savor things." My eyes go to my food. The deep purple eggplant skin. The pale brown rice. The thin slices of deep green basil. The slivers of red pepper. "I did, sometimes, before mom got sick." After my first recovery. "I tried, after she went into remission. I'm not good at it, but I have moments. A night out with Lee. A run on a crisp day. A family trip to St. Barts."

"You went to St. Barts?"

"I did."

"And?"

"I worked the whole time."

"What did you enjoy?" he asks.

"Lee dragged me to the beach. Made me lie on the sand."

"And you hated it?"

"Of course? Why would I lie in the sun? For a tan?"

He laughs.

"Oh, are you tanning on the beach?" I reach for his hand. Run my fingers over his designer watch. "Is there a white line under here?"

"I don't tan in my watch."

"You're darker than Adam."

"When did you last see Adam?"

"The wedding," I say.

"Ah." He nods. "That was something."

"It was." Lee and her husband Harrison had a huge wedding planned. A secluded beach in the Hamptons, near the Pierce manor. They were set for a big to-do. Then Harrison's father, Preston, collapsed at the rehearsal dinner.

He was hiding his illness.

Hiding the ugly truth to protect his son.

He's dying.

He's okay for now, but he's probably not going to be around for long.

Harrison was furious. Lee tried to talk to him. To remind him what it was like for me, for her, for the two of them, attending treatments with my mom. Watching her fade. Wondering if it was the end.

What it was like for Mom, having that attention, feeling like a fragile vase.

He understood, but he didn't shake the betrayal.

They kept the wedding date, but they moved the ceremony

into the chapel at the hospital. No one believed it was Lee's idea, but it was.

She was demanding as a bride, sure, but that's Lee. She knows what she wants. She doesn't accept less.

She had specific ideas for her dress, flowers, cake, but she knows what matters: family.

That's probably why they're trying now, so soon after getting married. They want their kid to meet his paternal grandfather.

Harrison is good friends with Simon's younger brother, Liam. Their fathers were good friends. After Simon's dad died, Preston helped out, suggested sending Liam and Bash to the secluded all-boys boarding school Harrison attended.

Harrison and Liam are good friends. They have been since they were kids. It's strange—Liam is all trouble, all the time, and Harrison is dead serious—but it makes sense too.

They get each other.

They respect each other.

They're practically brothers. Preston is practically Liam's father.

Is this hard on him too?

On Simon's other brothers?

On Simon?

"Are you close?" I ask. "With Preston?"

"No. I was older when our father died. I didn't appreciate him trying to fill that role."

"Do you now?"

"Yes. I didn't realize it then, but my brothers needed it. I needed the help."

"You admit it?"

"Our secret." He smiles.

My heart thuds against my chest. That smile. Fuck. "He's a warm guy, Preston."

"Different than my father."

"More like mine," I say. "My adopted father."

"Do you call him that?"

"No. I call him Daddy."

"You do?"

"I know. I'm in my thirties and I still call my father Daddy. I'm a Freudian nightmare."

"It's sweet."

"I'm not sure I can take your word for it."

He raises a brow.

"Not if you're into that."

"Women calling me Daddy?"

I nod.

"No. Not my thing."

"What is your thing?"

"Do you want to talk about sex?"

Yes. No. Maybe. "I should probably finish dinner first."

"Probably." He lobs the ball back to me. Pauses. Waits.

I can discuss family, film, finance.

Or I can talk about my desire to mount him.

Ask him his favorite position.

Push the conversation to X-rated areas.

"Why not?" I ask.

"Why don't I want to be called Daddy?"

I nod.

"I picture my kids calling me Daddy. Not—"

"An eighteen-year-old with daddy issues?"

"Is that what you think of me?"

I motion *a little*.

He smiles, not offended, but not above it all either. A real smile.

A panty-melting smile.

"Do you really picture kids?" I ask.

"I did. I've always thought about family. My brothers. Then Opal. But I never asked if I wanted it. I assumed I'd get married and have children, because it was my duty."

"Have you ever come close?"

His eyes flit to my bare ring finger. "Not as close as you."

Right. I was engaged. And I called it off, even though he was perfect, and we looked perfect together. People still ask why, even though it was years ago.

"What happened?"

"With Sol?" I uncross and recross my legs. It's strange talking about this with him. Why is it so strange talking about this with him? "He was a sweet guy. Giving and kind."

"Handsome."

"You noticed?"

"Of course."

"Were you jealous?"

"I told myself I wasn't." He takes a long sip of his tea. "But I was."

"Why?"

"My father didn't want me to marry you."

"How did that come up?"

"He had… old-fashioned views."

Oh. "He actually said that?"

"He used the right words, but I knew what he meant."

"But how…" Why was Simon's dad talking about the possibility of us getting married? "Why did he consider it?"

"I liked you."

"He knew?"

"I didn't hide it. He was old-fashioned about women too. He commented on whether or not a 'young lady' was 'marriage material' or not."

"What did you say to him?"

"Nothing." He looks to his food. "I should have stood up to him. Told him he was wrong. I told myself it didn't matter. I was seventeen. I wasn't thinking about marriage. And you hated my guts."

"I did."

"So what did it matter if my father objected?"

I swallow hard.

"That was what I told myself. But it did matter. I should have said something. If I was a better man, I would have."

"Now?"

"He's gone. He can't offer his input anymore."

"So you would…"

"Marry you? Is that a proposal?"

"Marry a black woman?"

"If I loved her."

I take another bite of my food. It's still good, that mix of oil and herbs and fresh eggplant, but it's different, somehow. Deeper. Richer. Tinted with our conversation.

"I expected to be married by now. I expected to have my father's life. I didn't question it."

"Pretty blond wife who stayed home?"

"My mother wasn't blond."

"Even so."

"You have a fixation," he says.

"Maybe."

"Why?"

"I just see it for you."

"Ah."

"What? What ah?"

"The captain of the swim team," he says. "She was blond. We were crowned homecoming king and queen."

"It wasn't that."

He raises a brow *wasn't it.*

"You just seem like a guy who marries a blonde."

Again, he raises a brow *really?*

Maybe I'm stereotyping now. It's not fair. Lee is blond, and she's a force of nature. But she's also the kind of woman Simon would marry in every but one—her personality.

"Did you want a wife who stayed home?" I ask.

"You know how it is for women who marry wealthy men. They have to look the part. They have to play the part. They don't earn a salary, but they're working."

"Like being a politician's wife. All smiling at assholes and support your husband." I swallow another bite. "Is that what you wanted?"

"No. It was inevitable. My duty. Like having children to carry on the family name."

"Now?"

"Is *that* a proposition?" he asks.

"What if it was?"

"I'd say take off your clothes."

"Really?"

"No. Not after my father… You know Opal's history."

Yes, his father knocked up his secretary. Paid her off to keep quiet. Kept them living a luxe life, even after he died, so long as her mom kept the secret.

Then her mom died, and Opal discovered the truth and walked into Simon's life.

It's almost as fucked up as my history.

"If I have kids, I'm giving them my name," I say.

"A hyphen?"

"Moyer-Pierce."

"Fair." He offers his hand.

"We're negotiating."

"We're fucking. It's a possibility."

That's true. But he's kidding.

Isn't he?

I shake. Try not to consider the implications. Or imagine our hypothetical children.

He's tall and broad. My biological father was the same. My mom is tiny.

I'm in between.

Would our kids be tall?

Would they have his blue eyes? My tight curls? Is that even possible, genetically?

Fuck.

I need to discuss something else. Something less dangerous. "Opal seems like a good kid."

"She is. You'd like her. When she's not meddling."

"We both have fucked-up families."

"You're both strong and demanding."

"And we love art?"

"I'm not sure she loves it. She's taking the class because I insisted she do something productive with her summer."

"What does she love?"

"Besides making my life difficult?" he asks.

"You're the one giving her a curfew and mandatory summer classes."

"I don't want her getting into trouble."

"Rules give her something to rebel against."

"So she comes home at twelve thirty and takes an art class she doesn't care about. Better than taking ecstasy and sleeping with strangers."

"You give her minor rules on purpose?" I ask.

"How do you think I got my position?"

"Negotiating with your own sister." I shake my head. "Cold."

"Smart." He smiles.

My heart thuds against my chest. He has such a handsome smile. It lights up his blue eyes. It turns the world into a beautiful place.

It sends desire straight to my core.

I want to mount him.

Right here.

Right now.

Can he go again? It's been a while now. Almost an hour.

Some guys take longer.

Some guys are faster.

Knowing Simon—

He's probably Super Cock. Ready in an instant, ready for as long as I want, completely and totally in control of every part of his body.

Can I make him lose control?

How would I do it?

I don't usually think about sucking guys off. I don't mind it. I even enjoy it with guys I like.

But I don't get off on it.

I don't think about it.

I don't recall the act or envision future opportunities when I fantasize.

So why am I thinking about dropping to my knees and trying to make Simon lose control?

Here.

In a limo.

While he's on a conference call.

Or something else that demands his composure.

Ahem.

"You're off somewhere again," he says. "But it's different this time."

"How?"

"Something you want. Before, it was bad. Something that hurt."

How can he tell?

"It was."

I take another bite to buy myself time to explain, but I don't have an explanation. Only the truth. And I'm not ready to admit that. "You have this signature expression. This amused half-smile." I try to copy the gesture, but it's hard without a mirror. "Like you're so above it all, you're amused by other people's effort."

"Is that really what you think of me?"

Not right now. "Sometimes."

"Sometimes, I am. You are too."

"It's not a happy thing."

"For me either."

It's not?

"It's lonely. Being removed."

"You're lonely?"

"Yes."

"I didn't think you'd say that." I take one last bite. The food is great. Filling. Sex may not be exercise, but it shares plenty of traits. I don't want to be stuffed. "Why aren't you married?"

"Fuck, Vanessa? Am I lonely? Why am I not married? What are you going to ask next?"

"Your biggest regret."

His eyes flit to the window. The view of midtown. "Not protecting Bash."

"Wasn't he in an accident?"

He doesn't answer the question. "I knew he was doing something stupid. I didn't stop him. Maybe I couldn't have stopped him, but I could have tried harder."

Huh?

"As for the marriage... I thought I'd follow my father's model. Find someone who fit the role of Mrs. Simon Pierce. I tried, for a while, but I never felt anything. I went on dates. I got to know women. I asked some to be my girlfriend. But I always knew, deep down, I didn't feel what I was supposed to feel. I enjoyed their company, I enjoyed the sex, I even liked knowing who I'd take to events, what I'd do on Saturday night. But I never wanted more."

"What more?"

"My housekeeper had a test—"

"Your housekeeper taught you about relationships?"

"Who else?"

True.

"If you come home, and see someone's car, are you glad it's there? Or disappointed."

"You live in Manhattan."

"See their coat on the rack. Their keys on the table."

"Am I glad I see my boyfriend's coat?"

"Are you relieved, when it isn't there?"

I am. I was. With Sol. I cared about him, I did, but I was relieved when he had to work late.

"I was always relieved to come home alone. I never felt a desire to fall asleep next to someone. Or tell her my secrets. Or plan a life together."

"Never?"

"Never. I didn't even miss women when they went on business trips. Or crave them when we went weeks without a night together."

"You went weeks?"

"Sometimes."

"I never craved Sol."

"Did you love him?"

"I thought so, at the time. Now, I don't know. He was all right on paper, but I couldn't trust it."

"So you're here."

"So I'm here." I take my last sip. "And you?"

"Why am I here?"

I nod.

"Because I find you irresistible." He stands. Offers his hand. "And I want to spend as much time as possible listening to you come."

Chapter Fourteen

SIMON

Vanessa excuses herself to clean up in the washroom in the bedroom.

I use the one in the hall.

Once again, standing here, trying to find a hint of sense.

I still hear my brother's voice. Only, this time, he isn't chiding me for my inability to love.

He's offering a high-five. And a hug. And pontificating on the brilliance of love.

You think you enjoy sex, Simon, but try making love. Go ahead. Roll your eyes. I don't care. It's because you don't know.

That's how it feels.

Like you really are making love. Creating it. Bringing it into the universe. Taking as much as you can and still having more to share.

Who wouldn't want that?

I wash up. Then wash my hands and face again, for good measure.

My reflection is strange. Barely recognizable.

The same deep eyes, square jaw, broad shoulders.

Everything else is different.

No suit jacket. No tie. No defenses.

It's ridiculous. I'm six inches taller than Vanessa. In every external way, I'm stronger.

But she's a million times stronger than I am.

She's here. Trying.

Not escaping to the bathroom to talk herself into facing intimacy.

Or maybe she's doing the same thing in the bedroom.

She's like me. In too many ways.

I take a deep breath. Roll my shoulders with my exhale.

My desire for her is overwhelming.

But I'm facing it.

For Bash.

And for me too.

The lights are off in the main room. The curtains are drawn. The soft blue of the city streams through the windows. The pockets of yellow light. All the steel and glass of the city.

Beautiful.

For a moment, I keep my eyes on the skyscrapers around us. Then I turn to the bedroom door. Closed.

For Vanessa's privacy?

Or something else?

I knock.

"Come in." Her voice is a low purr.

Soft light fills the room as I pull the door open. The scent of wax and roses. Candles line the space. Petals cover the bed.

"Was this you?" she asks.

"By proxy."

"By proxy?" She steps forward, into the light, still in her cocktail dress and heels.

"I didn't arrange the flowers."

"But you asked?"

"I did."

"And you had specific ideas for how it should go?"

"I always do." I offer her my hand.

Her fingers brush my palm.

I pull her body into mine.

Her arm hooks around my neck.

It's strange being this close while we're both dressed.

New.

Terrifying.

Maybe Bash was right. Maybe I'm not single because I'm busy or broken.

Maybe I'm single because I'm a coward.

Too afraid to face this kind of intimacy. Risk.

I haven't done it in a long, long time.

"And people are who they are." Her fingers dig into my skin. "When they work, when they play, when they fuck."

"They are."

"You're a man who knows what he wants."

I nod.

"And you want to adorn the place where we fuck?"

"Yes."

"Who did you ask?"

"Danielle."

"Your brother's girlfriend?"

"She's a photographer." An erotic photographer. She takes sensual images. She knows how to set a mood.

"Your future sister-in-law is helping you get laid?"

"It was a trade. This, for permission to use the room for a photo shoot."

"Right. The naked pictures." Her fingers brush my collar. "Do you like them?"

"Not in particular."

"She's an attractive woman."

"She's my brother's girlfriend." Among other things. "She's not mine."

"Has anyone been yours?"

"You." I bring my hand to her lower back. Pull her closer. "For tonight."

"Does that mean you're mine?"

"For tonight."

"Would you take pictures?"

For anyone else? No. "For you."

"Take pictures of me?"

"Yes."

"Look at them when you fuck yourself?"

"Yes."

She releases me. Steps back. Runs her fingers over the rose-petal covered sheets.

She pushes her strap off her shoulder. Pushes the dress over her hips.

The fabric falls at her ankles.

"You like to watch," she says.

"Yes." My eyes pass over her slowly. Her wavy hair. Her dark eyes. Her lips—freshly painted that deep shade of red.

Her bare shoulders, chest, stomach, thighs.

Naked except for her heels.

Every inch of her dark skin on display.

I take a step toward her.

She shakes her head. "Watch from there."

My eyes pass over her again. Faster this time. Taking in every inch.

She sits on the bed, spreads her legs half an inch.

Then another.

Another.

Until her knees are against the sheets.

Until I can see every sweet inch of her cunt.

Fuck.

My breath leaves my body.

My blood rushes south.

I'm usually patient. It's one of my greatest strengths.

But right now?

I need to touch her, taste her, feel her.

I need to bury my head between her legs and lick her until she's coming on my face.

I press my palms into my slacks. Force myself to stay in place.

She looks me in the eyes as she slips her hand between her legs.

She doesn't tease. She goes straight to where she needs stimulation. Rubs herself with two fingers.

For a moment, her eyes stay on mine.

Then they flutter together.

Her chest heaves.

Her fingers claw at the sheets.

She works herself with steady strokes.

Again and again.

Pushing closer and closer.

She's there fast, moaning and tugging at the sheets as she comes.

Pleasure spreads over her expression.

Her entire body tenses and relaxes.

She nearly melts into the bed.

Somehow, she doesn't. She stands. Crosses the space to me.

Brings both hands to my chest. The button. "The mirror is right there." She nods to the wall across from the bed.

"I know."

"It wasn't there last time."

I nod.

"You moved it for me?"

"For both of us."

"Good." She undoes the first button. The second. The third. She pushes the shirt off my shoulders. "I like the way you watch." She undoes my belt buckle and tosses it aside. "You're the same as always. Patient and intense and irresistible." She kisses me as she unzips my slacks.

I wrap my arms around her. Back her against the bed. Kick off my shoes and socks.

She pushes my slacks off my hips.

I step out of them and lower her onto the bed.

She reaches for something. A condom. She already has it in place. It's fucking genius.

But this first.

I pin her legs to the bed, drop between them, place my lips to the inside of her knee.

I kiss a line up her thigh.

She shudders as I get closer—

Closer—

"Simon." She reaches for something. My hair. My shoulders. "I haven't. It's been a long time."

"I'll start slow."

She murmurs a yes as my lips brush her clit.

Her head falls back to the right. The side with the mirror.

She's watching.

Is there anything sexier?

I take a moment to take in the sight of her splayed wide on the bed, unfolding for me, then I dive between her legs.

Slowly, I explore every inch of her. The soft strokes that make her thighs shake. The quick flicks that make her nails dig into my back.

Then harder.

Higher.

The spot where she needs me.

She gasps as I flick my tongue against her. "Fuck. Simon." Her thighs fight my hands. Her hand knots in my hair. "Don't stop."

I'd die first.

I stay where she needs me. Work her with those same steady strokes. Again and again.

Pushing her closer and closer.

Until she's there.

She digs her nails into my skin, rocking against my lips, shaking as she comes.

She gets sweeter, wetter, even more irresistible.

I need to have her here.

I need to have her everywhere.

She tugs at my hair. Reaches for something. The foil package.

She tears it with her teeth.

It's almost absurd enough to knock me off my feet. Beautiful, elegant queen of the world, Vanessa Moyer tearing a condom wrapper with her teeth.

A high school fantasy come to life.

How many times did I fuck myself to her?

A hundred?

A thousand?

She rakes her nails over my chest, hungry and impatient. She doesn't wait. She wraps her hand around me. Pumps with firm, steady strokes.

Fuck.

My eyes fall closed.

My thoughts tune to her.

The feel of her palm. The sound of her groan. The smell of her skin.

She pumps me one more time, then she rolls the rubber over my cock, wraps her legs around my hips.

I lower my body onto hers.

Chest, stomach, pelvis.

My cock brushes against her.

Fuck. She feels good. It's almost too much to take.

Different this time.

Her skin against mine.

Her need against mine.

I can't look away. Not even to watch in the mirror.

"Fuck." She claws at my skin. Her head tips back. Her lips part with a groan.

I need more.

Every ounce of her pleasure.

Every scrape of her nails. Every second of her groan. Every shudder of her thighs.

She's right. I know hell.

But this, this is heaven.

I'm not slow or patient.

I pull back and drive into her again.

Again.

Her eyes go to the mirror.

I watch her watch.

Until it's too much to take.

Then I bring my gaze to her, take in all the need on her face one more time.

I close my eyes and bring my lips to hers.

She kisses back with reckless abandon.

Hard and hungry.

Demanding every ounce of my attention, need, devotion.

I want to give it to her.

I want to give her everything.

Her hips rock to meet mine.

Every thrust pushing her closer and closer—

But not there.

I untangle our bodies. Flip her over. Push her knees apart.

"Touch yourself, sweetness." I nip at her ear. "I want to feel you come."

She groans as I enter her again.

No warm-up.

I fuck her hard and fast.

She slips her hand between her legs. Works herself with those perfect circles.

She comes fast, pulsing around, tugging at the sheets, mumbling curses into the bed.

It pulls me over the edge.

With my next thrust, I come. I rock through my orgasm, spilling every drop, consumed with every inch of her.

My entire world is Vanessa.

Jagged breaths. Soft skin. Pure bliss.

For once, I unfurl.

Release something deep and aching.

Something I can't articulate.

She's heaven.

But there's more too. More than the pleasure spilling through my body.

Something warm and supple.

An affection I've never felt before.

Not like this.

Not even close to this.

I pull back, do away with the condom, help her clean up as I catch my breath.

She rolls onto her back, stretching her arms over her head with a sigh. "You wore me out."

"Is that a compliment?"

"Will it make your ego bigger?"

"Of course."

"Even so. I have to admit it." She smiles, all softness. "You did."

———

SHE SHOWERS FIRST. THEN I TAKE MY TURN.

When I emerge, she's in bed, in the pajamas I bought her.

She traces the neckline of the slip and raises a brow. "Is that why you asked if I always wear silk?"

I shake my head. "I invited you here."

"To your hotel room."

"To spend the night." I cup her cheek with my palm. "I'd rather you sleep naked. But…"

"You're such a great host you brought pajamas?"

"Exactly."

"What bullshit."

"It's true."

She laughs. Tugs at *my* pajamas. Pulls me into bed. "Of course you wear silk pajamas. Top shelf-whiskey. Designer watch. Three-hundred-dollar pajamas. Simon Pierce, King of New York, man of luxury."

"New York now?"

"You don't want to lose the throne?"

"Never."

"Both." She smiles. "Darkness. And New York."

"And man of luxury?"

"Absolutely," she says.

"What do you wear at home?"

"You want to picture me there?"

I do.

"Picture me naked."

"Is it accurate?"

"Maybe."

I run my fingers over the strap of her nightgown.

She turns and melts into my chest.

"What do I have to wear to sleep? To prove I'm not a stereotype?"

"A Taylor Swift t-shirt and boxers."

"Taylor Swift?"

"Don't tell me you're unaware?"

"I live with a teenage girl."

"Is she a fan?"

"A die hard."

"She seems the type. Sweet and energetic.

"I took her to a show."

Vanessa laughs. "You did not."

"Two years ago."

"You wore a suit?"

"What else would I wear?"

"Jeans and a concert tee."

"I don't have any."

"Really? None?"

"I've been to shows." I pull her closer. "With people I loved. Never for myself."

"You don't like music."

I nod into her back.

"There's something sad about that. I don't stop and smell the roses"—she plucks a petal from the bed—"but I know what I love. What brings me pleasure."

"Beethoven and opera?" I ask.

"Have you seen opera? It's transcendent."

"For work."

"You weren't moved?"

"No."

"Because you don't like art."

"I never paid attention. But I will. Preston is trying to convince Liam to go. If I suggest it—"

"Our entire families will be there watching us." She laughs. "But it would be nice. To go with him. And Lee. She loves it."

"She does?"

"She only acts tough." She drops the petal. Nestles into the pillow. "No, she is. But she's like you. She loves her family. She just does it ruthlessly."

"Ruthless."

"You like the sound of it, huh?"

"I do."

"I knew you would." She mumbles into her pillow.

"I am the King of Darkness."

"What's that make me?"

"A queen."

"I'll hold you to that," she mumbles as she falls asleep.

I expect to struggle to sleep, but I don't.

I rest easy. Wake early to the buzz of my phone, reminding me I need to check on my sister.

I slip out of bed, dress, check on Vanessa before I leave.

She doesn't rouse.

I'm not relieved.

I'm disappointed.

The feeling deepens as I leave, make my way back home. I already miss her. I already want to see her again.

I already want to lose myself in her.

Is that even possible?

I don't know.

But I know one thing: I need to make her come again.

Chapter Fifteen

VANESSA

This time, I leave the pajamas and the same note.

> Thanks for the hospitality.
> - V

I smooth my dress. Step into my heels. Apply a coat of lipstick.

Men have it easy. They can wear last night's suit without telling the world they spent the night in someone else's bed.

Or is this Simon's bed? A home away from home?

Hell, he might have a spare suit in the closet. Or at least a fresh shirt and tie.

No. The closet is empty.

No signs of clothes. No signs of him at all.

But then it is a hotel room. Supposedly, one for important clients. Why would Simon leave his clothes?

Why am I overcome with the desire to steal his shirt and tie?

Wear them home, leave them in my bed, lounge.

Smell like him all day.

Good sex.

It's too fucking intoxicating.

I slip out of the room before I get ideas.

Sure, I get a few looks on my way out of the hotel room, but I call on Daddy's advice to hold my head high, and I ignore them.

The drive is quiet. It's early, before rush hour, and all the traffic is moving in the other direction.

The cabbie drops me off with a *hope he was worth it* look.

I try to shrug it off. Copy Simon's calm composure. Strong, intense, above it all.

And, soft, somewhere underneath his defenses.

Someplace I want to find, study, hold close.

Fuck.

No feelings. I'm not falling for him. He's not falling for me.

We're having fun.

And last night was fun.

Period.

The end.

The doorman looks at me funny.

I force a smile. "Yes, Sam?"

His eyes flit to my bare legs. "There's someone waiting for you, Ms. Moyer."

Huh?

"A woman. In the lobby. I told her I didn't know when you'd return, suggested she leave a note, but she was insistent."

The same as the woman at the office.

Either she's scared and desperate or—

No, no matter what her role is, she's scared and desperate. I need to be careful.

"She says she knows you, but she won't give her name." He motions to the lobby inside.

The pretty blond woman in designer sunglasses and a linen shirt, hands around an expensive stroller.

An Upper East Side mom on her day off. Wearing clothes that hide bruises.

Poised, despite the circumstances. Used to keeping up appearances.

"I can ask her to leave," he says.

"No. She's a friend."

He shoots me another funny look. *A friend like the friend who kept you out all night, huh? This is a nice building, you know.*

But she looks more like she belongs than I do. Especially given my current outfit.

I smile, thank him for his help, step inside.

I'm not giving him the satisfaction of riling me.

I had sex last night.

The US might not be at our peak of civil liberties, but it's still a free fucking country.

My personal life is none of his business. Especially if it's happening outside the building.

The woman turns to me. Studies me with gentle grey eyes. "Ms. Moyer."

It's not a question, but I nod and offer my hand anyway. "Can I help you?"

"Celine." She doesn't give a last name. "We threw a gala together a few years ago."

We did. "Arts in public school?"

"Yes."

"That was a nice event."

"Thank you."

The details are fuzzy. Spring weather. Hotel ballroom. Pink and blue decor. Understated elegance.

She was on the board of the charity. Did most of the planning.

We met briefly. Two or three times, maybe, and never alone. But I remember the champagne toast. The way she looked at me.

The curiosity in her eyes. Like I was a knight in shining armor.

But then I see possible victims everywhere. They are everywhere—domestic violence is disturbingly common—but I can't help people until they ask for help.

If she's here—

"Can we talk upstairs?" she says.

"The office is more secure," I say.

"Even so." Fear slips into her voice, but just barely. She's good at hiding it. Used to hiding it. "The office on the second floor. The CEO is a friend of my…"

Her husband.

Even if the friend means well, he might give her away by accident. It happens all the time.

I try to remember the event. There was a man with her. He was older. Graying but still good-looking.

Not as beautiful as she is.

Or as handsome as Simon.

But who is?

If she spends her free time throwing galas, she must be married to someone rich and powerful.

And she's here, in my building.

I can say no. Insist we go to the office or a hotel or somewhere else far from my home.

But she might get scared. Run away. Run to a less trustworthy person. Or right back to the arms of her husband.

I can't risk that.

"Follow me," I say

"Thank you." Her shoulders fall with relief.

"Do you need help?" I motion to the stroller in front of her. Not that I know how to help. Despite all Lee's fertility talk and the day-to-day details of my job, I don't have much experience with babies.

"Just quiet," she says. "He's finally sleeping."

She looks at his round face with adoration.

She's leaving for him.

Because she's afraid for him.

A lot of people who won't raise a hand to protect themselves will die for their children.

My mom would have died for me. She protected me so many times, but it still took her years to leave.

My head spins as I lead Celine to the elevator.

I push the button. I force a smile. I try not to let my thoughts make it to my expression.

This is why I don't interact with survivors often.

Everything is loaded.

I'm not objective or smart or safe.

My memories come to the surface.

The feelings come to the surface.

And feelings are contagious. My fear and anger spread around the room.

There's something to be said for group therapy. For finding people who've been through what you've been through, people who understand.

But there's a reason why those sessions are led by a professional.

They know how to help.

They know how to wade through deep water without drowning.

I flail so hard I drag others down with me.

The elevator doors slide open.

I step into the hallway.

"Your dress is lovely." She follows me. "The shoes too."

"Not my usual morning gear."

"No? It suits you."

"Thank you." I unlock the door. Hold it open for her. The security in the building is good, top-notch, but if her husband is the kind of man who exists in this world—

Rich, powerful men find ways to break the rules.

"Give me a minute," I say.

After she steps inside, I check the bathroom—empty—and the bedroom—my second and third choice outfit are still sitting on the bed—then I return to the main room. Slip out of my shoes.

"Can I get you something to drink? I have tea. Coffee." Whole beans. The regular Lee used to drink. And the decaf she drinks now. "I'll have to grind it."

"Tea is fine."

I move into the kitchen, fill the kettle, find two cups in the pantry.

She sits at the dining table. Folds her hands in her lap. "Late night?"

"With a friend."

"He's a lucky man." She smiles softly. "Or woman. I shouldn't assume."

I check the tea selection. Not a lot of variety. I know what I like. "Do you prefer English Breakfast or Earl Grey?"

"Do you have milk?"

"I do."

"English Breakfast." She glances at her son, still sleeping in his stroller. "I'm sorry. I don't mean to pry. It's just been a long time since I've talked with girlfriends."

"I imagine you have your hands full with your son."

"Yes."

Neither of us adds *and your husband probably tried to isolate you from your friends. Did he do it by manipulating you into believing they didn't have your best interests at heart? Or did he use actual threats?*

Maybe that isn't it.

Maybe it's something else. Something normal.

I've never had a team of girlfriends. I've always kept to myself. Spent my free time studying, reading, working.

Lee is my best friend. She's all the girlfriend I need.

But then Lee is a lot of girlfriend. She aces all the stereotypical tasks: Sunday brunch, boy talk, shopping, makeup, attire.

And she's my sister.

What's better than hanging out with your sister?

Lee is a force of nature. She's the one who insists I have girl talk in my life.

She shows up here every Sunday, without fail.

She sees me upset and demands an explanation.

I can't hide many things from her. But I can.

She knew about my eating disorder when we were kids. And, after, we'd laugh about how she was supposed to be the one with a fucked-up relationship to food.

She was the ballerina. How could I get on her turf?

And we'd laugh.

And then last year…

She doesn't know about that. But then it's not bad. It's just…

It is.

"My sister is better at girl talk," I say.

"Sisters always are."

"Do you have any?"

"A younger sister back home." She doesn't say where. "But we haven't been close in a long time."

She's not just scared.

She's lonely too.

I don't know what to say. Even if things were normal, if she was an acquaintance looking for company, I'd be out of my depths.

I try to channel Lee. A softer version of Lee.

"She asks about my love life too," I say. "She's a newlywed. Wants to see the entire world in love."

"I remember that time." She smiles sadly. "I'm sure you hear it all the time, but my husband, he was sweet when we met. He showered me with love."

That's common. The intensity. The obsession.

It happens so fast, people don't realize they're cut off from their friends and family.

Even if they can leave without danger, they have nowhere to go. No support. No affection. No love.

"I'm sure you can guess why I'm here," she says.

"No one's come to the front door."

"Never?"

"Never."

"Is it an imposition?"

Yes, and it's scary that she knew where to come. I try to be hard to find. It's necessary with my work. "How did you find the address?"

"A friend."

"Of your husband's?"

"No, no. He… I suppose there's no reason to dance around it, is there?"

The kettle hisses. Not a full steam, but warm enough, and I don't want to wake the baby. I pour water over the pyramid tea bags. Bring both cups to the table. Then a small carafe of milk. Honey. Spoons.

"Thank you." She wraps her hands around the ceramic mug, soaking in the warmth. "My friend knew your family."

"He knew them?"

"He passed."

A million possibilities fill my head, each more horrible than the last. Her husband, catching them in the act, strangling him with her bare hands, forcing her to watch, to clean after, to become an accomplice to his crime.

Finding him some other way.

Stalking him.

Hurting him.

Killing him.

Torturing her with his old clothes, letters, gifts.

I shouldn't be here.

Regina should be here. Regina can sit across from this woman and stay calm and helpful and not jump to conclusions.

"It was an accident," she says. "A car accident."

"In the city?" I bite my tongue. Not the question. I'm not a lawyer investigating her husband. I'm not here to pry.

"On Long Island." She smiles sadly. "I always said I'd die if I had to live on Long Island, but he…" She shakes her head. "He gave me your name. If I ever needed help. I told him we'd met at an event. He said all the better. That I could go to someone I know."

"My address?"

"No, I put that together. I… before. I used to follow him. To see what he was doing when I wasn't around. Who he was visiting. I thought… I don't know what I thought."

A man who visited my building?

No one visits my building.

Only Lee. And sometimes Harrison. But Harrison is still here. And Harrison isn't the type to cheat.

He can't lie. He's physically incapable.

"It was a fantasy," she says. "Watching his life. Imagining myself as a part of it." She pours milk into her mug. Stirs with a teaspoon. "I almost believed it sometimes. I almost saw the possibility."

I follow her lead. Pour milk, stir honey, sip my tea. It's not as strong as it normally is, but it's still rich, warm, sweet. Comfort —and energy—I need.

"Sorry. I shouldn't ramble. It's bad enough I showed up announced. Terrible manners."

"It's okay." I know how scared she is. How much she needs a friend.

I can't discuss her husband without making things worse.

But I can talk about this.

"It's nice to chat sometimes," I say.

"Are you sure?"

"Yes." For a few days. After that, I don't know. But I can figure it out.

"Thank you." Relief floods her expression. "I used to talk to him. My friend. About everything. I was like a lovestruck teenager, sharing my hopes and dreams. Then he was gone and I…"

"What was he like?"

She smiles, all warmth and softness, no memories of ugly things. "Sweet. Romantic. Reckless. He didn't care that I was older. He didn't care I was married. He wanted to save me. Even before he knew I was in real trouble. When he thought it was only a loveless marriage."

"That is romantic."

She nods. "I never doubted his devotion, but he was young. Naive. He thought I was a princess in a tower. He thought he could slay the dragon. At first, I didn't believe him, but after a while… he convinced me." She looks to me. "Has anyone ever loved you that way? Openly? With his entire heart?"

"I don't know. I don't think so."

"It was like the *Wizard of Oz*. When Dorothy first lands in Oz and everything goes from black and white to technicolor. I didn't know I was living in black and white. I didn't know what I was missing."

"He sounds like a great guy. I'm sorry."

"He was." She smiles. "Strong without being hard."

"My dad is the same way."

"Your adopted father?"

My shoulders tense.

"I'm sorry. I didn't mean—I looked into you, that's all. I know it's not my business, but I…"

She's scared. She wants to know she can trust me.

It's understandable.

I understand.

But I still want to tell her to fuck off. My past is mine. My fucked-up family is mine. My fucked-up history is mine.

Not a stranger's.

Even a stranger who desperately needs help.

"He… his father…" She looks to her son. "He didn't know I was pregnant. I didn't know yet. It was early. My husband thought it was a miracle. We had tried before, but we hadn't… He was happy, for a time. He was peaceful. I'm not sure what changed, what made him wonder, but something did. He started acting suspicious. Hostile. It was a matter of time, so I… I was staying with a friend, but that's no longer an option."

"So you're here?"

She nods.

"Do you know what my company does?"

"Of course."

"We don't run a shelter. We don't have the resources to house anyone long term."

"I know."

"I can recommend one—"

"Then what?"

"We need to find somewhere safe for you to live."

"There isn't anywhere. My husband… he's a powerful man."

"We help lots of people with powerful spouses."

"He's not afraid to play dirty."

I won't tell her she's not in danger. She is. Leaving is dangerous. For everyone.

It doesn't matter how much money or power an abuser has—

They're dangerous.

"If it's necessary, we can help you disappear." It's off the books. Rare. Illegal. The government frowns on fake identities.

She stays apprehensive.

"That's the nuclear option. A new name, a new country,

never contacting old friends or family. Your sister won't be able to see—"

"Seb."

"She won't be able to see Seb again. If he has any other aunts or uncles, godparents, nannies, teachers... No one."

She nods with understanding. "How long would that take?"

"A few weeks."

"Could I stay here?"

"In my apartment?"

She looks around the room. "I understand it's unusual, but I... I trust you."

It's hard to say no to that. Especially when I know it might send her into the arms of a dangerous man. "This building isn't as safe as others."

"Please."

She's scared.

Desperate.

Maybe her husband did kill the other man.

Maybe he's going to come here to kill her son.

I'm good at a lot of things. Running fast, wooing donors, running a nonprofit.

Defending a woman and her child against a violent man?

Not so much.

"Until we find a better option," I say.

Her shoulders fall.

"And only if I bring in extra security."

"You trust them?"

"Yes." Xavier is one of the few people I trust completely.

Him, Lee, and Dad.

Dad knows danger, but he's too old to stand guard. And he's like me.

He's too close.

It's not smart.

"Are you sure you don't want to come to the office?" I ask. "It's more secure."

She shakes her head.

"You'll have to stay inside until I'm home tonight."

"It's not a problem."

If she got here okay, she should be safe. As long as she stays out of sight. "Keep the blinds down. Stay away from the windows. It's a small place, but you're welcome to the couch."

She nods.

"There's food in the fridge," I say. "I get a meal delivery service. There should be a week of dinners. I can pick up something on my way home. Take out. Or if there's anything you need for Seb. I don't host babies."

"I have everything I need."

"Are you sure?"

"Yes. Thank you, Vanessa. I don't know how I could possibly repay you."

I want to ask her to promise she'll never go back to him, but I know better. "Stay safe. That's how."

She nods *of course*.

I don't know why I believe her, believe this is the best option, but I do. "If you need anything—" I scribble my number on a Post-it note. Leave it on the table.

Then I get ready, and I leave her in my apartment.

I try to focus on work, but it weighs on my mind.

Who the hell told her to find me?

Chapter Sixteen

VANESSA

All day, I struggle to focus. When I ask the front desk what time Xavier arrives. During lunch with a donor. After I tell Regina to secure space for a high-profile client.

It's not what we do officially.

But we don't turn anyone away unless they're dangerous. We always send them to someone else who can help.

And we can help Celine. Whether it's our normal resources —job training, counseling, assistance in finding housing or employment—or something out of the ordinary.

It doesn't surprise me to see an elegant Upper East Side woman on the run. But it is close to home.

My mother and I didn't come from money, but we were always close to it. There were a few years after she left when we stayed in shelters and shitty apartments.

Then she met Daddy, and we fell right into his big, beautiful world.

Celine's world.

Simon's world.

She's the kind of woman he marries in my head.

Quiet and demure.

Understanding of her station.

Beautiful.

Did she believe she married someone like Simon? Someone rich, powerful, protective.

Someone who had enough money and power to lavish her with love.

Only he didn't use his resources to keep her safe.

He used them to hurt her. To hide it.

To scare her lover.

Maybe even kill him.

It's not as common as it is on TV. Murder is a step too far for most. Especially premeditated murder.

But something about her voice—

No. It's me. My history. What I wish happened to my father.

I need to pass this to Regina. She knows what to do. How to help. How to counsel Celine to make the best choice.

I send her another email, check on Xavier, finish an hour of work, look up tips on entertaining babies.

But I have no idea how old her son is.

I need to find calm, clarity, peace.

Normally, work soothes me.

Today, I'm too close.

I can't break for a run. I don't want to tally the week's calories in my head. But then I have another way to pause.

A shiny distraction. A man who sets my senses on fire.

After I fix a cup of tea, I grab my cell to text Simon.

But he's already beat me to it.

Simon: Did you make it home?

Vanessa: Are you checking on me?

Simon: If I am?

My stomach flutters. A lightness.

For a second, I feel guilty.

There are too many pressing concerns.

A million items on my to-do list.

A thousand emails to send.

A woman in my house with nowhere else to turn.

And I'm flirting with my fuck buddy.

But I need this. I need the lightness. I need relief.

Vanessa: It suits you.

Simon: Should I take that as a yes?

Vanessa: You bought me pajamas.

Simon: I did.

Vanessa: But not a change of clothes. I rode home in last night's dress.

Simon: I'm imagining it now.

Vanessa: Which part?

Simon: You didn't wear anything under it.

Vanessa: I took my panties off in the bathroom at the hotel. They were in my purse.

Simon: I'll remember it my way.

My lips curl into a smile. My stomach flutters. Simon Pierce is imagining me naked under my dress.

He's thinking dirty thoughts about me.

He's so fucking sexy.

And I don't care that it's wrong. Not now.

Vanessa: Did you wear the same thing home?

Simon: What else would I wear?

Vanessa: Did anyone look at you funny?

Simon: I see your point.

Vanessa: You do?

Simon: We can meet at your place next time.

My place. That would be scary under normal circumstances. Right now—

Well, I can't tell him about my new house guest. But then he's not inviting me.

I'll cross that bridge when I come to it.

Simon: Or you can come here.

Vanessa: I can? What about Opal?

Simon: She noticed the lipstick again. And the scratches.

Vanessa: You asked.

Simon: I'm not complaining.

Vanessa: You don't mind?

Simon: Her knowing? No. But I won't be able to fuck you properly if I know my sister is in the next room.

Vanessa: She has a late curfew.

Simon: If I know she might come home any minute.

Vanessa: No? It might be fun. Staying quiet.

Simon: Exhibitionist.

Vanessa: Voyeur.

Simon: It might be possible sooner.

My sex clenches.

Vanessa: Oh?

Simon: Liam must have read my mind. He invited us to the opera Friday. Preston's balcony.

Vanessa: With the two of them?

Simon: Yes, but Liam will leave at intermission. We'll have the balcony to ourselves.

Vanessa: I can work with that.

Simon: I'll pick you up at seven.

Vanessa: No. I have a late meeting. I'll meet you at the venue.

Simon: Dinner first. If you have time.

Vanessa: The four of us?

Simon: I understand if you don't want to deal with him.

He's inviting me to dinner with his family.

That means something.

But I can't consider it.

Not now, when the other concerns are heavy in my mind.

Simon is my shiny distraction. My strong, handsome release.

I need it.

I'm going to enjoy it.

After I figure this out.

I may not be able to save the world on my own. But I can help this woman. Right now, that's what matters.

Right now, it's the only thing that matters.

Chapter Seventeen

SIMON

Between meetings, calls, projections, my thoughts flit to Vanessa.

The arch of her back.

The scrape of her nails.

The taste of her lips.

Her body, stretched over the bed, unfurling as she comes.

Her laugh, low and hearty, filling the room as she teases me.

I like her.

I want her.

I had her last night, but I can't stand the thought of waiting until tomorrow.

All afternoon, I try to focus on work.

All afternoon, my thoughts drift to her.

Even when I finish and meet Opal at her art class.

The lesson is running late.

A figure drawing session.

There's a beautiful young woman, lying on a couch, but I barely see her.

Instead, I picture Vanessa on the red leather. In that long

wine-colored gown, pulling her dress up her thighs, parting her legs, inviting me to taste her.

This isn't the time.

This isn't the place.

And there isn't a single part of me that cares.

I need her tonight.

I can't wait until tomorrow.

I pull out my cell. Call her.

Three rings. Voicemail.

She texts back a minute later.

Vanessa: Did you actually call me?

Simon: Yes.

Vanessa: Is everyone okay?

Simon: I want to see you.

Vanessa: We're firmly in the middle of the millennial generation.

Simon: We are.

Vanessa: We don't call.

Simon: You're on the phone at work all day.

Vanessa: With older people.

Simon: I'm out of date?

Vanessa: It suits you, I suppose. An old-fashioned way of contacting a woman.

Simon: A cell phone?

Vanessa: It's not a stamped letter, sure.

Simon: Do you want one?

Vanessa: What would it say?

A million dirty demands flit into my head.

All the things I can write on paper.

All the things I want to say to her.

I'm not a writer. I've never been a writer. Never seen the appeal of the art.

I don't read poetry. I don't look for beautiful words or clever phrases.

I say what I need to say to make a point.

Nothing more.

Nothing less.

All of a sudden, I'm filled with the urge to find beautiful words. Something that matches the poetry of her groan. Or the sheer bliss of her body against mine.

How do I express that?

Is it even possible?

Simon: I won't ruin the surprise.

Vanessa: Is it going to be formal? One of your emails? "Vanessa, I wish to share your bed. I'm available Saturday evening and Sunday afternoon. Two hours should be sufficient time. Best, Simon."

Simon: Is that an invitation?

Vanessa: No.

Simon: Too bad.

Vanessa: I can't this weekend.

Simon: You can't...

Vanessa: Host you.

My stomach churns.

Vanessa: I'll be there, at the opera tomorrow. And the restaurant, if work doesn't run late. But I can't invite you back here.

Simon: You don't want me in your place?

Vanessa: I haven't thought about it.

I can't stop thinking about it. Vanessa Moyer, in her home, comfortable, happy.

How does that look?

What color are her walls? How big is her couch? What does she wear to sleep? What does she drink in the mornings? What does she eat for dinner?

I want everything.

I want too fucking much.

Vanessa: It would be nice to wear my pajamas for once.

Simon: Not a silk nightgown?

Vanessa: I don't want to ruin the surprise.

Simon: Fair.

Vanessa: I'd like to have you here sometime. But I have a guest.

Simon: A guest?

Vanessa: A friend from college.

Vanessa went to the Sorbonne. She knows a lot of worldly people. It makes sense.

But it doesn't sound like her either.

She's like me.

Guarded. Private.

Simon: From Paris?

Vanessa: Grad school.

Simon: A fellow MBA?

Vanessa: Will you be jealous I've invited another business expert to my house?

Yes.

Simon: A man?

Vanessa: You are jealous.

Extremely.

Vanessa: We're monogamous.

Simon: We are.

Vanessa: You don't trust me?

Simon: I do.

Vanessa: But you're jealous someone else sees me in my pajamas.

Simon: In your real pajamas.

Vanessa: Right. My real pajamas.

Simon: How long is your friend staying?

Vanessa: To be determined. Why? Are you counting the hours?

I will be. If she gives me a deadline.

Simon: I want to make plans.

Vanessa: To come to my place?

Simon: To make you come at your place.

Vanessa: Not bad.

Simon: That's all?

Vanessa: That's all.

Simon: Brutal.

Vanessa: You're a creative man. You can do better.

Simon: Is your friend keeping you busy?

Vanessa: No more than usual.

Simon: Come over tonight.

Vanessa: What about Opal?

She's right. Opal and I have a routine. One I insist we follow. Tuesdays, she meets me at the office after class. Thursdays, I meet her here. We go to dinner. Go home. Watch one of those ridiculous shows she loves.

I can't cancel on my sister.

Vanessa: It's okay. I don't want to leave my guest alone.

Simon: Your male guest?

Vanessa: Maybe. Maybe not.

Simon: Are you trying to make me jealous?

Vanessa: Is it working?

Simon: Yes.

Vanessa: I've never seen you jealous before.

Simon: You have.

Vanessa: When?

Simon: Senior prom.

Vanessa: You had a date.

Simon: You were dancing with the captain of the soccer team, staring into his eyes like you were madly in love.

Vanessa: You liked me that much?

Simon: I did.

Vanessa: You never asked me out.

Simon: You hated me.

Vanessa: Is that really what stopped you?

Maybe Bash was right. Maybe I've been afraid of a real connection all this time.

I never pursued Vanessa.

Even though I wanted her.

Even though she saw me in a way no one else did.

She hated me, yes, but that isn't what stopped me.

It was something else.

I always had a reason. She was seeing someone. She was on the opposite side of mock trial. She was going to school in Paris.

They were all excuses.

The truth is, I was scared.

I was scared I'd fall in love with her.

Fuck, I can hear Bash laughing. See him rolling his eyes, calling me on every ounce of my bullshit.

He always saw through me.

He was good at that.

How was he so fucking good at that?

Simon: No.

Vanessa: What stopped you?

Simon: I imagined a different future.

Vanessa: Now?

Simon: Now, when I imagine the future, it's Adam coming to work again every day. Opal graduating from school. The four of us, together.

Vanessa: You see your family.

Simon: I do.

Vanessa: And you, with a family?

Simon: It depends on the day.

Vanessa: Cute blue-eyed kids?

Simon: First, it was blondes, now this?

Vanessa: You don't need a blue-eyed woman for that? Do you?

Simon: I'm not a geneticist.

Vanessa: Is that what you imagine?

Simon: I did. When I was younger.

Vanessa: The blond, blue-eyed wife?

Simon: You're obsessed.

Vanessa: A little.

Simon: Is it projection? Should I wear a wig next time?

Vanessa: You'd wear a wig?

Simon: Yes.

Vanessa: You have a wig?

Simon: I live with a teenage girl.

Vanessa: Okay. Next time. Wear the wig.

Simon: Only if I keep it on.

Vanessa: Send me a picture then. So I can judge.

Simon: You think I won't?

Vanessa: I don't know.

A murmur fills the hall. Opal's class ending.

A student slips out of the room. Rushes to the stairs. To work or another class.

Or maybe to the bed of the woman he's desperate to fuck.

I should put my phone away now. Before Opal sees me.

That's the smart thing.

But I need to say this first.

Simon: Are you staying in tonight?

Vanessa: Maybe.

Simon: I don't have to come over to make you come.

Vanessa: You don't?

Simon: You've never had phone sex?

Vanessa: An actual call? Of course not.

Simon: Texts?

Vanessa: Pictures?

Simon: Yes.

Vanessa: Is that safe?

Simon: Cyber security wise? No.

Vanessa: But you'll send one anyway?

Simon: Yes.

Vanessa: I wouldn't turn that down.

Simon: Sweetness, you're gunning for my ego.

Vanessa: Not on purpose.

Simon: If you don't want a picture…

Vanessa: I do. But only if there's context. Not just the money shot. The posture. The expression. It's riskier, including your face, I know, but that's what I want.

Fuck. My thoughts are in the gutter.

Simon: Done.

Vanessa: Really?

Simon: I'll warn you first. Make sure you're alone.

Vanessa: I look forward to it.

She's an exhibitionist. Pictures will turn her on.

Not that my intentions are pure.

I want to savor the sight of Vanessa Moyer, naked, for me.

And I want to fuck myself to it.

The door swings open.

Footsteps and conversation fill the hall.

Simon: Until then.

Vanessa: Until then.

I slide my cell into my pocket, but I'm not fast enough.

Opal is already in the hallway, hugging her sketchbook to her chest, tapping her fingers against the yellow surface as she smiles. "Talking to someone?"

"Making plans."

"Plans to…"

"Let's get dinner."

"It was Vanessa!"

"Do you want Thai or sushi?"

"Is that even a question?"

Of course not. She loves spicy stir-fried noodles more than anything. I offer to take her sketchbook.

She hands it to me. And the backpack.

I carry it over my shoulder.

One of her classmates looks at me funny. Like I'm a disgusting pervert dating a teenager.

Usually, I don't mind the judgment. I'm not old enough it's clear I'm her father. We both have Dad's blue eyes, but otherwise, we don't look like brother and sister.

People see a thirty-something guy in a suit with a teenage girl and they assume.

It isn't going to stop me from helping my kid sister.

I still carry her backpack, walk her out of the building, try to change the subject as we find seats at the restaurant.

But it wears on me today.

Is that how people see me, as the kind of asshole who dates teenagers?

No, not people.

Vanessa?

I care about her opinion.

As more than a friend.

More than a fuck.

Something else, something deeper and infinitely more terrifying.

Chapter Eighteen

SIMON

"This might work with Liam." Opal folds her menu. Sets her hands on the table. Looks me dead in the eyes. "But it won't work with me."

"What won't?" I ask.

"Really, Simon? You think I don't see the bait you're throwing at me? 'What are you wearing tomorrow?'"

"It's an honest question."

"You care what I'm wearing to the opera? Really?"

"I'm responsible for you."

"I'm eighteen. I'm responsible for myself. And Briar is coming over early to help me pick out an outfit."

"Isn't that what you did last night?"

"We picked finalists. Obviously. Nice try, though. Asking me about last night so I don't ask you where you were. Or *who* you were doing?"

"It's not interesting."

"Then why are you hiding it?" She shakes her head *try selling that story to someone who buys it.* Looks to the server as he drops off our drinks. Water. And Thai iced tea with coconut milk instead of sweetened condensed milk.

Opal hates when I "interrogate" the server, chef, or manager, but I don't let that stop me. If we go to a new restaurant, I'm going to make sure they take allergies seriously.

I call ahead. Spare her the horror of my concern.

But I still check when I arrive.

After we order, hand over our menus, thank the server, she reaches for her drink.

I stop her.

She sighs in that *you're so annoying, Dad* way of hers. I'm not her father, but I'm the closest thing she has. I don't mind the irritation.

It's my job. As her older brother. "Humor me."

She nods *go ahead*.

I test my drink. The unique flavor of Thai tea, creamy coconut, a hint of sweetness. "Perfect."

She nearly dives into hers. "Mmm. That is perfect." Once she knows food is safe, she eats and drinks with gusto.

With new foods or at a new place, she hesitates.

She doesn't think I notice, but I do.

"It's not a big deal if I accidentally have some milk," she says. "I carry Benadryl and an epi-pen."

"It's not a big deal to test drinks and talk to staff."

"Okay, fine. It's not a big deal. Now, you, hiding your activities last night… could be a big deal."

"Which dresses are your finalists?"

"The long black one, with the off-the-shoulder sleeves. But Bri got me opera gloves. So I'm leaning more toward the black dress with the thick straps."

"The short one?"

"You have my closet memorized?"

"I notice things."

"Uh-huh." She shoots me a *get real* look. "Are you going to pull out a ruler and check if the skirt is too short too?"

"No." I'm going to think it's too short. And hate the way men stare at her. But this isn't a fight I'm going to win.

"You're just thinking it hard."

"I didn't say anything."

"What was Vanessa wearing last night? Something short?"

I return her *get real*.

She laughs. "You look so weird when you do Liam expressions."

"Do I?"

"Yeah. It's just… off."

"Did you decide on hair and makeup?"

"Really? You want to talk about how I'm doing my hair?"

"Do you need help?"

"With…"

"I learned to braid."

She laughs. Looks to her long, dark locks hanging over her shoulders. "You're not bad. French. Dutch. Reverse Dutch. Maybe a crown braid." She drifts into the land of fashion.

I had no idea how much women think about hair, makeup, attire. I knew they put in effort. I appreciated the effort.

But I didn't notice they were held to high standards.

Expected to look polished without looking overdone.

Judged by the shade of their lipstick and hemline of their dress.

Of course, Opal spends a lot of time thinking about what she wears. To the rest of the world, that's who she is.

She's young. Still figuring out who she is. Still trying on different identities.

The sleek socialite.

The stylish artist.

The casual student.

The girly girl.

She pulls her hot pink backpack onto her lap. Finds her cell phone. "If you really want to talk about hair and makeup, I'll start pulling tutorials. Bri can do a great smoky eye, but she rocks her short hair. She doesn't know updos."

"I'm always ready to master a new skill."

Opal groans. "Simon… come on… Vanessa is coming tomorrow. Are you really going to make me wait twenty-four hours?"

"Wait for what?"

"You're not as sly as you think. I've seen you with women you were *ahem* before. It's always obvious."

It is?

"You look at them like you're picturing them naked. Which would be gross if I didn't know you were already getting naked."

"Who was this?"

"Did you already forget their names?" She shakes her head *sad*.

"I want to hear your observations."

"Okay, but if I'm right, you tell me about Vanessa…"

"If you're right."

She holds out her hand.

We shake.

Opal taps her chin with her finger, thinking carefully. "The last time, we were at some event. My shoes were killing me. Those silver heels. I picked them because my dress was short and I wanted to show them off. And this woman came up to us to say hello, as if she was a colleague. But the way she looked at me was five-alarm jealousy. She thought I was your date."

"You were my date."

"You know what I mean. She thought we were… it's gross. I can't even say it." She sticks her tongue out *yuck*. "She had this non-nonsense look to her. A slick-straight ponytail, a navy suit, loafers. She was the event planner or something. Katy. Katrina. Kathleen. Something with a K."

Accurate.

Opal first-pumps. "I knew it. Katy, right?"

"Katy."

"How long were you two…"

"Friends with benefits."

"Is that what you called it?"

"Yes." It's not entirely accurate. We weren't really friends. But I don't want to explain that to my sister. "Six months."

"A long time. What happened?"

"She met someone."

"Ooh. That's gotta hurt."

"No."

"Really?" Curiosity spreads over her expression. "I know Liam loves to go off on you being an unfeeling robot."

"An alien from another planet studying humans."

"Yeah, whatever. But he's just being an asshole. I know better. You have feelings. You just hide them behind that ten ton safe." She motions to my expression. "That. The poker face. You're good, but not as good as you think." She draws a circle around my face. "Is it about Vanessa?"

Maybe. I try to stay present, especially with my family. "Katy invited me to her wedding."

"When?"

"A few months ago," I say.

"You didn't take me?" She folds her arms. "You know I love weddings!"

"It was twenty-one plus."

"Okay, fine. It was twenty-one plus. What happened?"

"She thanked me for teaching her what love wasn't."

"Shit, really?"

I nod.

"That's a lot."

"It was fair. I enjoyed our time together, but it wasn't romantic. I didn't realize it then, but she was trying. Even though I'd been clear about the terms. She was trying to find more, and I wasn't interested."

"And you were sad about that?"

"Surprised, but not sad."

"You still look… something. Is it about Vanessa?"

Maybe it is.

"She'll be there tomorrow. That's big. Coming to dinner with the family. With Liam."

"Preston, Harrison, and Lee are coming too."

"Not to dinner."

True.

"You must like her to subject her to Liam. Or hate her. One of them."

"I like her."

She squeals in that teenage girl way. "What about Katy's wedding? Did you take her?"

"No. We weren't seeing each other yet."

"You're seeing her?"

"That's the easiest way of putting it."

"Dating?"

"No."

"Sex?"

"Yes, sex."

"So it's a recent start." She motions to the marks on my neck. "It must be recent. Or she recently let loose. Or you recently stopped trying to hide it."

I take a long sip. Try my best shrug.

It's not good. I don't have Liam's casual ability to not care.

Mine is sterner. As Vanessa says, above it all. A tone I don't like to take with my sister.

"Yeah, recent," she says. "How recent?"

"My sex life isn't your business."

"Uh-huh. You, Bri, and Danielle try to help me with masturbation tools. Like your generation invented the practice. If the three of you can take turns offering to buy me vibrators or find me classy videos, where I can trust all the performers are working consensually—"

"Danielle?"

She nods *of course.* "I swear. She probably thinks I'm on fire when I look at her pictures. They're hot, yes, but she's my brother's fiancée. It's weird."

"It is."

"You look at her pictures?"

"I looked into her." At the same time Adam did. Because the man who tried to destroy our family was obsessed with her. That's why Adam found her. That's why he convinced her to marry him.

I'm not sure if it was charm, money, love, some combination of the three.

They're happy.

He's functioning.

Maybe I should have more concern for her welfare. Maybe I should be more skeptical.

I can't.

I need my brother to be okay.

I'm willing to do whatever it takes to make sure he's okay.

"Like hiring a private eye?" she asks. "Or just using your secret software?"

"Our software is cyber security. It's the opposite."

"Yeah, but you work with that company that digs up information all the time. You're natural allies. The harder they work, the more you can charge. And the better you do, the more they can charge."

"Shrewd."

"I am a Pierce."

"You really are."

She smiles, won over for a moment. Then she shakes her head. Remembers her mission. "Did you hire a PI?"

"I did."

"How did Adam feel about that?"

"I didn't ask."

"Overprotective with him too?"

"It was necessary."

She raises a brow *was it?* "I guess… he was alone a long time. He wasn't doing well. It would be easy for someone to take advantage… but more likely he'd be taking advantage of her."

Maybe, but—"I'm trying to protect him. Not her."

"That's kinda fucked up."

"I didn't know her."

"Now that you do?"

"Of course," I say. "She's family. I'll do anything to protect her."

"Really? Bri too?"

I nod.

"I should warn them."

"Hey."

"What? I should. Are you going to investigate every one of their friends and coworkers too?"

"Only drastic changes."

"And with Vanessa? Did you investigate her?"

"It's not serious."

"She's having dinner with the family."

"She's a family friend."

"Mm-hmm." She shakes her head *sell that story to someone who buys it.* "You like her."

"I do."

"More than you liked Katy. Or the woman before that."

"I've known her a long time."

"And liked her a long time. That's what Liam says. He says she's been the number one spot in your spank bank since you hit puberty."

That sounds like Liam. "I had a crush on her in school."

"Simon with a crush… I wish I could see that. It's hard to imagine. Or maybe I'm seeing it now. Quick, think about her."

"Not in front of you."

"Are you excited to see her tomorrow? At the opera?"

"Not the way you mean."

"Oh my god, you are! You totally like her. Get a ring, pronto. You'll never do better."

I won't. She's right there.

"Why don't you talk about it with me?"

"I don't talk."

"You do." She folds her arms. "You did, with Bash. I know it's different now, but… do you really think this is what he'd want? For you to hold on to everything, all the time?"

No. Of course not.

"He was always trying to draw out your romantic impulses. Even when he talked about sex. He made the dirtiest things sound romantic."

"Should I be concerned?"

"So you do remember."

"He had a way of speaking."

"Seriously. He could be in one of these." She pulls a paperback book from her backpack. A romance with a swirling sheet on the cover. Something illicit.

The really dirty books have the sleekest covers.

Rings, ties, lace, silk sheets, feathers, heels.

"But more vanilla." She catches my stare. Drops the book in her backpack. "No shame."

"Should I be concerned now?"

"What do you always say? Don't be ashamed of your desires? Well, I'm not. So I'm sure you support me in wanting to do two guys at once."

Fuck.

"There's this cute guy in my art class who's really close with his friend. They're always talking about it…"

She's trying to kill me.

"Oh my god, your face." She laughs. "See, it's not that bad. We're not talking about whether or not I'm going to plan a threesome—"

"Are you?"

"Not right now, but—"

"Opal."

She doubles over laughing. "Oh my god. You're too easy."

I am. She knows how to push my buttons.

The server interrupts with our food. He looks at us funny. Shrugs *weird rich white people* and leaves.

"We don't need to talk about whether or not you and Vanessa are planning threesomes." She stirs hot sauce into her already hot noodles. "We don't need to talk about anything specific. But we should talk about it. What it means."

"It's just sex."

"That's not true."

She scoops noodles to her mouth. Chews. Swallows. Groans. "Oh my god, this is so good." She motions to her plate. "Try it."

"I know what that means."

"What?" She plays dumb.

"It's too spicy for anyone but you."

"You can handle it."

I can't, but this is part of our routine too. I take a bite of her noodles, bring them to my lips.

Fuck.

Already, my tongue is on fire.

I push through it, but it's hotter with every bite.

There.

I manage to swallow.

"Good, right?" she asks.

Fuck, it's hot. The Thai iced tea helps. Not enough to soothe my tongue, but enough I can talk. "You're super-human."

"Thanks." She takes another bite. Shrugs at the spice level. "It's more than sex."

"We're back to that?"

"We never left." She sips her tea. Sighs with pleasure. "What would you say to Bash?"

"If he was here, I'd have more pressing questions."

"If he hadn't… if things were different."

I wish he were here. Everything would be easier. Even this.

"I'm not Bash. I know. I'm younger, less experienced." She clears her throat *way less experienced.* "And I'm a woman." She doesn't add *I know that's it, but I won't call you on it,* but we both know it's there. "But I can be romantic too." She taps her chin, trying to recall our late brother. "Were you with her last night?"

"I was."

She squeals in a very Opal way. But when she smiles—

That's Bash's smile.

Warm, affectionate, wanting the entire world as in love with love as he is.

"You spent the night with her," she says. "Actually spent the entire night. What was that like? Being in her bed? Holding her? Having this vision of a life you could have together?"

"Intense."

She looks at me, that Bash mix of love is serious business, and love is joy. "You were texting her. You didn't wipe off her lipstick. You didn't cover her marks. And now, she's coming to the opera with us. To dinner. Two days after you spent the night with her. That means something." She takes another bite. Then she channels Bash perfectly. "You don't have to admit it to me. But you should admit it to yourself. You deserve to be happy, Simon. Why are you always fighting that?"

———

171

WITH EVERY BITE, MY THOUGHTS SCATTER. OPAL IS GOOD AT channeling Bash.

Too good.

It hurts. Calling on those memories of him. Feeling his presence here. Seeing him in her.

It's a necessary pain.

But a pain still.

Eventually, Opal declares me madly in love with Vanessa, moves on to other concerns.

The freshness of the mango in her mango sticky rice.

The warm air on our walk home.

Whether we should watch an old show or a new one. The mix of sentimentality, and above it all, cleverness makes *Dawson's Creek* the perfect Simon watch, apparently.

But it's not the same without the original theme song. And what's she going to do? Buy a DVD?

She pulls the theme up on YouTube to start the episode. Watches from the beginning. Stops me from lecturing her about the horror of sixteen-year-old Pacey pursuing his thirty-something high school teacher.

The show frames it as him pursuing her.

Him, wearing her down.

Fucked up on every level.

This show was on when I was Opal's age. No, younger.

I didn't watch. We didn't have a TV growing up.

But my classmates did.

Did Vanessa watch?

Did she think anything of it?

Or was she more fixated on the main character's obsession with sex?

I don't usually think of the past. Better to move forward. To build a future.

But, as we finish the second episode, I think of Vanessa. The girl I knew in high school.

Activities kept her busy. Track, mock trial, debate team. She aced her classes. She studied a lot.

And her family was, is, prominent. She made a lot of appearances. Gained a lot of press as a Cinderella story. Her mother and her coming from nothing, meeting the biggest trial lawyer on the East Coast, marrying into this family of money and esteem—

Her dad mostly fights big corporations who abuse their power.

He believes in fairness and justice.

She takes after him.

She's a part of this world now. She belongs in it. Knows how to work it.

But does she feel that?

Or does she still feel out of place?

When the episode ends, Opal gets ready for bed, wishes me good night.

I try to stay busy with work, but my thoughts keep going to Vanessa.

After an hour, I give up on resisting her. I slip into my room, lock my door, pick up our conversation from earlier.

Simon: Are you alone?

Chapter Nineteen

VANESSA

My cell blinks with a notification.

It's there, on the end table, three feet away.

Usually, I keep it in the living room—that's the only way to stop myself from working in bed. But I don't want to wake my guests.

They're asleep in the main room. Celine has been asleep all night.

She roused, briefly, when I got home, but only for long enough to tend to her son, say hello, thank me for the hospitality.

He's like her. Quiet.

I haven't heard him cry once.

Maybe he's past that age. Or maybe that's what happens in a house with abuse.

He learns not to express his needs.

Can a child that young learn?

I try to push the thought aside. They're safe. She feels comfortable enough she's sleeping soundly. Right now, that's what matters.

The injustices in the world are infinite.

I can't solve those.

But I can help her and her son escape her husband.

I use the bathroom, wash up, brush my teeth one more time for good measure. Then I slip into my room, and I give in to the temptation of my cell.

Simon.

Simon: Are you alone?

Vanessa: It's late.

Simon: It is.

Vanessa: You made me wait.

Simon: I did.

Because he was busy?

Or because he's trying to make me wait?

No. He wanted to see me today. I said no.

He wants to be here.

In my bed.

Maybe in my life too.

I can handle the former. The latter?

I have too many other things on my mind. I can't begin to contemplate that.

But this—

The shiny, sexy break from my life—

I need this.

Vanessa: I'm alone. In my bedroom. You?

Simon: Same.

Vanessa: I've never seen your bedroom.

Simon: You'd hate it.

Vanessa: I would?

Simon: This apartment belonged to my father.

Vanessa: Didn't you live at the mansion?

Simon: Yes, but he stayed here when he had business in the city. Or "business."

Vanessa: Affairs?

Simon: He was loyal to our mother. But they were young when she

176

passed. He had a long time to secretly sleep with other women.

Vanessa: Now Opal lives in one of those rooms?

Simon: I'm in the master.

Vanessa: Oh, he only slept with women in the master bedroom?

Simon: Is that really what you want to talk about?

Right.

Simon isn't his father. I shouldn't compare them.

If someone compared me to my biological father—

I'd never forgive them.

Vanessa: I get distracted by the possibility of men abusing their power.

Simon: You do.

Vanessa: Even calling the bedroom the master. There's a natural power imbalance.

Simon: Colonialist language.

Vanessa: Right.

He's aware of this concept?

Simon: You sponsored a talk last year. I listened.

Vanessa: Is this your foreplay now?

Simon: Is it working?

Vanessa: Absolutely.

Simon: What should I call the bedroom?

A place I want to fuck him.

Vanessa: Call it your bedroom. There's not a good alternative.

Simon: You're right. It belonged to my father once. I have a new bed. New frame, new mattress, new sheets, but that won't erase the history.

Vanessa: I don't want to talk about your father.

Simon: Me either.

Vanessa: What does it look like?

Simon: Hardwood floors. White walls. Exposed brick on one side. Lattice windows. Three long, rectangular ones.

Vanessa: Sounds modern.

Simon: I painted.

Vanessa: Over?

Simon: A hideous wallpaper. It belonged at Versailles.

Vanessa: You would know.

Simon: You studied in France.

Vanessa: You grew up in a palace.

Simon: Wait until you see the upstairs.

Vanessa: Are you inviting me to your room?

Simon: I am.

Vanessa: When?

Simon: Soon.

Vanessa: Okay. Soon.

After I figure out how to help the woman sleeping on my couch.

But I'm not worrying any more tonight.

I'm sinking into my shiny distraction.

Simon Pierce's teenage room.

How many times did I imagine myself there?

Way too many.

Simon: The apartment isn't as massive as the Pierce mansion, but it's big. The bedroom is the size of a hotel ballroom. It's all open space. Closet. Dresser. Bed. Mirror.

Vanessa: Mirror?

Simon: I put in a new one. For you.

Fuck.

Vanessa: Show me.

A moment later, my phone buzzes with a picture message. Simon, standing in front of the four-poster bed in midnight blue pajamas.

His shirt is open.

His chiseled torso is on display.

And there, above his hip, a tattoo. Black letters in a curving script.

Something in Latin.

Why didn't I notice before?

Vanessa: What's it say?

Simon: Flectere si nequeo superos, acheronta movebo.

Vanessa: In English?

Simon: If I can't move heaven, I'll raise hell.

Vanessa: That suits you.

Simon: Is that a compliment?

Vanessa: You used it to permanently mark your body.

That quote is pure Simon, but actually getting a tattoo? That's surprising.

Vanessa: Don't you see it that way?

Simon: I do.

Vanessa: I can't imagine you with a tattoo.

Simon: You've seen it.

Vanessa: I was otherwise occupied.

Simon: Were you?

Vanessa: You know I was.

Simon: I got it with Bash. When we were kids. He was like you. He teased me about being the Prince of Darkness.

Vanessa: He used those words?

Simon: Similar.

Vanessa: He didn't seem combative.

Simon: He meant it with love.

Vanessa: You miss him?

Simon: Of course.

Vanessa: You talked to him? Confided in him?

Simon: I did.

Vanessa: Do you have anyone now?

Simon: Opal tries, but she's young. She doesn't have the perspective, and I don't want to be the person who convinces her the world is a cold, hard place.

Vanessa: Is that really how you see it?

Simon: Don't tell me you think otherwise.

No. The world is a cold, hard place.

But it's warm and soft sometimes too.

Now.

Here.

Vanessa: There's good and bad. But I understand the focus on the ugly parts. With what happened to your brother.

It's been a year now, a little longer maybe.

But how can Simon ever truly get over the loss of his brother?

If I lost Lee…

I might move on, but I'd always carry that wound. I'd always have that empty space in my heart.

Vanessa: Will you let me offer condolences this time?

Simon: Yes.

Vanessa: I am sorry. If I lost Lee… I don't know how I'd function.

Simon: You would. It's the only choice you have.

Is that really how he felt?

Simon: Your family needs you. Your work needs you. The world needs you. There isn't time to stop and fall apart.

Vanessa: Do you want to fall apart?

He doesn't reply.

I wait another minute.

Still no reply.

Is he busy? Or thinking?

Vanessa: I do sometimes. I want to be somewhere safe, where that feels possible. Where I can let go, stop trying to hold myself together, trust someone to catch me, to help me put myself back together.

Simon: Do you trust anyone?

Vanessa: I haven't, before.

Do I now?

No, I still don't know Simon well. But I want to know him. I want to climb into his bed and melt into his arms.

It's not the same.

But it's something.

Vanessa: I have a hard time trusting people. It's been… interesting with you. I trust you with my body. It might not sound like much, but it is.

Simon: That means a lot.

Vanessa: Really?

Simon: *Yes.*

Vanessa: *Is this where we bring it back to sex?*

Simon: *If that's what you want.*

Vanessa: *It's not what you want?*

Simon: *I want to go to your place and bury my head between your legs.*

Fuck.

Simon: *I want to have you every way I can, Vanessa. But I enjoy talking to you too.*

Vanessa: *I enjoy talking to you too.*

Simon: *I don't hear that often.*

Vanessa: *You're a good listener. And a good conversationalist. You just hide it.*

Simon: *Most people don't interest me.*

Vanessa: *I'm special?*

Simon: *Extremely.*

Vanessa: *Are you still standing at the mirror?*

Simon: *In my armchair.*

Vanessa: *You have an armchair?*

Simon: *Sometimes, I sit in my suit and drink whiskey.*

He's teasing me.

It used to be annoying.

Now?

It's fucking intoxicating.

Vanessa: *Now?*

Simon: *It's too late.*

Vanessa: *Show me.*

Simon: *It's your turn.*

Okay. It's my turn. I'm pushing it back to sex.

Because I want him.

Because this is our arrangement.

Not because I'm scared of falling apart in his arms.

Or telling him my secrets.

Because I want to send a picture that drives him out of his fucking mind.

The lights in the apartment are off, but I don't need them. I have the soft blue glow of the city.

I draw the blinds. Position myself in front of the window. Put my camera in selfie mode.

There it is, my reflection. No makeup. Hair in natural curls over my cheeks. Comfortable cotton tank hanging low over my chest.

It's not sexy. Not the way his silk pajamas and four-poster bed are.

But it's me. My room. My life.

I snap a picture, from the nose down, send it to Simon.

He replies a moment later.

Simon: You look gorgeous.

Vanessa: Thank you.

Simon: Take off the shorts.

Vanessa: It's your turn.

He replies a moment later, back at the mirror, now clad only in his boxers.

Fuck, Simon Pierce in boxers.

The picture is dark and grainy. A stranger wouldn't recognize him.

But I do. The posture. The broad shoulders. The sculpted v-shape of his torso.

And those muscular thighs—

Fuck.

I don't reply with words. I don't have them.

I slip my shorts off my hips. Snap another picture from the nose down.

Simon: Fuck, I love your thighs. I want to die between them.

My cheeks flush.

My chest too.

I can see the need in his eyes. I can hear his low, deep groan.

I need that.

I need more.

I toss my tank top aside. Turn to the camera.

Click.

For once, I don't think about my not quite flat stomach or stretch marks. I think about the desire in his eyes.

And I send him a picture of my breasts.

He replies immediately.

Simon: Fuck.

Then a picture message.

Him, at the mirror, from his chest to his thighs.

No more boxers.

His hand wrapped around his hard, thick cock.

Fuck.

I slip my hand into my panties. Take another picture.

Send it.

This is dangerous and foolish, and I don't care.

It feels good.

For once, I want to feel good.

I slip into my bed, push my panties to my ankles, take one more shot—of the underwear falling off my feet—and send it.

My eyes flutter closed.

I picture him here, in bed with me, tossing my phone aside, diving between my legs, licking me until I'm groaning his name.

In his bedroom, in some massive leather armchair, pulling me into his lap, sucking on my nipples as he plays with my clit.

Driving down on him again and again.

The tension in my sex winds tighter and tighter.

So tight I can barely take it.

I come fast. With intense pulses.

I have to put my hand over my mouth so I don't wake my guest.

Pleasure spills through my body.

I sink into the bed.

Soft and spent.

After I come back to my senses, I text him.

Vanessa: Perfect.
Simon: Better.
Vanessa: I'll see you tomorrow.
Simon: Sweet dreams.

I fall asleep fast.

Wake rested.

And naked.

With my guest awake in my kitchen, singing to herself, waiting to find me in sweaty, spent, post-orgasmic bliss.

Shit.

Chapter Twenty

VANESSA

I slip into my clothes, clean up in the bathroom, attempt a casual smile. Something that says *I didn't spend the night masturbating with my fuck buddy, and I'm glad you're here, but I'm still on top of the whole keeping you safe thing.*

Celine smiles as I step into the main room. It's friendly but awkward. She's trying as hard as I am.

She motions to the kettle on the stovetop. The mug in her hands. "I hope you don't mind."

"No. Help yourself."

"The water is still warm." She rises from her spot at the kitchen table. "Can I pour you a cup?"

I'm the host. I should fix her something. But I should be gracious too. "Thank you."

"You like it with milk?" she asks.

"Strong, creamy, and sweet."

"It's best that way."

"It is."

She moves into the kitchen nook, pulls two tea bags from the box, places them in a mug, pours hot water over them. She's already comfortable in the kitchen. Graceful. The way Lee moves.

"Are you a dancer?" I ask.

"How did you know?"

"My sister did ballet for years."

She presses her hand to her chest. "I thought you might say my feet." She raises her leg with perfect control. "Dancer's feet."

"My sister has them too." The crooked toes, bunions, bone spurs. "She had bruises on her feet until she was sixteen."

"She stopped?"

"An injury," I say. "She was devastated."

"People who don't dance think of ballerinas as soft, gentle, beautiful. We are. On stage. But the practice is brutal. It doesn't sculpt you into a long, lithe beauty. It destroys your body."

"How long did you dance?"

"I was in a company for a few years. Until I met my husband."

He wanted a gentle, beautiful dancer.

Or maybe he knew the truth. Knew she could take a beating without complaint.

"Did you miss it?" I ask.

"Yes. I still do. There's something about the control. The discipline. It's calming."

I know exactly what she means. "It can be."

She checks the tea again, deems it ready, pours milk, sweetens with a spoonful of honey. "Try this." She drops it on the table. "Can I make you something? Breakfast? It's the least I can do."

"I can."

"No. Please. Allow me."

I need to accept her offer. "That would be great. Thanks."

She nods and finds the eggs in the fridge.

"Did you eat last night?" I ask.

"A pesto dish," she says. "It was fantastic."

Fantastic is overselling it. The meal service I use is good, but the meals are mass-produced and delivered frozen. Still, I take the compliment. With a smile.

"My husband introduced me to pesto. He loved the finer things… He laughed then, me thinking pesto was the picture of refined dining."

"I did too," I say. "I felt grown-up the first time I ordered pesto for myself."

"The basil and pine nuts." She smiles. "Good in eggs."

"I don't think I have any."

"Salt and pepper is plenty."

"You like simple?"

"I do."

Like Simon.

"Hmm." She makes the same noise Lee does when I'm lost in my head. Only lower. Softer. "You're glowing."

"I am."

"Your friend?"

"He enjoys simplicity."

"A woman in silk?"

My cheeks flush. "I couldn't believe it when he ordered drunken noodles. It didn't sound like him."

"Green curry is more refined."

"Is it?"

She nods. "Red is obvious. Green is subtle."

"I'll keep that in mind."

She smiles. "My husband loved to try new cuisines. Always the best. Always the most unique dish. Even green curry… that would be too obvious for him. But he would laugh if I ordered it." She pauses. Takes a deep breath. Composes herself. "I guess you've heard it all before? The charm. The explosive temper. The desperate apologies. Chocolates, flowers, promises."

"A lot of people stay."

"It wasn't just that I was scared. I loved him. And he loved me. I believed him when he told me he was sorry. He did mean it. He just… I guess you've heard that before too?"

"It's a familiar pattern."

"He was sweet most of the time. Until I miscarried…" She studies her mug of tea. "He was different after that. He blamed me. No, deep down, he knew it was him."

For a few minutes, she's quiet, focusing on cooking breakfast.

I take a seat at the dining table. Try to treat the morning as if it's any other.

I help bring everything to the table. Sit across from her. Raise my mug to say cheers.

She offers that same soft smile. The *this is strange, but I'm making the best of it* smile. Then she picks up her fork, motions *enjoy*, and eats with dainty bites.

I spread orange marmalade on my toast. Let the sweet citrus melt on my tongue.

It tastes better than usual.

Is it the circumstances? The act of actually sitting down to eat? Or is it a sign I'm actually recovering?

In touch with my senses.

Accepting pleasure.

"How is it?" she asks.

"Amazing. Thank you."

"It's the least I can do."

I don't know what to say to that, so I smile and nod and focus on the pepper in my eggs.

We drift back into awkward silence.

Then the baby cries. It's not the high-pitched scream I expect. It's quiet. A little more than a coo.

She rises immediately. Lifts him from his bed. Brings him to the bathroom.

A few minutes later, she returns, lays him in his crib, watches him fall asleep.

She goes to the sink and washes her hands again. "He's quiet. Somehow, he learned he had to be."

"I'm sorry," I say.

"Don't be. I'm here. He'll be okay. He'll learn it's okay to cry or scream or laugh. He'll take after his father."

"Oh?"

"Seb's father. The man I was… seeing."

"It's none of my business."

"Do you mind if we talk about it?"

No. Girl talk is easier territory. "No, go ahead. The man who turned your life to technicolor?"

She smiles. "For a long time, I was faithful. I buried myself in my charity work. I convinced my husband it was necessary for appearances. But I was lonely. I found men who were happy with a physical arrangement. Then I met him at a gallery one night. I was looking for new art, trying to find something beautiful. My husband loved to brag about my taste. How I brightened the space. That was the only way to describe Seb's father. He brightened every room."

She's a woman in love.

Still in love, even though he's gone.

That must hurt somewhere deep.

"You know those spring days when it suddenly pours rain?" she asks.

"I do."

"The sky turns dark and grey. Then, as fast as it started, it stops. The clouds part for the blue sky. The sun shines. That was him. He was the sun and I didn't even realize I was soaking wet until I met him." She laughs softly. "I didn't mean… but that was true too. I didn't know what I was missing there."

"It happens."

She nods. "He was everything. Handsome. Radiant. And charming, but not in a witty or sarcastic way. Not removed. Honest, vulnerable, romantic."

It's a beautiful image.

Almost the way Simon describes his brother.

He uses "romantic" because he sees himself as a realist.

Is that why she uses it?

Or is it something else?

The warmth he brought to a cold, hard world.

What was she like before she met her husband? Was she like Simon and me?

Or like the man who won her heart?

She continues, "he agreed to my terms to keep things physical, even when he fell in love with me. He didn't ask me to reciprocate. He didn't ask me to leave my husband. He let me know he wanted that. He wanted to run away with me. But if he couldn't have that... he said he'd rather have me an hour a week than not have me at all."

"Did you believe him?"

"Not at first. Eventually... it didn't matter. I fell in love with him too. One day, I woke up, and I saw it. The possibility of a life filled with love. I believed I deserved it. I was ready to fight for it... Then he..."

"I'm sorry."

She nods. "I was grief struck for a long time. I lost that strength. But when Seb was born, I found it again. I owe him that much. Both of them."

"Leaving is the hardest part."

"Is it really?"

And not going back.

She seems sure, but I've seen plenty of determined people return.

Then it gets worse and worse. Until someone is dead.

But I'm not here to scare her. I'm here to keep her calm and comfortable until we find a safer place.

It's not my skill set. I run numbers. I charm donors. I schedule meetings.

Regina is good at this.

But Regina isn't here. I am.

"Leaving and sticking with it," I say.

She nods. "Listen to me… all dread all the time. Tell me about your friend."

"My friend?"

"The one you left in a cocktail dress."

"He's a friend, that's all."

"Really? You came home at seven for a friend?"

"It's physical. Like your previous arrangements."

"Is that how you want it?"

It was. But now? I'm not sure. "It makes sense. We both work demanding jobs. And he's all wrong for me."

"In what ways?"

He's a spoiled rich boy turned stuck-up suit. That's my usual line.

And it's true in some ways.

Simon did grow up with a silver spoon. And he did grow into a stuck-up suit.

Only he's not stuck-up. And he looks as sexy as fuck in his suit.

"We want different things," I say.

"What do you want?"

"To save the world. He teases me about that."

"What does he want?"

"Money."

"That's all he wants? Money?"

"You wouldn't believe that?" I ask.

"Plenty of men only want money. But I can't imagine you with one."

"You barely know me."

"I could tell the minute I met you," she says. "Years ago. I could tell you're the kind of person who cares."

I am. I can't object.

"You wouldn't be with someone unless they cared too. Even for sex. He must care about something."

He does. "His family. His brothers. His sister. A future wife and kids."

"Is that what you want too?"

In theory. If I can find someone I trust. If I can hear the word "wife" without seeing my mom covering her bruises. "Only if I find the right person."

"And he's not the right person?"

Simon wouldn't hurt me. I know that.

Why?

I'm not sure. Because I've known him since he was fourteen, I guess. Because I've never seen a hint of anger in his posture.

Or is it because I want to believe it?

He's handsome, skilled, caring.

A gentle lover.

But plenty of gentle men are cable of roughness.

That doesn't necessarily mean anything.

"You like him?" she asks.

"I do." But I'm scared.

She can tell, but she doesn't call me on it. "Am I, uh, what do they say? Cock-blocking you?"

"Maybe a little, but it's good. He's jealous."

"Oh?"

"I told him a friend from school is staying with me. From my MBA program."

"A man?"

"I didn't specify."

"But he assumed."

I nod.

"Do you like him jealous?"

"Certain things." As long as it's that light tug. And not possession. Or rage. Or anything that reminds me of my biological father.

"There's an idea of jealousy as romantic," she says. "I felt it with him, Seb's father. This jealousy of the other women in his life. The people who could love him freely. But we know the ugly side of that, don't we?"

"We do."

"Do you see that in him?"

"No," I say.

"But it could be there," she says. "You never know if it's there."

I swallow hard.

"It's hard to trust sometimes."

It is.

"Are you jealous? Of the women in his life?"

"Not usually."

"But you have been?"

"A few times."

"Was it ugly?"

"No." Not the way she means. Maybe he's the same.

No, he is.

There's no reason to doubt Simon. No good one.

Only the fucked-up shit in my head.

"It's not serious," I say, but neither one of us believes it.

"You trust him?"

"Yes."

"You can invite him here."

There's not enough space. And I don't want to lose the line separating work and life. It's thin enough as it is. Even without Celine in my apartment. "He can wait a few days."

"Spend the night there?"

"Maybe. My head of security wants me to stick with my normal routine as much as possible."

"Do you normally meet your friend?"

"No. But he thinks it would be better to err on the side of

leaving the apartment. So it doesn't seem I'm going out of my way to return."

She nods.

"Friday out. Saturday gala. Sunday brunch."

"Is that your normal week?"

"Most of my job is asking for money."

"I was on the board of a nonprofit," she says.

"Right. You know. Sorry."

"Don't be."

"My mom ran an art's charity too. My mom would love you, actually."

And my dad has the best security money can buy. It's necessary, after years of going after corporations with deep pockets.

But what would I say?

Hey, Mom, hey, Daddy, can I drop a survivor off at your door? Did I mention she has a baby in tow?

Fuck, maybe I can. If I don't come up with a better plan.

"If she raised you, I'm sure she's a wonderful woman," she says.

"I'll pass on the compliment." I stand. Find my phone. "I should get dressed."

She nods *of course.*

"Will you be okay alone?"

"I won't be alone."

"You and Seb?"

"Yes. We'll appreciate the quiet."

"I'll text before I head home." I motion to the burner on the table. "The code. So you know to expect someone."

"Or if you're staying at your friend's place?"

"No." I bite my lip. "Only when I'm on my way home."

She smiles. "Maybe at eight a.m. Or sometime Sunday? Or Monday evening?"

"Maybe."

"Do me a favor, Vanessa?"

"Yes?"

"Don't use me as an excuse. If you want to go home with your friend, do it."

————

I LEAVE MY PLACE LATE, HEAD STRAIGHT TO LUNCH WITH A donor, smile as she talks about her tech company changing the world.

My thoughts drift to Simon, sure, but I pull them back. All afternoon, I work.

Until my assistant, Tammy, knocks. She holds up a dry cleaning bag and a pair of designer heels. "Half an hour to deadline."

"Thanks."

"There's a limo downstairs. Talk about all out." She mentions the CEO of a company sponsoring a gala tonight. "He's romancing you."

"He's not."

"Are you kidding? He practically stuffs checks between your tits."

"He's not the only guy who ogles."

"Do you think the universe appreciates the irony?" She sets the clothes on a hanger. Does away with a bag. "You're going to knock 'em dead, at—" She checks the calendar on her phone. "Oh."

I play dumb.

"Dinner with Pierce. Really?" she raises a brow. "Which Pierce?"

"It's for Lee. Her father-in-law is hosting."

"Interesting how it says 'Pierce.' And not 'Preston Charles.'"

"The reservations are—"

"You're fucking him."

I say nothing.

"Holy shit. Simon Pierce? Really. He's the devil." She doesn't wait for a response. She barrels forward. "A handsome devil though. And that ego… does he back it up?"

I clear my throat.

"You really think I'm asking about his dick?"

That's a good point. "He's precise, controlled, and goal-oriented in everything else he does. What do you think?"

"Goal-oriented. That's hot."

"It is hot."

She laughs. "Good for you, Vee. You deserve it."

"Thanks." I think.

"You can invite him back home again Tuesday." She winks. "If your guest is ready to transfer to another secure location."

"If she wants to go all in?"

"A few more days," she says. "But we can always rush it."

"Does she?"

"She has a sister."

"Can you imagine?" she asks.

I can't. Saying goodbye to Lee forever, even if it was the only way to stay safe, keep her safe, keep her hypothetical child safe.

That would kill me.

"I want to find out what we're dealing with," I say. "If her husband has that kind of reach." Abusers are dangerous, no matter how much money they have. Especially when someone is leaving. But if her husband was the type to keep her around with apologies and charm—

He might chase her across the country. In his mind, he'll do it with good intentions. He'll go to apologize and beg for forgiveness.

That's still dangerous. He still might hurt her if she says no.

But that's a crime of passion. Anger in the moment.

If he had her lover killed?

That's a totally different ballgame.

Especially with a kid in the picture. A kid who isn't his.

"No way, Nancy Drew. That will end poorly," she says.

"We know people to ask," I say.

"I know people. I will ask. But it's not your decision, Vee."

Her husband isn't my father.

This isn't about me. Or my baggage. Or my choices.

It's about her and what she wants.

This is why I don't work with survivors.

I'm not objective.

"You're right," I say. "But see what you can find. For my own peace of mind."

"If you promise to talk to Regina."

"I will."

She shakes her head, not buying it, but she doesn't call me on it. "Now go. Get laid. Forget about saving the world for the weekend. Bring back details Monday."

"In your dreams."

"My dreams don't include your sex life. They include Scarlet Johansen in her *Black Widow* costume."

"You're verging on fetish."

"I like redheads. Sue me."

"You just called me Nancy Drew."

She laughs. "You got me. If you go ginger, I won't be able to control myself."

"I don't think you're teasing."

"Did I say I was?" She blows me a kiss and leaves with a smile.

Easy.

Normal.

Like I don't have a woman and her son spending the weekend in my apartment.

Of all the weird shit I do in this job—

This really is a first.

I try to take Tammy's advice. To push thoughts of Celine and Seb aside. To enjoy my weekend for once.

I change into my dress, fix my hair and makeup, slip into my shoes.

With every step, I let the week fall away.

I let my thoughts drift to Simon.

By the time I step into the restaurant—a secluded place a few blocks from the theater—my mind is in the gutter.

And it's obvious.

Because everyone here—Simon, his kid sister, both his brothers, and both their girlfriends—are staring at me like they know I'm picturing Simon naked.

Chapter Twenty-One

SIMON

"**V**anessa Moyer, as I live and breathe." Liam offers the first handshake. "You look even more gorgeous than the last time I saw you."

"Thanks." She shakes. Looks to his girlfriend with a friendly smile.

"Briar West," she offers. "I've heard a lot about you."

Vanessa shoots me a *what does that mean* look, but she holds her poker face. "How is it, living with Liam?"

"Exactly as difficult as you'd imagine." Briar brushes a purple hair behind her ear.

Liam's assistant turned girlfriend wears her rebellion on her sleeve. Short purple hair, punk rock makeup, visible tattoos, all black attire.

He hides his. Not just the tattoos—he thinks I don't know about most of them. The lack of desire to fit into the world our father wanted him to join.

He didn't just revel in his pre-engagement nickname. He's the one who dubbed himself the Playboy Prince.

"You mean even more amazing than anyone could imagine," Liam says.

"Uh, no," she says.

"And so many orgasms I can barely walk straight," he says.

"Why would orgasms make it hard to walk?" she asks.

"Because he's trying to sneak in a mention of his girth," Danielle says.

"Me? Never? Why would I want everyone to know I'm locked and loaded?" Liam asks. "It's enough I'm handsome, brilliant—"

"Brilliant?" Briar asks.

"Handsome, charming?" he counters.

She nods *yes*.

"Handsome, charming, successful. A big dick on top of it all… they'll stop admiring me and start feeling jealous," he says.

"What a cursed life you lead," Briar says.

"It's hard, yeah," he says. "And speaking of hard—"

Briar shakes her head *how is he saying this* even as she smiles *and I love how ridiculous he is*.

He is ridiculous. He's been ridiculous for a long time.

But his level of absurdity is directly proportional to his audience. A dinner for seven?

We'll be lucky if we manage to go two minutes without hearing about his sex life.

Danielle shakes her head *this again*. She smiles *and I like it* too, but not with the same enthusiasm Briar does.

It's clear her feelings are platonic.

"My brother is exactly like Liam," Danielle says. "The only way to stop him is to ignore him."

Liam mimes being stabbed in the gut.

Danielle does as she suggests and ignores the gesture. "Danielle Bellamy. It's nice to meet you." She offers Vanessa her hand.

Vanessa shakes. "The photographer?"

"You've seen me naked then?" Danielle laughs.

"Your work is beautiful," she says. "You helped Simon decorate the room?"

Danielle turns to me and raises a brow.

"She did," I say.

"I did," she agrees. "He picked the roses from memory. Were they right?"

"Perfect," Vanessa says.

"Hold up." Liam moves on to his new method of attack. "Simon asked you to decorate his fuck room?"

"He didn't say what he was using the room for," Danielle says.

"Uh-huh." Liam shakes his head *yeah right*. "Roses and…"

"Candles," Danielle says.

"Roses and candles for a business meeting?" Liam asks.

"Sometimes women enjoy men with an intellect," Briar says.

Liam makes a show of scratching his head.

"They have scintillating conversations," Briar says.

"Baby, you know what those SAT words do to me," he says.

"You're a college graduate," she says.

"And the MBA," he says.

She laughs. "Are you bragging about being educated while implying you're brainless?"

"As long as we agree I know what matters," Liam says.

Danielle shakes her head. "Look what the attention does." She laughs and turns to Vanessa. "Whatever you were doing in the room, I'm glad you liked it."

"I did. Thank you," Vanessa says. "You have quite the eye."

"The room or the pictures?" Danielle asks.

"Both. The set you took with…" Vanessa looks to Adam. "The anonymous model. Those were…"

"They were fire," Liam says.

Briar nods *they were*. "And emotional too. But I don't think Vanessa is here to talk about seeing you or Adam naked."

"Why not?" he asks. "Everyone's seen my spread in Manhattan Magazine."

"You weren't naked," she says.

"I was too," he says.

"But it didn't show anything," she says.

"So you were looking?" he asks.

She blushes.

Danielle laughs. Shoots Adam her own coy look. One loaded with history.

"They won't stop," I say.

"We really won't," Briar agrees.

"Can I get you a drink?" I offer Vanessa my hand.

"Thanks." She takes it.

"We'll grab the seats," Danielle says. "Catch up when you're ready."

Liam raises a brow *interesting.* Shoots me a *make me proud, kid* look and turns to the rest of the party.

He looks between Danielle and Opal, deciding who to torture.

Settles on Danielle.

I leave them to it. Lead Vanessa to the bar.

It's only fifteen feet away, but it's in the corner, behind a half-wall. Secluded, but not especially so.

It was one of Adam's favorites before the accident. He's always appreciated privacy. But he didn't need it.

After the accident, he spent months locked in the house. He didn't leave his cage until he found Danielle.

It's a fucked-up story, but it's what Bash would want.

And Adam is getting better.

He's here, in public. He's attending the opera. He's staying in the city all weekend.

He stays most weekends.

That's progress.

That's everything.

My family is okay. Vanessa is here.

What else matters?

"Whiskey?" Vanessa runs her fingers over the bar.

She's staring at me like she wants to devour me. Why am I thinking ugly things?

"What else?" I turn all my attention to her.

Fuck, she's gorgeous. More every day.

The tight curls, the dark eyes, the long champagne dress.

A goddess.

A queen.

"Do you have a cigar this time?" she teases.

"Are you inviting me to the balcony?"

Her eyes flit to the back of the restaurant. The wide windows. "I don't see a balcony."

"If you did?"

"I would," she says.

"There isn't."

"Too bad."

Would she really sneak away for sex?

It's tempting.

Sure, this restaurant is without a balcony. But there's plenty of space in the single-stall bathroom. The hallway. The hotel across the street.

I need to touch her.

I need to watch her come.

But I need to savor it.

I can't rush it.

Her fingers brush my watch. My shirt. The cufflinks. My silk tie.

"Do you have plans for it?" I ask.

"If I did?"

Whatever they are, yes.

"If I wanted to tie you to the headboard?"

"Who says I have a headboard?"

Her laugh breaks the sexual tension. "It was in your picture." Her chest heaves with her inhale. "The four-poster bed."

"It was."

"Have you ever used it for that?"

"No," I say.

"Never?"

"Never." If a woman wants to be restrained, I'm happy to oblige. I am, above all, goal-oriented, but it's not an interest.

And I've certainly never considered allowing someone to tie me up.

If it was what Vanessa wanted—

Anything she wants, as long as I watch her come.

Is there anything better?

"Would you?" She runs her fingers over her tie. "Let me?"

"Yes."

"Really?"

"Are you offering?" I ask.

"One day." Her eyes flare with surprise. She didn't expect to say that.

But I don't underline it.

I let the words fall.

Sometime.

She thinks about the future.

About fucking me in the future.

"As long as I can watch," she says.

"My thoughts exactly."

"Voyeur."

"Exhibitionist."

Her chest heaves with her inhale. She turns to the bar. Hails the bartender.

He arrives quickly. Shoots her a flirtatious smile. "What can I get you, doll?"

"An Aviation," she says.

"Haven't heard that in a while," he says.

"I know what I like," she says.

He looks to me *is this guy with her*. "And you, sir?"

"My friend will have a whiskey," she says. "Neat."

He looks at me *that kinda guy*. "Anything in particular?"

I name the brand.

"I'll have those in a minute." He shoots her that same sweet smile and turns to the shelves of liquor.

I lean close enough to whisper. "He likes you."

"He's just being friendly," she says.

"He's staring at your chest."

"You're projecting."

I do want to savor the sight of her all fucking night, but that isn't it. "He was."

"Are you jealous?" Curiosity drops into her voice. And something else. Something I can't place.

"No," I say.

"Why not?"

"You're mine tonight."

"And you're mine," she says.

I pull her closer. "Come over after the show."

"All night?"

I want her to stay the night, fall asleep in my bed, wake up in my arms. It's strange. Thrilling. "All night."

"Maybe. My guest offered their blessing. I think they want the place to themselves."

"Their blessing?"

"They don't want to be a cock-block."

"They said that?"

"They did."

They. Not she. Not he.

Some people use the pronoun now. But that's not it.

Vanessa doesn't want me to know who she has at home.

She's not inviting me into that part of her life.

That's our arrangement.

Sex.

No strings.

No feelings.

But that's not the case anymore. For either of us.

"We don't have to go to the opera," she says.

"Would you really leave?" I lean into her touch. "Go to my place? The hotel across the street? The bathroom?"

"Would you really ask?"

Not usually. Not with anyone else. With her? "Yes."

"Then ask."

"What are you wearing under that?"

"Nothing."

Fuck me.

She pulls back right as the bartender drops off our drinks.

"Thank you." She smiles politely. Wraps her fingers around her glass. Brings it to her lips. Lets out a soft groan. "Perfect."

"I'm glad you like it." He smiles *and there's plenty more where that came from* at her. "Should I keep it open?"

"No. We have a table." I slide him my credit card.

He takes it. "Happy to serve from here." He runs the card. Drops off the receipt. Shoots her another *let's fuck after this* grin.

She waits for him to leave. "We don't have to stay."

"I know." I'm tempted to call her bluff. I want to leave with her. I want to go straight to my place and spend the entire night in my bed.

But I want to do this with her too.

Talk to my family.

Watch the opera.

Wait until the perfect fucking moment.

"The show ends at ten thirty," I say.

"You can wait that long?"

"The balcony is private."

"Oh." She holds up her glass. "To balconies."

I raise mine. "To balconies."

I raise my glass.

She toasts. Sips. Sighs. "What do we tell them?" She looks to the group, at a long table in the middle of the room, discussing something with enthusiasm and verve. Then Opal catches her looking and whispers to Briar.

"The truth."

"What's the truth?"

"It's none of their business."

"That will make them more curious," she says. "We need to tell them something boring."

"Sex isn't boring. Not with you."

Her chest heaves with her inhale. "With someone else?"

"Yes."

"You can pretend."

"No." I slip my hand around her waist. Lean close enough to whisper. "I can't."

She leans into my touch. "They're watching."

"I know."

"We should say something."

"Your call."

She nods *okay*, leans into my chest, soaks in the gesture for a moment. Then she pulls back, takes her drink, turns to the table with a casual smile.

At once, all five of them look at us.

Vanessa freezes. But she pushes past it. Walks to them casually.

I pull out her chair. Place her drink on the table. Sit across from her.

Danielle studies us.

Opal whispers to Briar.

Liam looks Vanessa right in the eyes. He smiles, holds up his bright green apple martini to toast, and says, "To you and Simon fucking."

Vanessa nearly spits out her drink.

Briar clears her throat.

"What?" he asks. "You are fucking, aren't you?"

Chapter Twenty-Two

VANESSA

"It's a reasonable question," Liam says. "And we know the answer. But we can keep pretending we don't notice. And you can keep pretending you don't notice we notice."

"It's none of our business," Briar says. She's not as devil-may-care as her fiancé, but she has the same zest. The same willingness to fuck convention and go after what she wants.

"Aren't you curious?" Liam asks. "Simon is good at keeping women silent. Well, not during the act. There were a few times at the house... the walls are thick, but they aren't thick enough." Liam winks at his brother.

Simon's kid sister, Opal, rolls her eyes. "Why does everyone say young people are obsessed with sex? You're obsessed with sex."

"We're young people," Liam says.

"No. You're almost thirty!" Opal says.

Briar doubles over laughing. "She called you old."

"I'm twenty-eight," he says.

"Old." Her laugh gets louder. "Oh my god, that's perfect. Liam Pierce, creepy old man."

"Only four years older than you," he says.

"Briar is young." Opal motions to her. "Look at her hair." She turns to Briar. "Unless you want to lecture me about safe sex or intimacy. Or some other topic you all seem to think you understand better than I do."

Liam shoots Simon a *that means you* look.

Simon shrugs but it's not indifferent. It's *I know you're trying to rile me. It's not going to work. I love you anyway.*

"If you're so wise, why do you care about the details of your brother's sex life?" Opal asks. "Shouldn't you realize relationships are about more than sex." She lowers her voice. "Not that you'd know it. From talking to the three of you."

"Really? The three of us? Even Adam?" Liam asks.

"Especially Adam," she says.

"What did you say to her?" Liam asks his brother.

"Danielle and Briar too," she says.

Danielle laughs. "Sorry. I get carried away." She looks at Adam lovingly. "Love does that to you."

"Love? Or lust?" Liam asks.

Opal motions to me *see what I mean.*

Simon chuckles.

"You too," she says. "And you lecture me about making smart choices." She shakes her head *ridiculous.*

"But you are curious about Simon's boning habits," Liam says.

"Is it the alcohol?" Opal motions to Liam's bright green drink. Briar's deep red martini. The empty cocktail glasses in front of Danielle and Adam. "It must be the alcohol."

"You're right," Briar says. "We're idiots."

"She wants to know," Liam says.

"But we know how to mind our own business," Briar says.

Liam makes a show of scratching his head. "We do?"

"I'm not sure we do," Danielle agrees.

Adam interrupts them. "I'm sorry, Vanessa. They don't

know how to hide their surprise. We haven't seen Simon this soft in a long time."

Liam jumps on the opportunity. "Soft, huh? Is that it? If you're having trouble rising to the occasion—"

"No one wants to hear about your dick," Opal says.

Danielle laughs.

Briar too.

Liam shoots his girlfriend a look that's heavy on the *I know you want to talk about my dick.*

He is obnoxious. I can see why he and Simon struggle.

But there's something about it. This playfulness aimed directly at his oldest brother. This is for Simon's benefit.

"We are," I say. "We're seeing each other. There's nothing exciting about it."

Adam is right. None of them hide their surprise, him included.

He and Danielle are kind of like Liam and Briar. Exactly the same, yet completely different.

They're both well-dressed in a way that doesn't call extra attention—a simple charcoal suit for him, a black wrap dress for her.

They have the same thoughtful aura.

But she's animated and artistic.

He's stoic and scientific.

He has pale skin, short hair, and deep blue eyes.

She has light brown skin, long wavy hair, and warm eyes. Not just the flecks of amber. The expression too.

They're both gorgeous. Even with his scars. Or maybe even more.

There were a lot of rumors at the time of the accident, but I never paid much attention. I only know Adam disappeared for months.

The first time I saw him after he lost his brother, he was with Danielle, and he was happy, the way he is now.

Free.

He spent months locked from the world, grieving. And he emerged free of the pain he was carrying.

Simon hasn't done that.

What was it he said?

He survived because it was the only choice he had.

But was it that simple?

He's still hurting.

All that pain is going to catch up with him eventually.

The same as mine.

Liam interrupts my train of thought. "You're not *just* fucking?"

Briar's face turns red. "Why are you asking her?"

"She said they're 'seeing' each other. I want to clarify the terms," he says.

Simon's eyes meet mine.

They ask for something, but I don't know what it is.

Does he want more?

Or does he want me to understand there isn't going to be more?

I swallow hard. "We're dating."

"It's serious?" he asks.

Briar puts her hand over his mouth. "Sorry. The only way to shut him up is a gag."

"Do you know from experience?" Simon asks.

Her blush deepens.

Simon raises a brow, but I'm not sure if it's *maybe it's true what they say about executives.* Or *I'd like if you gagged me by sitting on my face.* Or—

I'm kind of stuck at sitting on his face.

"She knows," Liam muffles.

Briar releases her hand.

"We do all sorts of freaky shit," Liam says. "But nice try on changing the subject."

"I think you volunteered that information," Opal says.

Danielle motions *sorta*.

"You all want to know," Liam says. "You're dying to know." He turns to me. "What kind of stuff is Simon into? Biting? Bondage? Humiliation? Feet?"

"Feet?" Danielle asks. "That's… specific."

"Maybe I know something," he says.

"When have you ever known anything?" Briar asks.

He nods *true*. Snaps right back to me. "How much of a freak is he? One to Rick James?"

"Where does that scale end?" I ask.

"At Rick James," he says.

"Who's at the other end?"

"Oh, that's good. No one's ever asked." Liam taps his chin. "Gonna have to think on that one." He looks to Simon. "Smart woman. She's a keeper."

"And willing to put up with you," Opal says. "She must really like him."

"That is a big sacrifice," Briar agrees.

"You too, baby? That hurts," he says.

"Maybe you'll find a way to make it up to me," she teases.

"Maybe I will," he says.

"Weren't you complaining she's the rude one," Opal says. "Shouldn't she be… gross. Never mind."

Briar laughs.

Danielle too. She mouths *sorry, they're crazy*.

They are.

But it's sweet. Surprising.

Simon's family loves him.

It's warm enough to fill the restaurant.

After a few more rounds of refining Liam's *Super Freak* scale, we order dinner.

Opal and Liam fight for control of the conversation. She tries to move it away from sex. He tries to move it back.

Eventually, she wins, changes the subject to the show.

We talk about the opera. We finish dinner, walk to the venue across the street, greet Lee, Harrison, and Preston (thankfully, my parents are busy tonight. I don't have to discuss my sex life with them).

The lights flicker, warning us the show is about to start.

We head to our expensive, semi-secluded seats.

Liam steps in front of us. Leads us to the top balcony. "This one is yours. Just the two of you."

"There are ten of us," Simon says.

"And, damn, I forget we were using Preston's tickets, so I went ahead and bought this." He motions to the balcony. To the curtains at the side, blocking it from view of the other balconies. "Enjoy the privacy."

Simon shoots him a *really* look.

Liam nods back *really*. He pulls his older brother into a hug. Whisper-talks, "Make me proud, kid."

"I'm older than you," Simon whispers back.

"Less experienced in this area."

"Which area is that?"

"I'll leave it up to you to decide." He pulls back. Shoots his brother a wink. "You have two and a half hours of privacy. Use them wisely."

Chapter Twenty-Three

SIMON

"**I**'m sorry about Liam," I say, once he's past the curtain. "He's an idiot."

"He is." Vanessa takes her seat. "But he's sweet."

"Sweet?"

"In his way."

"Telling me to fuck you on the balcony?"

"He's trying to help you get laid."

"Do I need the help?"

She smiles. "No. You don't." She looks from the stage. "Did you know we'd have this to ourselves?"

"No," I admit. "He arranged that."

"That's going above and beyond."

"That's Liam."

She laughs. "He reminds me of Lee. I know they'd both hate the comparison, but... they're pushy in a well-meaning way that other people find obnoxious."

"I find him obnoxious."

"I know."

"You adore your sister," I say.

"You adore Liam. And you find him obnoxious."

"I love him. I don't adore him."

She looks to the opera section below us. "I like seeing you with him. With your family. I never see that side of you. Soft. Caring. On defense."

"Defense?"

"You're still aloof, but in a loving way. It's hard to explain, but it's… I like it. That's all."

She likes it.

And she didn't insist this is casual to Liam.

It's none of his business.

But—

Is that still what she wants?

Or does she want more?

I sit next to her. "I have to admit. I didn't invite you here to make you come on the balcony."

"You didn't?"

I nod. "I want to watch *La Traviata* with you."

"To actually watch it?"

"Yes."

She presses her lips together, considering it. Asking herself if she's willing to break her own rules to touch me.

It's thrilling.

Intoxicating.

Sexy as fuck.

But I know her now. And I know where she draws her lines.

"Briar and Liam got into an argument once," I say.

"Only once?"

A laugh spills from my lips. Eases the tension in my shoulders. I'm nervous. Even though she's already spent two hours with my family.

She endured dinner with Liam and stuck around.

That's dedication.

It's terrifying.

And this—

The way my heart is racing, the desire to know her, deep in my bones, this need to prove I'm not the heartless bastard she sees me as.

I've been to the opera before. Sat in the balcony with a client. Or a date.

I appreciate the theatricality, the technical prowess, the historical context—

But I never feel anything.

Vanessa might not care about opera, but she cares. Her ability to care is infinite.

She doesn't want a heartless bastard.

She wants someone who feels.

"Many times," I say. "One of them, she was debating the term 'Netflix and chill.'"

"People still say that?"

"It was a few years ago. Before they were together."

"At work?"

"A work party. They agreed it was a useless term. Liam thought it was sad to need a euphemism. She thought it was ridiculous. If someone wanted to come over to watch TV, they were watching TV. Who hooks up in the middle of a perfectly good TV show? That's insulting to the show."

"What was the argument?"

"Liam trying to push her buttons."

"Of course."

"Saying she must not know good sex if she thought a TV show could compare."

"Rough."

"She pushed back. Said he must not have enough brain cells to follow the story, so of course he needed to switch to sex."

Vanessa laughs. "She's tough."

"She is."

"Was she right?"

"About Liam? No. He's smarter than he looks."

"The TV part?"

"I don't know. We didn't have a TV growing up. We read, went to the theater, listened to records."

"Classical?"

"Mostly, but Dad had a soft spot for new wave."

"Really? Mr. Pierce listened to Depeche Mode?"

It's strange, her referring to my father as Mr. Pierce. Familiar and foreign at once. "Mostly The Cure."

"Your dad was rocking out to The Cure?"

"He was."

"Did he wear eyeliner too?"

"There's one picture."

"That he found and burned?"

A laugh spills from my lips. "It was in his desk, in his study. He brought it out when old friends came over. Preston especially."

"That's hard to imagine."

"I didn't believe it the first time I saw it. It's always strange seeing young pictures of your parents, realizing they're human the way you are. But it was more than that. I'd never seen him in jeans."

"He went to our school?"

"No. Liam's. Mom didn't want us at an all-boy's school."

"Why did he go?"

"Liam and Bash? It was Preston's idea, but I was quick to agree. I needed someone watching them carefully. Every weekend."

"A proper boarding school?"

I nod.

"That's why Liam was always sleeping around. The rebellion to the all-boy's school?"

"Tell him that. He'd like it."

"Do you regret that decision?"

"No. It was good for them."

"Do you ever wish it was you?" she asks. "At the all-boy's school."

"Never."

"I did." She smiles. "When we were younger, I wished you'd gone to the all-boy's school my dad discussed."

"So you could win mock trial."

"You still think about mock trial?"

"Not the way you mean?"

"Not your victory?"

"No. I'm not gaining nutrients from the memories."

"Does it work with memories?"

"Only fresh victory."

She laughs. "Of course."

"It was the first time I saw you in a pencil skirt and heels."

"Oh."

"I wanted to roll the wool up your thighs and bend you over the table."

She swallows hard. "I wanted to kiss you to shut you up."

"Just a kiss?"

"To start."

"Innocent."

"No." Her voice drops. "And it wasn't sweet either. It was sweaty and angry and hot as hell."

"How did it go?"

"You want to role play our high school competition?"

"I want to roll your skirt to your waist and peel your panties to your ankles."

"I'm still not wearing anything under my dress."

Fuck me.

"Do you still listen to The Cure?"

The what?

My body begs me to relent. To toss our conversation aside, drop to my knees, dive between her legs.

But that isn't what she needs.

Not yet.

"Sometimes," I say.

"When was the last?"

"Six months ago."

"On purpose?"

"No." I rarely sit and remember. Better to move forward. To let go of the past.

Is that what I've done with my father?

With Bash?

I'm here to honor him.

But the rest is still a tangled mess. I haven't released my desire for revenge. No matter how much I try to let go, for him, for the people he'd want to protect, I crave justice.

But I try.

I wait. To protect the people who need protecting.

That's what matters.

Action.

"Opal had a playlist on the speaker in the kitchen." I need to protect her too. To protect my entire family.

And I need to think of something else.

Not the loss of my father. Or my brother. Or my ability to live a completely free life.

My desire to connect with Vanessa.

The present waiting for her in my bedroom.

The sound of her groan bouncing around the walls.

"You have a speaker in the living room?" she asks.

"I do."

"Since when?"

"A week after she moved in." This is why I'm here. Love. Not what Bash meant, but what he'd want.

Vanessa smiles. Part big sister pride. Part *I want to mount you.* "She was fifteen?"

"She was."

"Playing Taylor Swift all day?"

"And all night."

Vanessa laughs. "I would pay to see that."

"Come over and offer her DJ power. You will."

"Soon." Again, she smiles. "I interrupted you."

"I don't mind."

"I want to hear the story."

Fuck, where was I? "When *Lovesong* came on, I froze. I thought about him. How hard he tried to hide the side of him that loved new wave and Bond movies."

"Bond, really?"

"What's wrong with Bond?"

"It's a guy cliché."

"I've never seen one."

"Really?" she asks.

"Really."

"Well, why would you, when you could watch *Killing Eve*?" She notes my blank stare with a smile. "You have no idea what I'm talking about?"

"A movie?"

"TV show."

"Spies?"

"That's part of it. And sexual tension between two women. Women weaponizing other people's perceptions of them as cute or pretty or soft or sexual even. It's a popular show. Opal might watch it."

"I'll ask."

"You might like it. Or… do you like anything?"

"I don't watch TV on my own," I say.

"But you watch with Opal."

"I do."

"Is it just being a good brother? Or do you secretly love the drama on… what are you watching now?"

"*Dawson's Creek*?"

Her eyes light up. "That's what we watched in school. How

did she even find it?"

"Streaming."

"Did you ever watch?"

"No. You?"

"A little. Lee loved it. She was obsessed with the love triangle."

"Who wins the girl?" I ask.

"I can't ruin the surprise." She laughs.

"What if I want to know?"

"Do you?"

The characters are only vaguely familiar. The girl from the wrong side of "the creek." Her childhood best friend. The playful bad boy.

No one who resembles Vanessa.

Or me.

No, that's not quite right. A girl from the city shows up. She's banished to the small town because she got into too much trouble.

Not Vanessa's path—she went from having nothing to having everything, and she was never even a little bad—but a big enough change.

"Do you think it's sad? If they end up with someone they liked in high school?" I ask.

"It can be." Her eyes meet mine. "If they get stuck at sixteen, use that as an excuse to stop growing. But some people grow together."

I nod.

"Or they grow in parallel. Find each other when they're older and wiser and able to see past their preconceptions."

"It won't matter they used to hate each other."

"Not if they mature."

"Is that what happens?" I ask.

"I won't ruin the ending."

"A hint?"

She looks at me funny, like she's not sure what I'm asking. "It's not what you expect."

"Were you happy?"

"Some parts. But I wonder... do people really end up with someone who sees them? Sees all of them? Respects who they are now? Or do they give up a piece of themselves for love?"

Is that what she thinks of love?

Why she ended things with her fiancé.

Why she's been single as long as I have.

"You don't believe in true, honest love?" I ask.

"Sometimes. Lee and Harrison, maybe. He loves her. The good parts, the bad parts, the really ugly parts. And she's still her. She's still a force of nature."

"Harrison?"

"You think she overpowers him?"

"Does she?" I raise a brow.

A laugh spills from her lips. Breaks the tension in her brow. "No. I think she'd tell me. She's extremely detailed about their attempts to get pregnant."

"I'm surprised she told Liam."

"She told him to annoy him."

"It worked."

"It did?" she asks.

I nod. "Briar is afraid of commitment."

"Aren't they engaged?"

"Kind of."

"Kind of?"

"It was for Preston's benefit."

"Oh. I think the baby making is too."

Because Preston is dying.

They want their kid to meet his grandfather.

"It's fucked up, but it's sweet," she says.

"Is it likely?"

"No," she says. "But he'll probably be able to tape the sonogram to the fridge. Pat her belly. Well, if she lets anyone pat her belly. I can't see it."

"Me either."

"It seemed easy for her," she says. "Falling for him. Maybe it's easier, because she's so strong, and he's—he's strong too. But not the way you and I are. Not unyielding."

"I can be yielding."

"Can you?"

I don't know. But that's not what she's asking. Not exactly.

She's asking if I can fall for her.

And that—

That's a terrifying question.

———

THE LIGHTS DIM.

The curtain draws.

At once, every ounce of Vanessa's attention goes to the stage. She watches, rapt, as the performers take their place, fill the space with beautiful vocals.

Italian.

I don't know a single word.

But I'm still transfixed.

Not on the show.

On Vanessa.

Even when the first act finishes, when we break at intermission, meet my family—and hers—at the venue's bar.

Opal announces her plans to get coffee with Briar and Liam after the show. She won't be home until midnight.

One, if I make an exception to her curfew—which she really doesn't need to follow, since she's an adult.

I don't argue.

I give her an extra hour.

Then I fall into the show, into the spell of watching Vanessa watch the rest of the opera.

It's transcendent.

But not the way she means.

In a way that's much more exhilarating.

And risky as hell.

Chapter Twenty-Four

SIMON

We say quick goodbyes. Everyone—her family and mine—wants us alone.

Harrison is the only person with a hint of restraint. He shakes his head, suggests people let us orchestrate our sex lives on our own, even as Lee winks *you know you want it.*

Even Adam shoots me a *this is good, hold on to it* look.

He winks. The way Bash would.

If he were here—

He'd mock me for my inability to articulate feelings other than hostility. Then pat me on the back for finally finding the courage to do something brave.

Negotiating with a guy who's richer than you isn't brave, Simon. What's at stake? Money? You don't need money.

Pride, sure.

But you've got plenty to spare.

Your heart?

Now, that's risky.

That's brave.

Omnia vincit amor, et nos cedamus amori.

Love conquers all.

Let us cede to love.

That's brave.

Go get 'em, tiger.

My thoughts swirl, but there's no heaviness to them.

No ugly memories.

Or desire for vengeance.

Or twisted connections.

Only a wish to honor my promise.

To honor his memory.

This is what he stood for—

Love without fear.

He was wrong. He took it too far. Threw away any hint of rationality.

But, here, helping Vanessa into the limo, I almost understand.

Rationality is nothing in the face of passion.

My body is buzzing.

My heart is pounding.

My thoughts are long gone.

I only want her.

All of her.

Every way I can have her.

I slide inside.

The driver closes the door. Steps into the front. Rolls the partition.

"How far is it to your place?" Vanessa smooths her dress over her legs.

"Only a few blocks from yours."

"How long?" Her chest heaves with her inhale.

"Ten minutes." I turn toward her.

Her eyes meet mine. "Not long."

"Are you that impatient?"

"Yes."

"But you'll still wait." I cup her neck. Run my thumb over her soft skin. "Try to outlast me."

She nods.

"You're naked under here?"

"Only the shoes." She pulls her dress up an inch.

"All night?"

"All night."

"Show me."

"Help me." She turns so her back is to me.

I run my fingers down her spine, until they brush the curving backline of the dress.

Then the zipper.

Lower.

Lower.

Until my fingers brush the small of her back.

"Simon." It falls off her lips as a plea.

But I don't give her more.

I don't move faster.

I trace the same slow line.

Up.

Down.

Again and again.

Her breath hitches.

Her fingers curl into the soft leather.

I tease her again and again. Then I press my lips to her neck. She shudders as I scrape my teeth against her skin.

"Simon." She reaches back. Grabs my thigh. "Fuck. Like that." She tugs at my slacks. "Not harder."

"Nothing rough."

She nods. Repeats the words, like she's not sure where she heard them.

I tease her with soft scrapes of my teeth.

I trace the line down her spine.

Then up again.

Again and again.

Until the car turns onto my street.

And I slip my hand into her dress. Cup her breasts with my palms.

She groans as I run my thumbs over her nipples. "Fuck."

I draw slow circles.

She melts into me, surrenders to sensation.

To the feeling of being on the edge.

Her eyes flutter closed.

Her lips part with a groan.

Her nails dig into my slacks.

I tease her again and again.

Until I can't take it anymore.

Then I pull her into my lap, so her ass is against my pelvis, so she can feel me, hard against her.

"Simon." She rocks against me. "Fuck."

I kiss her neck as I toy with her breasts.

She melts into me, purring, groaning, clawing at my skin.

Wracked with bliss.

And desperate for more.

There aren't enough mirrors here. I can't see every inch of her.

Only the nails—painted the same champagne shade as her dress—digging into my slacks.

Her head falling back into the crook of my neck.

Her wine lips parting as she moans.

I tease her until the car stops.

The driver knocks.

She stirs. Still dazed but aware of her surroundings.

"We can stay."

"Fuck here?"

"Fuck here."

Her lips press together. "The driver will know."

"So he'll know."

"What do you say? Drive around the block until we're done?"

"Do you really want a cover story?" I bring my lips to her ear. "Or do you want him to know?"

"I do." She presses her hands to her chest, holding her dress against her skin. "But I don't want to be another rich asshole."

"The partition blocks sound."

She nods.

"There are other reasons to stay in the car."

"The comfortable bench seats?"

"The air-conditioning."

"Right." She laughs. "Air-conditioning."

"The privacy."

"It is for privacy."

"For conversation." I press my lips to her neck. "Have you never stopped somewhere and had a conversation in a car?"

"I have."

"A limo?"

She nods.

"With a donor?"

"Sometimes. Sometimes, with Regina. Or Lee. Or my assistant."

"It could be that."

She turns, so she's facing me. "Is that what you want?"

"I want to make you come."

"That's all?"

"All?" I raise a brow. "Should I stop?"

"No." She grabs my wrist.

I can't help but smile.

"Is there anything more specific?"

"I want to make you come here. And in front of the mirror in my bedroom. And in that leather armchair."

"While you're sipping whiskey?"

"While I'm licking whiskey off your thighs." I press my lips to the hollow of her neck. "You're an exhibitionist."

"I am."

"You want this."

"I do."

"He won't mind."

"How do you know?"

I don't, I admit. But I know men. And I saw the way the driver looked at Vanessa. "He wants to imagine you naked here."

"He does not."

"He does."

"How do you figure?"

"He looked at you."

"That's not—"

"It is. You're the most beautiful woman I've ever met." I press my lips to her collarbone. "Most men would kill to be here, with you."

I bring my hands to the back of her dress. Look up at her, waiting for her permission.

I want to fuck Vanessa here.

I want to fuck her everywhere.

At every time.

No. It's more.

I want to give her this.

Because she wants it.

Because it turns her on.

Because I want to be the one person who sees that side of her.

The one person who fulfills all her fantasies.

"I'm a patient man." I trace a line up her spine. "I can wait a long time."

She looks down at me. Bites her lip. Thinking. Deciding.

I trace the line back down.

Lower.

Lower.

Lower.

Her eyes close. Her lips part. "Yes." She curls her hand around my neck. "Tell him."

"Turn around."

She does.

I zip her dress and help her onto the bench seat—her skirt is too tight around her hips for her to maneuver easily—then I knock on the partition. "We're going to have another drink. Take us around the block until we're finished."

"Please," she adds.

The driver nods *whatever.* Looks at her like he's picturing her naked. "Would you like music?"

I name the opera we watched.

The driver nods *figures, rich people want to listen to foreign shit.* "Spell it."

Vanessa does.

A moment later, the car fills with the dramatic Italian vocals.

The driver rolls the partition.

The car pulls onto the street.

"He did," she says. "You're right."

"I know."

"Are you jealous?"

"No. It turns you on." I run my fingers over her shoulder.

She turns, so I can unzip her dress.

I pull it down her spine. "Being on display."

"For you."

"Only for me?"

"I only trust you."

Fuck. She only trusts me. It hits me everywhere. Sinks into my fucking bones.

I always want my partners to trust me. But this is different. Something deeper.

Truer.

She wants me to see her.

All of her.

Physically, yes.

And all the other ways too.

I want it.

I want it as badly as I want to fuck her.

And I really, really want to fuck her.

I peel her dress off her chest. Slip off the seat to peel it over her hips, down her legs, past her ankles.

She sits on the bench seat, naked except for her heels.

I kneel in front of her. Lift her right leg and place it on my shoulder.

Then the left.

"Simon." Her fingers curl around my neck. "Fuck."

I'm not in the right position to tease her, but I do what I can.

The soft brush of my lips on her inner thigh.

The sharp scrape of my teeth.

Not rough.

Not enough to hurt.

Only enough to drive her out of her fucking mind.

Her nails dig into my skin.

I tease my way up her left leg.

Then down the right.

Up.

Down.

Until she's scratching hard enough to draw blood.

Until I can't stand it anymore.

Then I bring my lips to her clit.

No more teasing.

Exactly what she needs.

I work her with long, slow strokes.

Then harder.

Faster.

The spot where she wants me.

Again and again.

I push her to the edge.

Then over it.

Her hand knots in my hair.

She tugs me into position, rocking against me, groaning my name as she comes.

I give her a moment to catch her breath, press my lips to high thigh, run my nails over her skin.

Then I pin her to the bench seat, and I dive between her legs.

No tease. No warmup.

Hard, fast strokes.

Exactly where she needs them.

This time, she comes fast.

She groans my name like it's a curse, tugging at my hair as she pulses against my lips.

"Fuck." She grabs at my suit jacket. "You're good at that."

My veins buzz with pride.

She offers her hand. Helps me up. Onto the bench seat.

"There isn't much." I motion to the sliver of the mirror across from us. "But there's something."

She nods, takes in the reflection—a sliver of her bare skin against my charcoal suit—and undoes my belt buckle. The button. The zipper.

Fuck.

She palms me over my boxers.

I should be fair. Let her tease me. Let her take her time.

But I'm not a fair man.

I'm a greedy motherfucker.

"Come here." I wrap my hand around her hip.

She pushes my boxers out of the way. "No."

"No?"

She wraps her hands around my cock. Presses her lips to my neck.

She runs her thumb over my tip. "I thought about this all night." She drops to her knees between my legs. Brings her lips to my cock.

She teases me with a soft brush of her hips.

A soft flick of her tongue.

But she's impatient.

Thank fuck.

She wraps her lips around me.

My hands go to her skin reflexively. One around her neck. The other to her breast.

I toy with her nipple as she explores me with her tongue.

Soft flicks.

Slow ones.

Left.

Right.

Slow circles.

Soft suction.

Fuck.

My nails dig into her skin.

It's too much, too rough, but she doesn't pull away. She wraps her hand around my wrist. Brings it to her chest.

And she takes me deeper.

Again.

And again.

She groans against my skin.

I toy with her as she takes me.

I look down at her. Take in the sight that served a million fantasies.

Vanessa Moyer naked, on her knees, in front of me.

Groaning against my cock.

Fuck.

I draw circles around her nipples.

I let my eyes fall closed.

I let my world turn to Vanessa.

The soft, sweet feeling of her around me.

All light and bliss and warmth.

With the next flick of her tongue, I come.

The world goes white.

Pleasure floods my senses.

I toy with her as I come.

She stays glued to me. Waits until I've spilled every drop, then pulls back, swallows hard, looks up at me with pride in her eyes.

She's naked, on her knees in a limo, and she's exactly where she wants to be.

What the fuck did I do to deserve this?

She holds out her hand.

I help her up. Help her into her dress.

She looks to the mirror. Pulls her lipstick from her purse. Applies another coat. "Ready?"

I nod and knock on the divider. "We're ready to go home."

The driver mumbles an agreement.

After another turn, we stop. Park in front of my place.

I open the door for her. Help her out. Wrap my arm around her waist.

She looks up at the building with wonder. "This is your place?"

"You've never seen it?"

"When would I?"

I'm not exactly the consummate host.

"Is it what I expect?"

"Worse."

She smiles *could you really be worse than I expect* and follows me inside.

Only it's not like before.

Not a judgment.

Or an insult.

It's an inside joke.

A sign of love.

Or something like it.

Chapter Twenty-Five

VANESSA

H oly shit.

This place is huge.

It shouldn't surprise me—of course, Simon Pierce lives in a massive brownstone—but it does.

Two stories.

Four bedrooms.

Winding balcony.

Airy foyer.

And the view of the park, the Empire State Building, the perfect deep blue sky—

It's gorgeous.

Old money meets new money. Old architecture. Modern decor.

All Simon. Well, Simon and Opal.

Her influence is everywhere.

Pink pillows on the black leather couch. A stereo system next to the TV. A bookshelf overflowing with an eclectic mix. Everything from Young Adult to extremely dirty erotic romance.

I recognize a few names. Authors known for BDSM, dark stories, edgy content.

A lot of survivors read romance. Some read syrupy sweet stories of unnaturally wholesome people with unnaturally good intentions. Others read tales of kidnapping and dubious consent.

I appreciate the potential coping mechanism. Even the really fucked-up books, the ones that romanticize abuse.

I understand why people read three hundred pages of a man intentionally inflicting harm on a woman then magically realizing the error of his ways and transforming into a loving partner.

I understand why the fantasy appeals to victims.

Some people need a glimmer of hope to survive.

But it's not true. It's not what happens with abuse. Patience and willingness to take verbal and physical beatings make things worse.

It's okay for people to indulge problematic fantasies.

But is that what happens?

Do people truly draw a line between real and pretend?

Or does the line fade? Does the pretend seep through?

Do young women like Opal grow up thinking it's okay for a man to stalk you? Ignore your boundaries? Keep touching you after you've said no?

Does every book they read, every episode of TV they watch, every song they hear impact their world view?

Maybe it's both.

I don't know.

Every genre is fucked up in its own way. It's just this one is closer to my scars. And I'm utterly unable to handle it.

I can't even read books about consensual bondage.

People ask me all the time. They see me as an expert. I try to offer a diplomatic answer, but it's not the truth.

The truth is, those books make me sick.

But it's worse than that.

It's the world.

How can we live in such a fucked-up world? One where so many women crave this fantasy of their willingness to endure pain curing an abuser?

How can we live in such a fucked up world and not spend all our time and energy trying to fix it?

But that isn't possible. No one can fix the world. Including me.

I devote my life to helping abused people, and I barely make a dent.

Fuck, I'm spiraling.

It's overwhelming, being in Simon's space. Feeling the affection in his stare. Hearing the desire for intimacy in his voice.

That's why I'm staring at this shelf, and not the shelf of sweet romantic comedies.

Because I need to tell him about my parents.

If I want this to continue, if I want it to ever be more than sex, I need to tell him.

About my biological father, my mother, my response to my lack of control.

How the fuck do I tell him?

"Where are you going?" Simon slides his arm around my waist. Pulls my body into his.

He's safe and warm and strong.

I want to dissolve between his arms.

Maybe that's enough. Maybe it's enough to touch him and kiss him and connect physically.

No.

That's bullshit.

I need to tell him.

But how the fuck do I start?

I try to find something. Chicken out instead. "Studying the room."

"Which part?"

"All of it." I motion to the pink rug. The framed modern art. The overflowing bookshelf. "Opal?"

He nods. "She's a paperback holdout. Refuses an e-reader."

"So she has to talk to her brother about sexy romances?"

"You heard her." He presses his lips to my neck. "Annoyed, all the adults in her life talk to her about sex."

"Do they?"

"I do."

"What do you say?" I ask.

"She was fifteen when she showed up here. She knew the technical details, but I explained them anyway. Told her to always be safe. To only be with people she trusts. To value her desires and pleasure."

"You said those words to your sister?"

"I didn't do it because it was fun."

"Was it?"

"Not at first. I was as awkward as she was. What the fuck was I supposed to say to a grieving teenager? But no one else was going to do it. It was my responsibility as the adult in her life. As her brother."

You were responsible and honest, even though it was hard. I can do that too. I can tell you this too.

I try to find the words.

But I can't. Not yet.

Soon.

After we talk about his sister and his home and his life.

"Did you discuss the books?" I ask.

"They're not the best education."

What does he see?

"Not anatomically correct." He half-smiles.

It eases the tension in my shoulders.

It warms the space.

This first.

242

Easy first.

Then I tell him.

"This is about your dick again?" The words are awkward on my tongue.

He notices, but he doesn't mention it. "Dicks in general."

"You object to the representations?"

"Strange, every man is above average."

"Writers aren't good at math," I say.

His smile widens.

My shoulders ease a little more.

My chest warms a little more.

He likes me. He really likes me.

And I really like him.

"Can I ask you something?" he asks.

I nod.

"You've been with other men."

"A handful."

"A range of sizes?"

A laugh spills from my lips.

Simon Pierce is asking me if I've slept with guys with small dicks.

It's high school and perfect and easy.

I push my ugly thoughts aside. Fall into the fun parts.

"I didn't bring a measuring stick," I say. "But there's been a range."

"Is there a correlation in satisfaction?"

"Are more... what was it Liam said?"

"Locked and loaded." He chuckles.

"Are more locked and loaded men better fucks?" The details of my past relationships are a mess, but I can answer this. "No."

"Any correlation?"

"Not really."

"Do you prefer it?"

"I knew it was about your dick."

He smiles. "I didn't ask if mine was your favorite."

"But you wouldn't mind if I volunteered the information?"

"I wouldn't complain."

"Honest answer?"

"Should I be concerned?" he asks.

My laugh erases the tension in my jaw. "No. You know you're well-endowed."

He raises a brow.

"Not the biggest I've seen. But that was too much. More painful than anything. And... I don't have the experience, myself, but I hear some men who are larger think their dick is enough. They don't try. They're not generous."

"Is that the honest part?"

"No. Well, yes, it's true." Again, I laugh. This is absurd. And perfect. "I don't think about it."

"No."

"I don't."

"Never?"

"If I'm imagining something." My hands slip to his hips. "The look. The feel. But I'm not counting inches. I'm replaying the sensation of fullness. Satisfaction."

"Fuck, Vanessa, was I supposed to take issue with that?"

"Did you?"

"No." He leans down and presses his lips to mine. "You're too fucking sexy."

My cheeks flush. "I am?"

He nods. "Yes."

"Thanks."

"My pleasure."

"You don't think that," I say. "Even though you're... gifted. You're still goal-oriented."

"I am."

"Generous even."

"I try."

"I appreciate that."

"Appreciate it?"

"It's sexy." My flush spreads to my chest. "I, uh… you're very skilled. In this department."

"Thank you." He releases me. "You are too."

"Thank you." I rise to my tiptoes. Press my lips to his.

He kisses back with intensity, drawing circles with his tongue, groaning against my mouth.

He's claiming my body.

And asking for my heart and my soul too.

This is it. I can tug at his tie, tell him to take off his pants, ask to go to his bedroom.

I can make the rest of the night strictly physical.

I can run from my confession.

Or I can stand and face it.

It's up to me.

Do I offer my body?

Or offer everything?

Chapter Twenty-Six

VANESSA

My heart thuds against my chest. My stomach flutters. My toes curl.

I pull back with a sigh.

The words form on my lips.

Let's go to your room.

I want to touch you.

I want to fuck you all fucking night.

They never make it to my lips. I'm too lost in his blue eyes. They're deeper than the ocean. And a million times more inviting.

Is this why people want to swim in their lover's eyes?

I want to swim in him forever.

His hand cups my cheek. His thumb brushes my temple.

He looks down at me, about to say something, then he stops. Smiles. "Do you want something to drink?"

He wants to talk.

And I want to talk too. I want to tell him my secrets and learn his in return.

I just don't know how.

"Do you have anything besides whiskey?" I ask.

"I do." His expression gets shy.

But that can't be possible.

Simon Pierce isn't shy.

Fuck, he's blushing.

He's actually blushing.

It's the hottest thing I've ever seen.

"I bought everything for an Aviation," he says.

"Really?"

He nods. "I tested the recipe last night."

"How was it?"

"It tasted like you."

"Good?"

"Fucking fantastic."

And, now, I'm so flushed I'm burning up. "Water first."

He nods and leads me around the corner to the kitchen.

It's beautiful. All new stainless steel appliances and shiny tile. Clean. Immaculate, actually.

Completely Simon.

Except for the touches of Opal.

The French Press on the counter is hot pink.

And there's a mug next to it. A pale pink printed with thick lashes and the words *good morning*.

There's another next to it. White with *Hello Gorgeous* in fuchsia.

"Opal's?" I nod to the cups.

"Mine." He holds up the *Hello Gorgeous* mug.

"Really?"

"You disagree?"

"No." I can't argue with the assessment.

He smiles. "We were at Target."

"You go to Target?"

"Where else would I go?"

"You wouldn't. You'd hire a decorator."

"I did, when I first moved in. But I wasn't going to ask her to rearrange the place for Opal when I could ask Opal what she wanted. She said Target. So we went."

"You in a suit?"

"What else?"

"Do you own other clothes?"

He smiles. "You want to see my bedroom already?"

Yes. "I want to see proof."

"You will."

"Not just the silk pajamas."

"If you stay until morning."

"Workout gear?"

"You're impatient."

"No." Yes. Extremely. "Do you really use the mug?"

"Every morning." He fills a glass with water and hands it to me. "Opal picked it up. She looked at me, looked right at my tie, and she said, 'this is perfect for you.' How could I argue?"

"The pink French Press?"

"I've had that forever."

"Really?"

"Years."

"You're fucking with me."

He nods. "I bought it for her."

"At Target?"

"No. They only had black at Target. Special order."

He's teasing again.

How did I ever find it annoying?

It's charming.

And sexy.

As sexy as other kinds.

I swallow a sip. Then half the glass.

He stands at the kitchen island. Sips slowly. "She wasn't comfortable here. Not just because the place was big and expensive. Because it was mine."

"Sparse and masculine?"

He nods. "She grew up with her mom. She was used to soft and feminine."

"Not leather and scotch?"

"Or cigars on the balcony."

"Do you smoke cigars on the balcony?"

"No," he says. "Our mother died of lung cancer."

Fuck. "I'm sorry. I didn't know that. And I'm sorry you lost her so young."

He doesn't fight me this time. He nods, accepting the condolences. "Thank you."

"Was it hard growing up without her?"

"You're going to laugh."

"I am?"

He nods. "Our housekeeper took care of us."

A laugh spills from my lips. "It's not that—"

"I'm a rich boy cliché. I won't argue."

"The hot pink French Press especially."

"Especially." He takes a long sip. Watches my lipstick mark the glass. "Is that where you went? Thinking about Opal?"

"Part of it."

"The other part?"

I'm not ready to talk about it. I want to be here. Where it's easy. "What is it like, having her here?"

"You have a younger sister."

"Three years younger."

"I try to do my best to look out for her. Teach her. Prepare her for the world. She doesn't always like it. She says I'm bossy and annoying. And she really hates my lectures. But that doesn't stop me."

"You don't mind if she's mad at you."

"I don't like it. But I understand. It's my responsibility to take care of her, even if that means she hates me."

He does.

He understands that with everyone in his family.

His employees too, probably.

Friends.

Lovers.

What does that mean about us?

Besides the fact, he'd be a great father.

Not that I'm considering it.

Only that I want to fuck him bareback.

"You're going somewhere again," he says.

Sex. But that's loaded too. "I admire that about you."

"You admire something about me?"

"You're willing to be disliked."

"You are too."

"I am. But I'm not fire-tested the way you are."

"Teenagers as fire testing." He smiles. "Accurate."

"You're a good brother. A good father figure." I add the last word too late.

It hangs in the air.

Expands to fill the enormous space.

"I was thinking about that," I say.

"Children?"

"Protection. I take the pill. And we're both safe. But if I… in the past, men have looked at me like I'm crazy for asking what they'd want if we had an unplanned pregnancy."

"Men don't consider it."

"Do you?"

"I'm careful."

"Accidents still happen."

"I don't have sex without a condom. Not usually."

Only with me.

He's only offering with me.

Fuck.

"Me either," I say.

"Your fiancé?"

"And a boyfriend in college."

"Did you talk about it?"

I nod.

"What did you say?"

"I couldn't be sure until it happened, but I wasn't ready. I didn't want that. Not with them."

"You added the last part?"

"No." I swallow a sip. "You?"

"No one's ever asked." His eyes go to the stereo. "There's this No Doubt song on one of the albums Opal plays."

"She listens to No Doubt?"

"She started with Gwen's solo career."

"That, I see."

"Gwen is interesting. She's a successful artist and business woman but she has a lot of songs about wanting marriage and family."

"Those aren't mutually exclusive goals."

"No. But they're in conflict."

"You can only have one top priority," I say.

"Mine is family. Always. But a younger sister and grown brothers require a different level of effort than a child."

"But you want that?"

He blushes again.

Fuck, it's so hot.

I want to mount him here.

Now.

"There's a song where Gwen talks about how she hopes for a mistake. I felt that way sometimes. But then I imagined my future with someone and it didn't fit. I wanted to be a father. I wanted a family. But I didn't see my partner in the picture."

I need to say something else. Before I say something I can't take back. "I work too much. We both do."

"It's who we are."

Maybe. "Do you love your job?"

"I love working. I love building a business with my brothers.

I even appreciate the purpose of protecting people's privacy. But I'm not passionate the way you are."

I am passionate, but that's loaded too. "I don't do as much as you think. I ask for money and balance budgets."

"Money to help abused women and children."

"And men."

"And men," he says. "Do you believe you don't do much?"

"No. But it's not what people imagine when they hear 'I run a charity.'"

"I know you, Vanessa. You're saving the world."

"Part of it."

"You're choosing to devote your considerable expertise to saving part of the world."

"What else would I do?" I ask.

"You could do anything. You could run a Fortune 500 company."

"I could not."

"You could," he says.

"The average CEO is a fifty-year-old white man."

"The for-profit world loves nonprofit experience."

"Would you hire me?"

"I wouldn't give you my job, but I would find a place for you."

I shake my head.

He smiles.

"What?"

"I knew you'd say no."

"It wasn't a sincere offer."

"It could be," he says.

"I like my job."

"You're good at it."

I am. "You're good at yours too."

"I am."

"Look at us. Two rich assholes stroking each other's egos."

His smile widens. "Would you rather stroke something else?"

Yes. Now. I need to touch him. Even if it's complicated. My fingers curl into my glass.

"More?"

Now. "Huh?"

"Water."

Oh. Right. "Thanks."

He takes the glass, fills it, returns it to me. "You're passionate about protecting women."

"I am."

"Reproductive rights."

"Yes."

"Honest conversations about birth control."

Right. That's how I started this.

Talking about unprotected sex.

"I am," I say.

"You're nervous?"

I nod.

"You want something else to drink?"

"This first." I swallow a long sip. "What would you want to do? If we had an accident."

"Honest answer?"

"Is the truth that ugly?" I ask.

"No," he says. "But you won't like it."

"Try me."

He does. "I'd ask you to marry me."

"That's old-fashioned."

"That's not why."

"Then why?"

"I respect you. I enjoy your company. I know you're responsible and you care about the world. I want to be a father. And I think you'd be a great mother."

He can imagine a future with me.

All of it.

Fuck.

"If you wanted something else, I'd respect it, but I wouldn't like it," he says.

"You'd really marry me?"

"I'd ask. I wouldn't expect a yes," he says.

"We're both adults."

"We know what we want."

Right. We know what we want. And he wants to have a child with me.

If we have an accident.

Not in general.

That's Simon.

He's responsible.

He steps up to the plate.

"It's unlikely." I say it for myself. Because his response is too overwhelming. Because I need to say something normal.

"I know."

I nod, agreeing with his agreement.

With my own statement.

And I agree.

At least, my head does.

But my body?

My heart?

I'm so far gone I'm lost.

Our rules?

Forgotten.

Replaced by a primal urge to feel his body inside mine.

And all the implications that come with it.

Chapter Twenty-Seven

VANESSA

For a few minutes, my thoughts stall. Grind to a halt, really.

I only hear half of what Simon says. Something about Opal wanting to try the Aviation. Insisting they buy a cocktail shaker.

Of course, Simon didn't have one since he only drinks whiskey.

Only there weren't cocktail shakers at Target. So they went to Bed, Bath, and Beyond, and Opal tried to buy half the store.

Simon made her narrow her selections to a few things. Since she's living here while she goes to school. And she doesn't need extra pillows for college. And no one needs the items sold on infomercials.

She called him mean, of course, but she eventually agreed.

I nod, finish my water, excuse myself.

I use the extremely pink bathroom in the hall, wash my hands with passion fruit soap, dry with a magenta towel.

Opal decorated this place.

And Simon envisions a future with me.

And I have to tell him about my parents. My issues.

My thoughts swirl. Another coat of lipstick fails to help. The bright bulbs of the vanity offer no clarity.

This is sex.

And it's more.

And I can do that. I can do more.

I step into the hallway—it's enormous, and it ends on a balcony—then return to the kitchen.

Immediately, all his attention turns to me.

But he doesn't look at me like he wants to consume me.

He looks at me like he wants to talk to me all fucking night.

"Aviation?" he asks.

"Yes. Thanks."

"Do you want dessert?"

"You eat dessert?"

"Not usually."

"Only chocolate as dark as your soul?"

"They don't make chocolate as dark as my soul."

"A hundred percent cocoa?"

"You tell me."

"I see you at eighty-five."

"My favorite," he says.

"Me too."

He grabs a bar from the shelf.

"Are you going to serve strawberries too?"

"If that's what you want."

I nod. Strawberries are good. Romantic and sexy.

"Sit." He motions to the couch. "I'll bring drinks."

It's a dozen steps to the couch, but it feels farther.

I sink into the supple leather. It's perfect. Sleek and smooth. Supportive but yielding.

A good place for a TV marathon.

A drink.

A fuck.

I smooth my dress. Check my cell.

An all-clear from my security team. Teasing from Lee.

Lee: How soaked is your dress by now? Pay the dry cleaner extra. XO.

"Work?" Simon sets the drinks on the glass coffee table. Slides into the seat next to mine. The way we sat on the balcony. Both times.

"Lee."

"Asking about me?"

"Do you really think the world revolves around you?"

"Does it?"

I show him my cell screen.

He laughs, really laughs. "She's a lot like Liam."

"Don't tell her."

"Don't tell him."

"Do you feel the same way?" I slide my cell into my purse. "About her?"

"Are you asking if I dislike your sister?"

"If you think she's mean."

"She is mean. It's not an opinion."

"She is," I admit.

"But I don't judge her for it. She's honest about who she is. She knows what she wants. She's willing to hurt anyone in her way. I understand that."

"You're both ruthless."

"You are too."

"Is that a compliment?"

"Of course." He lifts his drink.

I raise mine. "Are we toasting?"

"To ruthless women."

I tap my glass against his. Bring it to my lips. Take a long sip. Mmm. Gin. Lemon. Herbs. Sugar. The perfect mix of sweet and tart. "Simon, this is amazing."

"Thank you." He takes a sip. An Aviation for him too.

He looks strange, bringing the delicate martini glass to his lips, sipping the purple liquid.

But he looks right too.

Strong, powerful, in control.

"It took a few tries to get it right." He takes another sip. Sets the drink on the table. "Every time, it tasted like you."

"Did you drink them?"

He nods. "My new favorite."

"Will you stop ordering whiskey?"

"No." His eyes flit to the bedroom. "My plans haven't changed."

Right. Fuck. My chest heaves with my inhale. "I, uh, what were we talking about?"

"Sex."

"Before that."

"Sex."

"After that?"

"Opal," he says.

Everything complicated and fraught.

What's easy?

There must be something easy.

"You're a good brother," I say. "Watching TV with her."

"Lecturing her about the horrifying content?"

"Do you really?"

"All the time. I see something horrible and pause the show. She pouts and complains I'm no fun. I tell her what the problem is. This time, a teenage boy pursuing his teacher. I talked about the power imbalance. How it's never appropriate for a teacher. She tried to turn it around. Asked if it's appropriate for a boss. If I've ever pursued an employee. Or responded to an employee pursuing me."

"Have you?"

Something flares in his eyes. Hurt. "No. But I understand why you'd ask."

"I didn't mean—" I swallow hard. This is why I need to tell

him. So he'll understand it's not him. It's me. "No. I did. I'm sorry."

"It's a fair question."

"It's not you. It's the world."

"You don't believe I'd abuse my power?"

"I did when we were younger. Maybe even a few months ago. But not anymore."

"You were right. I was a spoiled rich boy. I endured a lot for my family, because it was my duty, but only the normal things."

"Losing both your parents before you turn nineteen isn't normal."

"No. I was unlucky. But I had plenty of advantages. I didn't think about them. I didn't think about how hard the world was for women until I had a sister. I know it's a cliché, a man caring about the plight of women when he has a daughter, but it's true. She's not my daughter, but she's—"

"She changed things for you?"

He nods. "It's not the same as death, as grief, but it's similar. All of a sudden, you see a new side of the world. One that was hidden to you before. You have no idea how you ever missed it. How you lived without this knowledge. How anyone does. You try to unsee it, sometimes, but you can't. You go back to something old, something you used to love, and it's the same, because you're not the same."

"Your mother?"

"No. I was too young. But my father. Bash… that was different. He was young and vibrant and…" He looks to his purple drink. "It was my failure this time. Not protecting my younger brother."

He said that before.

He's saying it again.

But wasn't it an accident?

What could Simon have done? Forced his brothers to take

classes on defensive driving? Installed better seat belts or airbags?

Whatever people do to make cars safe.

I've lived in the city my entire life.

I don't know how to drive a car, much less what constitutes safe driving.

"He turned everything to color. Without him, the world was grey again. For months. Even now"—his eyes flit to me—"there are things I see in color. In saturated shades. But it's different. I'm aware of the change in the air."

That's what I do.

I turn the world from black-and-white to color.

Because he likes me.

Or maybe—

Maybe Simon Pierce is in love with me.

Chapter Twenty-Eight

VANESSA

gain, my thoughts grind to a halt.

Again, only one thought flashes through my brain.

Only this time, it isn't carnal. It isn't images of his cock inside me.

It's that four-letter word in brilliant neon.

Love. Love. Love.

Neither one of us is good at it.

Neither one of us is saying it.

I'm not sure what to say, how to explain the feelings racing through my veins.

So I kiss him.

For a split second, he's still. Then he kisses back with hunger and need.

Asking for something deep inside my soul.

Offering something deep inside his.

When I pull back, I'm dizzy. I don't know what to say about love. I don't know what to say about my past.

But I need to say something about this.

"I'm sorry about your brother. Really, Simon. I wish I could do more than say I'm sorry. I wish I could do something to make it better."

His eyes fix on mine.

I don't know what I'd do. What there is to do. But I know I want to sit with him and listen and help him shoulder his pain.

And let him shoulder mine.

I'm capable.

I am.

"If you ever want to talk," I say. "I haven't been through that, but I can sit and listen. And say I'm sorry again."

"Thank you." He takes a long sip of his drink.

I don't know what to say, so I say, "You're welcome."

He sets his glass on the counter. "You're off somewhere."

I need to tell someone.

To tell him.

"It isn't you, Simon," I say. "My instinct to assume the worst. My obsession with the implications of fiction. My problems with intimacy. It's me."

His eyes meet mine.

"You probably know my history. My mom isn't private. And with my job, people assume. But I don't talk about it. Even with Lee."

"You don't have to talk about it."

"I know." I suck a breath through my teeth. I want to share things with him. So he understands. So I'm not fighting myself all the time.

"Whatever you want to share."

I finish my drink. I just need to start. To say it. "My father was abusive."

His eyes stay glued to mine.

"He never hurt me. Not physically. My mom swore he wouldn't, but I'm not sure she believed it. I didn't."

He waits.

"It's hard to explain to someone who hasn't been through it.

People think it's easy to escape. They think survivors are stupid for staying. Can't they see the signs? Can't they just... leave? But they don't see the other times. My father was violent and angry. But he was charming too. Loving. Sweet. Funny. He treated me like a princess. He tucked me in every night. Read from my favorite fairy tale. And he looked at my mom like she was the light in his life. When things were good, they were good. But when he was angry..."

He offers his hand.

I take it. Squeeze tightly.

I've never told anyone this.

Even in treatment, I pushed it away. Insisted it was something else.

"When I was really little, she shielded me. But I think, deep down, I knew something was wrong. I never complained. I never played music loudly or put a second helping on my plate or asked for candy. I was always easy. I never let myself have needs. Even then, as a kid, somehow, I knew that was the best way to keep the peace." I swallow hard. "I think I was seven or eight the first time I saw it. Saw him hurt her. I'd heard them fight before. I'd seen the bruises. But I'd never seen him hit her."

I take a deep breath. Push an exhale through my teeth.

I can do this.

I can.

"They were talking and he was the father I knew. Then, all of a sudden, he was another person, someone I didn't recognize."

He runs his thumb over the space between my thumb and forefinger.

"I still remember the rage in his eyes. The fear in her voice. The first time, she didn't know I saw. Or the next. When she did, she didn't ask him to stop, or tell him she was leaving. She begged, 'not in front of Vanessa.' She didn't want me to see. She didn't want me to know he hurt her. She wanted me to love him and love her and see love as a beautiful thing. But I… I already knew it was fucked up. Even though I didn't know what love was."

"I'm sorry."

"She was trying to protect me. But I still saw… I still knew. I didn't understand it. Why he did that. Why things changed. I just knew I needed to be quiet, to not ask for more than I was given, to do my best…"

"That's not fair to you."

"My mom would ask me what I wanted. She tried to draw it out of me when we were alone. One year she did. She took me to the zoo and offered me anything I wanted. I knew the tiger stuffed animal was too big an ask. Too much. But I wanted it. I wanted to be a tiger. Sleek and powerful and patient. And capable of destroying anyone who tried to hurt me. And… I liked Aladdin."

"The princess trapped in her castle."

"Waiting for someone to rescue her, show her the rest of the world, but still capable enough to break out on her own. I wanted that. And the pet tiger. It was too much, but she was happy I finally asked for something. For once, we were normal. All day. Until my father came home."

Simon nods.

"He'd had a bad day at work. A rude customer. I don't know. It happened so fast. He found the receipt for the toy and he exploded. He became someone else. A monster. He didn't stop. Even when she screamed. Even when she begged him to wait. It was always that. Never 'don't hurt me.' Always 'not in front of Vanessa.'"

He listens. Holds my hand. Waits until I'm ready to continue.

"I locked myself in the bathroom. I was terrified but, somehow, I fell asleep in the tub. Woke up to find her bruised and bleeding in the bathroom."

"It wasn't your fault."

"She was protecting me."

He doesn't explain or correct me. He sits with me, patient, understanding, open.

"Even then, even with a black eye, she still insisted he was a good man. He just got mad sometimes. He loved her. He loved us. He'd never hurt me." I suck a breath through my teeth. "She said that a lot. I believed her. That time, I didn't."

"Fuck, Vanessa. I'm sorry."

I don't know what to say, so I nod. "I hated her for staying."

"You were a kid."

"I still hate her sometimes. For putting us through that."

"Everyone resents their parents."

"Not like this. I... I blamed her, for a long time, for my decisions. My mistakes. I owned them when I was in treatment, but I never learned, really... I never learned how to express my needs. Or trust. Or let go."

His brow screws. "Treatment?"

"In school... do you remember the year I left a week before winter break?"

He nods.

"I learned my body was the only thing I could control. So I controlled what I ate. It was normal at first, then it wasn't, and I wasn't in control anymore. My disorder was. And everyone knew something was wrong. And my dad convinced her to send me to an inpatient clinic."

His eyes stay fixed on me.

"It was good, because it convinced her to get help too... for her PTSD. But I... Fuck, how much do you think I'm a mess?"

"You're not a mess."

"I am."

"No more than I am."

"I'm not sure that's encouraging."

His smile is sad. "Are you okay now?"

"Okay. But not better. I started restricting again when my mom got sick. Just a little. To feel in control. I know, I shouldn't, but it's the only thing that works."

"Vanessa—" There's so much packed into the word.

I care about you. I can't watch you hurt yourself. I won't let you resist help.

But Simon isn't in charge of me.

I can leave anytime. I can refuse help. I can lock him out.

I can choose control over love.

The way my biological father did.

Only different.

Self-destruction.

Better than hurting someone I love. But still dangerous.

"I haven't admitted it to anyone," I say. "I ended my last relationship because I didn't want him to know. Because I felt better controlling my body than…"

"Accepting pleasure?"

"Yes."

"I won't say I know what you've been through. I don't. But I know that feeling."

"You do?"

He nods. "After Bash… I…" He reaches for something. Doesn't find it.

It's strange seeing him tongue-tied.

Sweet.

Scary.

"Thank you for telling me. For trusting me. I'm honored," he says.

"You don't want to run away?"

"No."

"You promise?"

"Yes."

The word isn't a relief.

It's terrifying.

He wants to stay.

He wants to see my ugly parts.

He pulls my body into his. He's so warm and hard and safe.

There's a physical safeness. His size. His strength. His ability to protect me.

And something else too.

A soft place to land.

I let my eyes fall closed. Soak in the scent of his skin. "This is not a great seduction on my part."

He chuckles. "It's perfect."

We lie there for a long time. Until I can feel his heart pounding against his chest.

Slow and steady and comforting.

"We can wait until next time for the whiskey," he says.

No. I need this time. I want to feel good. "The whiskey maybe. But not the rest."

"Are you sure?"

Yes. I need to erase the ugly thoughts in my head. To replace them with something beautiful. "Yes."

"Do you need different?"

"Different?"

"Tonight. After talking about that. Softer. Slower. Or harder. I won't judge any reaction you have."

"You mean if I want you to hurt me, because I grew up seeing abuse as love?"

"No."

"No?"

"If you want to be in control."

"Tie you to the headboard?"

He nods into my neck.

"I'm starting to think you have an interest." My laugh is sad. But it feels good too.

"In watching you use me like a toy? Why wouldn't I?"

"Not tonight." I don't know what I need tonight. I just know I need him. "Maybe soon. To satisfy your dirty desires."

"For me?"

"Only because you want it, yeah."

"Considerate."

"Thank you."

"Is there anything else?" He runs his thumb over my temple. "Anything you need me to do?"

"No… The same. I… I don't like rough."

He nods. He doesn't ask if that's why. Or mention my need for control. Or ask what else I've done to cope.

He just holds me.

It feels so good.

Safe and warm and comfortable.

Like I really can collapse.

Fall apart.

Trust him to put me back together.

I'm not sure how long I stay there. Five minutes or two hours.

It's easy and steady. Almost a trance.

Until keys jingle. And the door creaks open.

His sister is home.

It's not just us, anymore.

It's not just sex, anymore.

He's inviting me into his family.

Into his life.

Into a real relationship.

Chapter Twenty-Nine

VANESSA

"**I**'m not looking." Opal steps inside, one hand over her eyes. "I'm minding my own business. I won't see anything."

Simon looks up at me, affection in his eyes. He leans close enough to whisper. "You can go."

"No," I whisper back.

"Are you sure?"

No. But I nod anyway.

Opal interrupts. "Continue your dirty talk at a reasonable volume. I know your generation is all sex maniacs. Briar and Danielle are technically in my generation, but they're on the cusp. And it shows. Less obsessive than you and Liam. But still thinking they invented sexy pictures. Especially Danielle." She pushes the door closed with her leg. Shrugs her purse off her shoulder.

"We're dressed," I say. "You can look."

She peeks through two fingers, like she expects to see us naked, in some acrobatic position. "You are."

I slide off Simon's lap.

He stands. Picks up the glasses. "Is it that surprising?"

"Yeah." She watches him bring the glasses to the sink. "Can I have one?"

"Do you want another?" He looks to me.

It's tempting, but it's a bad idea. "I'm good."

"The strawberries?" he asks.

Opal's eyes go wide.

He looks to his sister. "Yes?"

"Nothing. Nothing. I'm wiped. And it's hot. This is less breathable than I thought." She tugs at the neckline of her cocktail dress. "I'm going to shower. But after that... I had a lot of coffee, so I'm not really tired, but I—" She looks to Simon and motions *let's talk over here.*

He shakes his head *we can talk here.*

"You're not naked," she says.

"I'm aware," he says.

"Do you not have any game?" she asks.

"Game?" he asks.

She tries to whisper, but she's not remotely quiet. "Yeah. Is that why you don't have a girlfriend? Not because you're busy or emotionally unavailable, but because you can't close the deal?"

Oh my god. A laugh spills from my lips.

She looks to me and puts her hand over her mouth. "Sorry."

"We're obsessed with sex?" I ask.

She shrugs, guilty.

"Do I have game?" Simon asks me.

I motion *so-so.*

"No. It's worse. Anti-game. You're obscenely handsome. Isn't he?" Opal asks.

"He is," I say.

"Right. Like a guy who plays an evil CEO in a movie," she says.

I laugh. "She knows you."

"She does," he says.

"And tall too." Opal looks at her shoes, trying to gauge their rise. In her heels, she's eye to eye with him. "Women love tall guys."

"It's a popular feature," I say.

"Which is weird, right? If you're five-four, what do you care if a guy is five-eight or six-two? Either way, he's towering over you," she says.

"I'm supposed to know?" Simon asks.

"Seriously, Simon. I'm concerned. It's been two hours. Two and a half. I'm late. You didn't notice *and* you're not having sex. Do you need some dating tips? The strawberries are cheesy. Especially with whipped cream." She bites her lip. "Don't tell me you offered her the coconut whipped cream."

"It's what we have," he says.

"It doesn't spray. Look." She goes to the fridge and pulls out a canister of whipped cream with coconuts on it. Then she takes a plate, puts it on the counter, tosses the top aside. "Look at this." She puts her finger on the dispenser and pushes down.

It hisses. Sputters. Spits a few drops.

"You bring this out with a woman, and she's going to make the connection." She motions in the general direction of Simon's crotch. "Think you don't have the right stuff."

"Semen with velocity is the right stuff?"

"Oh my god, Simon! Don't be gross."

"I'm being gross?" he asks.

"Yeah."

"You sound like Liam," he says.

She looks at the melting drops of whipped cream on the plate. "I do."

"Horrifying."

"More horrifying is I'm right. He's right. Two hours and no sex. You're tall and handsome and you're wearing a suit. What's your excuse?" She folds her arms.

"Maybe we aren't sex maniacs," he says.

"At least come up with a plausible explanation," she says.

I laugh.

She raises a brow *look*.

"Maybe we had sex," he says.

"Then why are you wearing your clothes from the opera?" she asks. "I thought you—"

"That's a surprise," he says.

"Then you didn't," she says.

"Why do you care?"

"Three years, Simon. I've been here three years. And you've never invited a woman to dinner."

"Vanessa's been at dinners," he says.

"With Harrison and Lee and Preston, sure. Sometimes, her parents are there too. But never alone."

He actually blushes. It's quick—he snaps right back into concerned brother mode—but it's there.

And it's incredibly fucking hot.

There are a million things swirling in my head.

But this is clear; I need to fuck him.

I need to touch him and feel him and have him feel me.

Opal looks to me like she can tell I'm thinking dirty thoughts. "Is the suit a problem? Are you like Liam? He grew up a spoiled rich boy so now he's into grimy stuff." Her nose scrunches. "Teasing Briar about taking her to a trashy strip club and renting a private room. Of course, with Liam, who knows who's giving whom a dance. Or if a professional is involved. For all I know, he is a professional. Do you think he goes in as a cop? A doctor? A firefighter?"

"How much coffee did you have?" Simon asks.

"A firefighter. That's a stupid question." She shakes her head *obviously*. "With the hose and everything… that's Liam."

"How much?" Simon asks again.

She ignores his question. "Is that it? The gin? Liam says it happens to everyone."

"How did that come up?" I ask.

"It's Liam," Simon says.

"So it happens to him?" I ask.

"No, 'not me, I know my limits.'" She rolls her eyes. "I think it causes him physical pain to go ten minutes without talking about his dick."

"How much coffee?" Simon asks.

"Is that a new rule?" she asks.

"It's a question," he says.

"How many drinks?" she counters.

"One at dinner. One at the theater. One now," he says.

"They had coconut milk macchiatos," she says. "And raw vegan cheesecake. Chocolate mocha."

"You're going to be up all night," he says.

"See. This—" she motions from his position at the kitchen island to me on the couch. "You're trying to warn her off from having sex while I'm here."

"I'm being polite," he says.

"So, what, if you ever meet someone you like enough to ask them to move in, you'll never have sex when I'm home? What if you have kids one day? Is that the end of your sex life?" she asks.

She has him there.

"Who cares how much coffee I drank? It's coffee, not bourbon. I didn't rob a bank or sleep with a rando. Get a new hobby. Like learning how to make it happen," she says.

I can't help but laugh.

Opal shakes her head *sad*. "Do you not like guys in suits?"

"Does Simon own other clothes?" I ask.

"Supposedly," she says. "But he only wears them on Saturdays. If he's not going into the office. Sometimes Sundays, but not if we're going to brunch. And we're always going to brunch."

"You love brunch," he says.

"Yeah. But everyone else is wearing a suit ironically! Because the place is called Church. Sunday best."

He stares blankly at her.

She shakes her head *sad, he just doesn't get it.*

"What does he wear?" I ask.

"You don't like the suit. Ah"—she presses her hands together—"now, we're getting somewhere."

He looks to me and raises a brow *is that right?*

"I like it," I say. "I prefer him out of it, but I like it."

Opal squeals, somehow finding my obsession with sex charming instead of annoying.

Maybe it's only annoying when it's a lecture from an older person.

She's funny.

And I…

Well, I can't really claim I'm not consumed with thoughts of touching Simon.

Still. She's his sister. I'm not about to talk about how badly I want to feel his cock inside me.

"Does he own jeans?" I ask.

"Oh yeah, jeans, no shirt, no shoes." She looks at Simon. Realizes she's describing her brother. Scrunches her nose. "A good look, in theory."

"Where are you forming these opinions?" he asks.

"Newsflash. Your generation didn't invent attraction," she says.

"I'd like to see you in only jeans," I say.

She shakes her head *not going to happen.*

"You don't own jeans?" I ask.

"Oh, he does. Christmas present three years in a row. All with original tags attached," she says.

"You don't like them?" I ask.

"They're stiff," he says.

"Isn't that thing uncomfortable?" she asks.

"I'm used to it," he says.

"What does he wear on his days off?" I ask.

She shakes her head. "I'd tell you, but I don't think it's going to help his case. And I'm not a c-blocker."

He raises a brow.

"Equal opportunity," she says.

"Those are Liam's exact words," he says.

"And if Liam were here, he'd tell you to get the fuck on it. He's wise sometimes," she says.

"That's horrifying," he says.

"Yeah. But it's true." She looks at the whipped cream canister, shakes her head, turns to the hallway. "I am going to shower. After that, I'll be in my room, with the fan on. It muffles sound pretty well but don't make it a goal to test it." She walks toward her room with a wave. "Good night, Simon. Nice to see you again, Vanessa. I hope I'll see you in the morning."

"Good night," I say to her.

He waits until she's in her room, then he looks to me. "Is she right?"

"Your lack of game? Or the whipped cream?"

"The whipped cream, of course," he says.

"Absolutely. I only have sex on Spider-man sheets."

"That's how you decorate your room."

I stand and nod. "And I judge. Based on their ability to open a bottle of champagne."

"Reasonable."

My lips curl into a smile. "You never wear jeans?"

"She's exaggerating."

"What do you wear on Saturdays?"

"You'll see tomorrow."

If I stay all night. All morning. Through breakfast and coffee and whatever else they do all day.

I want to be there.

To see his love.

But that's terrifying.

This—

This makes sense.

This is pure.

"We can keep talking," he says. "Or sit here quietly. We don't have to—"

"I want to. If you do."

"Are you sure?"

"Yes."

He hesitates. He's worried about what I've said. What it means.

"We can talk tomorrow."

He nods.

"Tonight, I want this. Please."

His pupils dilate. "Tonight."

I move around the couch. "Are the walls thick?"

"I'll put on music."

"What kind?"

"A surprise."

"You won't tell me?" I ask.

"No. And I won't tell you what's waiting for you in my bed, gift wrapped, either."

Chapter Thirty

VANESSA

The space is all Simon.

Wide windows. Dark curtains. A leather armchair next to a mahogany end table.

His private space.

He's inviting me into it.

He's changing his space for me.

I want to consume every inch of it.

Every inch of him.

He points me to the white gift box on the grey sheets.

A present.

But it's not as exciting as the mirrors. They're everywhere.

So I can watch.

So we can both watch.

He catches me staring. "They're new."

For me. "What did you have before?"

"Something smaller." He motions to a mirror in the corner. "In case you need a reflection of a reflection."

Fuck.

He wraps his arms around my waist. Presses his lips to my neck. "Or something on the ceiling."

"You don't."

"Do I?"

No. He wouldn't.

Would he?

I check, just to be sure.

Simon smiles. "I can put one in."

"No."

"No?"

"Maybe."

"Maybe." He presses his lips to my neck. Points me to the gift box sitting on the bed. "Do you want to open it?"

"I do."

He releases me.

I move to the bed. Find the card tucked into the red ribbon.

A rectangle of cardstock in a white envelope, with a simple, cheeky message:

My pleasure.

- Simon

A response to my note, thanking him for his hospitality.

My lips curl into a smile.

This is perfect.

Easy, sweet, sexy.

I want it.

And the rest too.

I really like him.

Maybe even more. Maybe even the word that terrifies me.

I drop the card. Unwrap the gift.

Find purple lingerie sitting on wine tissue paper.

A plum bra and panty set and a long robe.

"The color suits you," he says. "It's regal. Intense. Sexy."

I pick up the robe. Study the way the soft light reflects the sheen.

"Is it too much?"

"It's beautiful." I lay the lingerie on the bed. Turn to Simon. "Thank you."

"My pleasure." His eyes fill with an intoxicating mix of pride, desire, affection.

The word rises in my throat.

Is this love?

I don't know. But it's something. Maybe even everything.

Fuck. I'm in so far over my head it's not even funny.

"There are pajamas too," he says.

"Purple silk?"

"Of course."

Of course. Because it suits me. Because it's regal and sexy, and he wants to fuck me and invite me into his bed.

For sex, yes.

And everything else too.

"I have something else first." He pulls his cell from his pocket. Taps a few buttons.

A speaker in the corner plays a familiar introduction.

A song from high school.

Played at every dance.

Slow, soft, romantic.

"Too much?" he asks again.

"Only if you're going to ask me to change into that lingerie now."

"After." He sets his cell on the end table. "We've never danced together."

"You've never asked."

"Let's change that." He offers his hand. "May I?"

I take his hand. Try to recall dance position.

One hand in his.

The other on his upper back.

He places his hand on the small of my back.

"This is a waltz," he says.

"Spoiled rich boy."

"I'm good at it."

"You're good at everything."

"Not everything." He presses his forehead to mine.

Warmth floods my body. Affection. Then the heat of desire.

I need him in every way I can have him.

"Do you know how to follow?" he asks.

"No. But I can try."

"We keep the waltz rhythm. But I set the steps. Guide you gently." He presses his palm into my lower back, pushing me forward as he steps backward.

Then the reverse.

Right to left. Left to right.

"We can start with a box step." He shifts forward.

I step back a little slowly. And not at all in time with the music.

But he's patient. Guides me through the next step until we're back at the start.

The second time, I get it a little better.

The third, I really have it.

There's something soothing about the steady pattern.

Every time, I ease into it.

My thoughts slip further away.

My body responds to his.

I follow his lead.

The song fades into the next. Another oft-played slow song.

"Did you pick these?" I melt into his movements.

"It was Danielle's suggestion. She asked if I needed music, to set the mood."

"When she decorated the room?"

He nods. "She went on about slow jams. I have a playlist."

"Simon Pierce fucking to sultry slow jams?"

"We'll see."

My stomach flutters. "I usually don't play music."

"Me either."

"But with Opal—"

He nods. "Now?"

"Now." He releases me, finds his cell on the end table, switches the song.

A steady rhythm fills the room. Soft, breathy vocals. I don't recognize the song—I'm not great with music either—but it's undeniably sexy.

"Perfect."

He motions to the lingerie on the bed. "Do you want to try it?"

"I do."

"I'll give you a minute."

"Help with this first." I turn. Pull my hair from my neck so he has access to my zipper.

He presses his lips to the back of my neck. Soft. So soft I can barely feel it.

He pulls the zipper down slowly. Traces the line of my spine back up to my neck with that same feather-light touch.

"Five minutes." He presses his lips to my neck again. "I'll knock once."

I nod. Wait for him to slip out of the room.

The door closes softly.

I slide out of my gown and shoes.

A million thoughts flood my mind.

Then I slip into the lingerie and they disappear.

It's my size—how the hell did he know—and it's perfect.

Sexy. Classy. Gorgeous.

My heart thuds against my chest.

My stomach flutters.

My toes curl.

My entire body is buzzing. Lust or love?

I'm not sure.

I only know I need him. All of him. As much as I can have.

The bra and panty are gorgeous, but the robe is better.

I do away with the set. Slip into the purple silk.

It's gorgeous. A gown out of an old Hollywood movie. Almost demure enough to be a dress. Except for the ease of removal.

Simon was right.

It's regal, powerful, sexy.

Is that really how he sees me?

As someone with as much authority as he has?

Someone as commanding?

It's different.

He's a man.

He's white.

He's from the right family.

But it's the same too.

We're both executives. Experts in our fields. People who know how to take control.

He sees me. He really sees me.

The vulnerable parts.

The strong parts.

The ugly and the beautiful—

He sees me, all of me, and he wants me.

It's overwhelming.

He knocks then slips inside.

It's there, in his eyes.

All that affection and desire. For my body, my heart, my mind.

My thighs shake. My knees knock. My toes curl.

I want the same thing. All of him.

"Fuck, Vanessa." He takes another step toward me. Looks me up and down, savoring the sight of me. "You are a queen."

I am.

That really is how he sees me.

How he makes me feel.

It's overwhelming.

Terrifying.

Completely intoxicating.

I turn toward him, but I let him come to me.

He moves with slow steps.

Closer and closer.

Until he's close enough to touch.

I look up at him. Wrap my hand around his wrist. Bring his hand to the delicate tie holding the sides together.

He pulls the strings.

The sides fall open, exposing my breasts, stomach, thighs.

All of me.

On display for him.

Because he wants to savor the sight.

Because it turns me on.

Again, he studies me, noting every inch of my skin with interest and delight. His eyes pass over me slowly, from the top of my head to my bare toes, then back up.

He looks me in the eyes as he brings his hand to my chest.

He pulls me into a soft, slow kiss. Then he turns me, so I'm in front of him, facing the mirror, watching him toy with my nipple.

Fuck.

I nearly come on the spot. It's almost too much. Too intense.

But I need more.

All of him.

I watch him toy with me.

Slow circles of his thumb on my tender flesh.

He brings his lips to my neck. Scrapes his teeth against my skin as he toys with me.

Again and again.

Winding me tighter.

Filling me with anticipation.

Again and again.

Until I'm sure I can't take it anymore.

Then, still, more.

I rock my hips against him. Feel his cock, hard against my ass. All that fabric in the way. Too many fucking layers in the way.

I need him inside me.

Now.

But, still, he teases.

I rock against him, again.

He groans against my neck. Brings a hand to my hip, pulling my body against his. So I feel him closer.

Fuck.

He slips his hand between my legs. Draws slow circles against my clit.

I need more.

But I need this too.

"Simon." It falls off my lips like a curse.

He moves to my other nipple. The other side of my neck. Teases me. Gives me what I need.

Soft brushes of his thumb.

Slow circles.

Winding me tighter and tighter.

Almost.

Fuck.

There.

I come fast, rocking my hips, tugging at his slacks, watching his hand move between my legs.

Watching him get me off.

He works me through my orgasm, then he brings his hand to my waist. Moves backward to lead me to his armchair.

He sits.

Pulls me onto his lap.

Looks up at me, cupping my cheek with his palm, staring with equal parts devotion and desire.

It means something.

Everything maybe.

But I'm lost in a haze of bliss and need.

I need him inside me.

I need his skin against mine.

I undo the buttons of his shirt, feel the soft skin covering hard muscles.

The tattoo above his hip. The Simon no one else sees.

I do away with the shirt, undo his belt, unzip his slacks.

He shifts his hips to do away with the clothes.

Simon Pierce, under me, in only boxers.

Then nothing.

Fuck.

He brings his hands to my hips, and he pulls my body into his.

No condom this time.

Only his body against mine.

My sex brushes his cock. It's only a tease, but it's so fucking intense this way.

All of him.

All of me.

I raise my hips to tease him again.

Again.

Again.

He presses his palm into the space between my shoulders and pulls my chest to his mouth.

His lips close around my nipple.

Soft suction.

Then harder.

Fuck.

I turn to the mirror. Savor the sight.

His lips against my skin.

The purple robe, falling at the sides, exposing my chest, stomach, thighs, but leaving me regal and powerful, while he's naked under me.

Right now, he really is mine.

I watch as I lower my body onto his. Watch as I take him.

Then I do it again.

Again.

It's already too much, the fullness of his cock inside me, the perfect pressure of his lips, the sight of our bodies joining.

I have to close my eyes.

I have to pull him back and bring my hips to his.

I kiss him as I ride him.

Harder.

Deeper.

With every fucking thing I have.

He brings his hands to my hips, guiding me over him again and again.

I break our kiss. Bring my hands to his shoulders. Use the chair for leverage.

He brings his lips back to my chest, toying with my nipple as I ride him.

The two of us moving together, bringing each other bliss, watching, finding more in the sight.

A perfect circle of pleasure.

Again and again.

It's intense.

Almost too much.

Then I look to the mirror, and I watch him slide into me, and I fall over the fucking edge.

My sex pulses as I come. It's hard, intense, so much I'm sure I'm going to push him out.

But I only bring him closer.

His fingers dig into my thighs. Hard but not rough. Only enough, I feel his need.

His bliss.

It's intoxicating.

I need more of it.

All of it.

I ride him again and again.

His eyes flutter together.

His lips part with a moan.

"Fuck me, Simon." I knot my hand in his hair. "Come inside me." The words surprise me.

I've never said them before.

Never savored the idea.

But I want it so fucking badly.

I drive over him again and again.

The rhythm he needs.

Until he's there, groaning my name as his cock pulses inside me.

It's different without the condom.

Closer, deeper, more intense.

He spills every drop.

I collapse on his chest.

He holds me close, like I really am his, like he really wants this to be forever.

———

I stay in his arms a long time. Until my legs are sore.

Then I pull back. Retie my robe. Help him up.

He pushes his clothes aside, takes my hand, leads me to the dresser, pulls the top drawer open.

"Pajamas." He points to the folded purple silk short set. "If you don't want to sleep naked."

If I want to stay the night.

If I want to stay in his life.

He doesn't say it, but it's there in his words, his actions, his posture.

"Something for tomorrow." He points to a simple black sundress. Comfortable and neutral enough, I won't look ridiculous in my heels. "There are shoes in the closet."

"There are?"

"Lee said you have the same pair at home."

"You asked?"

"She volunteered."

"After I came home in my dress?"

He nods. "I liked the idea of it. You, wearing the dress you were wearing when you came on my hand. But I understand it's impractical."

It sounds sexy that way. Not thoughtless or inconsiderate.

And with an entire outfit, I can stay longer.

All day, if I want.

"Do you want the first shower?" he asks.

"No. Join me."

He does.

The bathroom is as nice as the rest of the house. And it's Simon. A massive glass slower, marble floors, stainless steel accessories.

Plenty of space for both of us.

But we stay pressed together as we soap and rinse and kiss and touch.

After, I dry and dress in the purple silk pajamas, I crawl into his bed and fall asleep in his arms.

In his bed.

In his life.

Chapter Thirty-One

SIMON

Vanessa Moyer is in my bed.

A million fantasies in the flesh.

She's every bit as grand as she is in my head.

Grander, even.

But she's not a fantasy or a fairy tale.

She's a woman with her own scars.

And she trusts me with them.

Is this why Bash spoke of love poetically?

For once, I understand.

For once, I don't want to roll my eyes at his insistence on calling sex making love.

We are creating love, bringing more into the universe.

I've said the word before, but I've never felt it. I thought there was something wrong with me. That I was somehow incapable of feeling love. Understanding what it was.

If I enjoyed a woman's company, wanted a physical connection, wished for a happy future for her—

That's how people described love.

So I said the words, even though I didn't feel them.

My heart didn't thud. My stomach didn't flutter. My body didn't fill with warmth at the sight of her smile.

Just thinking of Vanessa's laugh—

Maybe I am in love with her.

Maybe this is how it looks.

I don't have her fucked-up history, but I have my own.

Love is dangerous.

Vanessa knows that. She'll understand if I explain.

But how the fuck can I tell her this?

I don't know.

But I owe it to her to try.

I want to trust her with my secrets.

And be the person she trusts to carry her burdens.

Soon.

There isn't a rush. I understand that, practically, but emotionally?

I want all of her, all at once.

But I can't rush her. Not after last night.

So I roll to my side, and I watch her sleep. I watch her chest rise with her inhale. I watch the morning light fall over her dark skin. Watch her purple pajamas shift with her exhale.

She's beautiful in the morning light.

Here. In my bed. In my life.

I savor the sight of her for one more moment, then I rise, wash, leave her sleeping.

Opal is in the kitchen, pouring coconut milk into a cup of coffee. She loves her drinks sweet and creamy.

She looks up from her mug. Takes in my outfit. "Are those silk pajamas?"

"Yes."

"You really slept in them?"

"No."

"Oh. Gross, Simon."

"You asked."

"Still." She smiles, not at all bothered, pours a cup of black coffee into my *Hello Gorgeous* mug, hands it to me. "How was it?"

"Could you hear?"

"Hear Danielle's sex playlist, yeah. I've heard it before." Her nose scrunches. "That's weird. Two family members with the same sex playlist. Three, I guess, since I heard it at Liam's place."

"What should I play?"

"Nine Inch Nails. No. Never mind. When I said that to Liam—"

"He said he had a nine-inch something?"

"Gross."

"And I'm going to say the same thing?" I ask.

"No. Maybe. I don't know anymore."

"You don't?"

She nods *of course not*, sips her coffee, slides onto a stool. "How was it?"

"Private."

"That bad?" She shakes her head *too bad* and takes another sip.

"That won't work."

"Are you sure?"

"I thought we were too obsessed with sex," I say.

"You are."

"Then why are you asking?"

"You've spread your diseases."

I can't help but chuckle.

"It was good, wasn't it?" She takes a long sip. "Really good."

"It was."

"You like her?"

"I do."

"Love her?"

I don't say no immediately. I don't know what to say. "It's new."

"Love isn't on a time line."

"I care about her."

"No, Simon, no. Care is a slap in the face. Don't even think about telling her that."

"What should I tell her?"

"That you love her."

"What if I don't love her yet?"

"Irrelevant question. You're totally into her." She draws a line around my head in the air. "It's all over your face."

Is it really?

"You bought her lingerie and pajamas. And an outfit for today. An entire outfit."

"So she can walk home."

"She lives around the corner."

"Four blocks."

"You don't want her to go four blocks to change. You want her here all weekend."

"She has a gala tonight."

"You already know her schedule?"

"She's a notable figure. I'm aware of what events she's attending."

"You cyber-stalk her."

"She volunteered the information."

"You cyber-stalk her and you're shy about it. I don't think I've ever seen you shy." She examines my expression. "Why aren't you blushing?"

"You're more like Liam every day."

She doesn't take the bait. "Are you going with her?"

"I wasn't invited."

"Please, Simon. You're like… The King of Park Avenue."

"We don't live on Park Avenue."

She bats the air *whatever*. "Everyone would be happy to see you and your big checkbook."

"Did you eat?"

"Why would I eat before coffee?"

"Do you want eggs?"

"Simon, if you don't want to talk, okay. But don't cook. Please. I can't bear that torture."

"Cruel."

"It would be cruel, yes." She looks to my bedroom. "I can go, if you want the place to yourself. I have plenty to do."

"When did you go to bed?"

"Late."

"Did you finish your homework?"

"I have class Tuesday. It's Saturday morning."

"Did you?"

"Yes, actually. The lines are a little shaky. Drawing while caffeinated. But it's a style."

I won't argue. She's right. I'm overbearing. "How was dessert?"

"Normal. Liam making sex jokes. Briar rolling her eyes in adoration. Raw cheesecake and coconut cappuccinos." She takes another sip. "It was really good, huh?"

"It was."

"In every way. Carnal and emotional."

"Did you just say carnal?"

"It's a word."

"An SAT word."

"Would you prefer tumescent?" she asks.

"My favorite word."

"You can evade if you want, but it won't change anything. You're glowing."

Am I?

"It's the glow of love. I saw it on Adam. I saw it on Liam. Now, I see it on you."

"How can you tell?"

"You too? Denial. Why can't men admit their feelings?"

"I would know?"

She sets her mug on the table. Smiles, channeling Bash. "Have you ever been in love?"

"No."

"Do you think about her when you're lying in bed?"

"I do."

"First thing in the morning?"

"That's lust."

"Is it though? Is it all sex?"

No.

She raises a brow *see*. "You think about what she needs, what she wants, how safe it feels to hold her."

"Where are you getting this?"

She ignores my question. "How much you want to be there, with her. How to make sure she's comfortable here, in your place, in your life."

"Conscientiousness isn't love."

"It's so obvious, Simon. I don't know why you can't see it. It really is all over your face."

The floor creaks behind me. My room.

Vanessa is up.

Opal squeals. "Are you going to tell her?"

"It's early."

"So you admit it?"

No. "Don't say anything."

"Please. Girl code." She offers her hand.

It was surprising, the first time she suggested girl talk. Even more when she suggested the girl code. But, now, I'm used to it. "Girl code."

She slides off her stool. "Does she drink coffee?"

"Tea. English Breakfast with milk and honey." I've seen her drink it at afternoon meetings. Holiday gatherings.

Opal looks to the electric kettle on the counter. It's always there.

But the tin of English Breakfast and the tea-strainer next to it—

Those are new.

"That." She taps the tin. "Love."

"I've got it," I say.

"No. I will. My mom drank tea. Focus on finding a way to verbalize those feelings."

"You're ridiculous."

"I am a Pierce." She turns, fills the kettle, gets to work making tea.

Vanessa steps into the hallway in her purple pajama short set. A button-up short-sleeve top and very short shorts.

She still looks strong, commanding, regal—she always does—but she looks soft too.

"Hey." She shoots Opal a smile. "Good morning."

"Good morning," Opal chirps. "Simon tells me you two had a good night."

Vanessa looks to me and raises a brow *what did you say?*

"He wouldn't offer any details about the sex, and I won't ask, but it's pretty obvious it was great. Look at him. Glowing," she says.

"You are glowing." Vanessa crosses the room to me.

I wrap my arms around her. "You're glowing."

She shakes her head.

I nod, pull her closer, press my lips to hers.

She melts into me for a moment. Realizes Opal is here. Pulls back. "Oh. Sorry."

"That's nothing. Liam is always talking about him and Briar's sex life," she says. "It's to annoy Briar, but it works to annoy me."

"They're always pushing each other's buttons," Vanessa says.

Opal nods *yep*. "You and Simon too. Only more stoically."

"Stoic. That is a good description of you." Vanessa smiles.

"I can go if you to want to be alone," Opal says. "I was thinking about going to breakfast anyway."

"There's nowhere nearby," I say.

"Nowhere in the three blocks surrounding us, yes," Opal says. "But we do live in Manhattan."

"I don't want to intrude," Vanessa says. "Do what you'd do if I wasn't here."

"We go to breakfast," Opal says.

"On Sundays," I say.

"Do you see what I deal with? If you look up routine in the dictionary, you get a picture of Simon." She shakes her head. "Most Saturdays, I drag Simon out of the apartment. Try to keep him from making an excuse about going to the office. And we do get breakfast sometimes. Go to the park. Then lunch. The ice cream place with the non-dairy flavors."

"Shopping," I say.

"I barely ever take you shopping." Opal finishes the tea. Presents the mug to Vanessa. "We don't have dairy. Only coconut and almond."

"Which do you prefer?" she asks.

"Coconut. Hands down. But it's intense. Straight from the can."

"Let's do it," Vanessa says.

Opal finds the can, fills the mug, hands it off to Vanessa.

"Thank you." Vanessa inhales the scent of the tea. Lets out a soft sigh. She takes a long sip. Lets out a longer sigh. "Intense. Good intense."

Opal beams. "I make breakfast too."

"You do?" she asks.

"My mom worked a lot. I cooked for us," she says. "And Simon… totally hopeless in the kitchen."

"You are?" she asks.

"Hopeless is overstating it," I say.

"Terrible," Opal says. "He can fry eggs, butter toast, maybe sear a steak. That's all."

"Lee can't cook either," Vanessa says.

"Can you?" Opal asks. "Or will you two hire someone to cook for you?"

I shoot her a *don't* look.

She shrugs *why not?*

"I'm okay," Vanessa says. "Not great, but not bad. I don't have time to cook. I use a service."

"We do too," Opal says.

"Simon told me."

"He gives me his dessert," Opal says.

"He told me that too." Vanessa looks at me with appreciation. "Let's go out."

"Can we do bagels?" Opal asks.

"I love bagels," Vanessa says.

"Good taste." Opal looks at her leggings. "I should shower. Then we can go. Or do you two need more time? I don't mind a solo bagel."

Vanessa looks at me expectantly. Asking what I want.

I want to spend the day with her.

I don't care about the details.

Is that love?

Or something else?

"Maybe later," Vanessa says. "I'm starving."

"Ten minutes?" Opal asks.

"Make it fifteen," Vanessa says.

Opal raises a brow *I know what that means*, but she doesn't say anything. She skips to the bathroom.

Vanessa rises to her tiptoes and presses her lips to mine.

She melts into me.

A long, slow kiss.

All need and affection.

She pulls back with a sigh. "She's sweet."

"Overbearing in her own way."

"Yeah, but not compared to you." She takes my hand. "Show me where these clothes are."

I lead her to the bedroom.

To the dresser filled with items for her.

"Shit. Is this why Opal takes you shopping?" She holds up a purple bra in her size. "This is a lot."

"Too much?"

"No." She checks the tag. "How do you know my sizes?"

"I asked your assistant."

"No wonder she knew we were fucking."

"She knew before I asked."

"Really?"

"Said it was practically written on your calendar."

"It did say Pierce dinner."

"Case closed," I say.

She laughs. "In her eyes." She looks up at me, searching for something, finding it. "I have work tonight. A gala. I have a plus-one. I was going to bring Lee, but she's ovulating, and she doesn't want to leave the apartment. Just in case."

"She told you that?"

"I wish that was all she told me."

I smile. "I'm your plan B?"

"More like plan D."

"Plan D, specifically?"

She laughs. "You sound like your brother."

"I do, don't I?"

She nods. "I kind of like it." She hooks her arms around my neck. "Simon Pierce, obsessed with his cock."

"I'm obsessed?"

"Yes."

"You don't care?"

"Not at all."

"If I decided not to use it for a while…"

"Don't say crazy things."

"Crazy, huh?"

"Simon." She lets out a soft squeal. "You're…" She kisses me again. "Go. Or I won't get dressed."

"You don't have to get dressed."

"I do. I want a bagel."

"Turned down for a bagel."

"You didn't mean it. You'd never ask your sister to wait."

I wouldn't. She's right.

"But maybe… no, I have to go back home tonight. Check on my friend."

"Is he okay alone?"

"They're occupied."

There's something there, something she isn't saying.

But I don't call her on it.

I trust her.

I give her the room to change. Then I put on my outfit for the day.

Join my sister and Vanessa in the living room.

Their jaws drop.

"No fucking way," Opal says.

Vanessa laughs. "I guess you proved it." She runs her fingers over my brand new Taylor Swift t-shirt. And my jeans. "Simon Pierce, man of the people."

"I try," I say.

"You're not really wearing that, are you?" Opal asks.

"Why not?" I ask.

"Really, Simon?" Opal asks. "I have the same t-shirt!"

"Your call." I turn to Vanessa.

"Sorry, Opal. It suits him," she says. "It really does."

Chapter Thirty-Two

SIMON

O pal glares at my outfit for the entire walk to the bagel shop. The second she sips her coffee, she drops the irritation and launches into a long story about a family trip to the Caribbean.

I spent the entire time working. I sat on the beach in my suit.

And when she finally convinced me to wear something else?

It was so horrifying she can't even speak of it now.

Vanessa listens with a smile. She's quiet, content to soak in the information and give Opal the floor.

She's like me that way.

No, she's better.

More considerate. More thoughtful. More willing to listen.

Not as patient when it comes to waiting to strike, maybe—

But that's another virtue. She's more willing to talk.

She told me about her parents, her issues.

I talked about Bash's death, yes, but not the gritty details. Not the truly fucked-up shit.

"Did he ever swim?" Vanessa asks.

"Liam pushed him off a dock," Opal says.

"While he was wearing a speedo?" Vanessa asks.

"Liam was wearing a speedo, yeah. But Simon?"

"In his suit?"

Opal nods.

"Weren't you hot?" she asks.

"I looked fantastic," I say.

"Oh my god, Simon. Please! Don't try to cop Liam's moves. You can't pull them off," Opal says.

"Can I?" I ask.

Vanessa smiles and motions *so-so*. "Tell me you had to strip out of your suit right there." She notes Opal's horrified stare. "After your family left."

"Left him to flail?" Opal asks.

"Simon is a strong swimmer," Vanessa says. "I've seen him in the pool."

I raise a brow.

She smiles. "In a black speedo."

"When was this?" Opal asks.

"High school," she says. "And one summer in college."

"Didn't you go to school in Paris?" Opal asks.

"I did. But I came home for a few weeks every summer." She looks to Opal. "I missed my family."

"If I was going to school in Paris, I'd stay for four years straight. Make them come to me," Opal says.

"Have you been to Paris?" Vanessa asks.

Opal shakes her head.

"No air-conditioning anywhere. And nearly as hot as New York in the summer," Vanessa says.

"Nearly as hot is a range," Opal says. "Are we talking eighty and humid? Or ninety-nine and humid?"

"We're talking Celsius. It's Paris," Vanessa says.

Opal smiles, charmed, completely in love with Vanessa and the possibility of me being in love with Vanessa.

"Opal," the cashier calls.

Opal jumps to her feet. "You two talk summer swim sessions." She puts her hand to her mouth to stage whisper. "It's still summer, by the way. So keep talking." She drops her hand. "I'll get the bagels."

She skips to the counter.

"It's still summer," Vanessa says.

"Do you have a pool in mind?" I ask.

"I've always wanted to dive into the pool at the house," she says. "Especially when we visited in the summer."

"And everyone was dressed to the nines?" I ask.

She nods. "At the rehearsal dinner… I wanted to push you into it."

"Then tear off my clothes?"

"And fuck you right there." She bites her lip. "I did."

"I can arrange that."

"Really?"

I nod.

"When?"

"Let's go for a weekend."

"You'll leave Opal alone?"

"I'll leave her with Briar and Liam."

"She's eighteen," Vanessa says. "You should give her a weekend alone."

"Is that really your concern?"

Vanessa's eyes flit to my chest. She eyes my shirt and smiles. "You look amazing."

"I know."

"But I want to tear that thing off."

"I know."

"Is she with us all day?" Vanessa asks.

"If you tell her you want privacy, she'll run away."

She stares into my eyes. "I want…"

Opal interrupts. Drops a paper bag on the table. Notes our charged chemistry. "I'm going to top this off." She grabs her mug, refills it, watches us as she adds sugar.

"I don't know if I'm ready to try your uh…" She draws an invisible tie on her chest. "But I know a private spot in the park."

Fuck yes.

She mimes zipping her lips.

I struggle to contain my thoughts.

Opal returns, not at all subtle or coy. "Thanks for ordering without butter or cream cheese. So Simon will allow you within fifteen feet of me."

"Is he that over-protective?" Vanessa asks.

"Worse." Opal shakes her head *he's ridiculous*. "Do you want some? I'll grab it."

"I'm fine," Vanessa says.

"Then more coffee." She grabs Vanessa's mug and skips to refill it.

"You are over-protective. I appreciate that trait, but I…" She watches Opal watch us. "I don't want to talk about it today. Okay? Not until we're alone, at least."

Protective energy fills my veins. Pride. Need.

Not the craving I expect, the desire for her touch. I want that, yes, but I need *her*. To know what's in her heart and her head.

To know where she hurts and how I can help her.

I want to hold her all day, whisper sweet nothings in her ears, heal her wounds.

How the fuck do I do that?

How does anyone?

"Deal," I say.

Opal returns to our tiny plastic table. Sets the paper bag in the center. Pulls out her cinnamon raisin bagel and her packet of almond butter. "Important question."

"Oh?" Vanessa's eyes meet mine. They ask for something.

For a promise to keep this normal. I nod. Yes.

I'm lacking my usual patience. I'm consumed with the need for her. All of her.

But I want to be what she needs. To wait until she's ready.

"Deal breaking question," Opal says.

"For my relationship with your brother?" Vanessa asks.

"No. I don't care about that," Opal says.

"Harsh," I say.

"He's completely smitten. There's nothing I can say to change that," Opal says.

"You think?" Vanessa's eyes meet mine. Her lips curl into a shy smile. The one she had as a teenager.

It's intoxicating.

"I know," Opal says.

"I'm not sure. Your brother has a high opinion of you. If you asked him to end things—"

"I would never!" Opal slaps her hand on the table. "I don't stand in the way of love."

"Hypothetically. If I wasn't the kind of person he deserved," Vanessa says.

"You are," Opal says. "You're better than he deserves."

Vanessa laughs. "She roasts you."

"She's right," I say.

Vanessa smiles. "I don't know. Simon has a lot of admirable qualities."

"It's the height again, huh?" Opal asks.

"He is tall. And handsome."

"And rich," Opal adds. "But you're rich too."

"Not in the same league," Vanessa says. "But I was thinking more… that he's thoughtful. Caring. Gentle."

"Sex?" Opal asks.

Vanessa laughs. "Aren't you tired of us talking about sex?"

"She wants what she can't have," I say.

"Probably," Vanessa says.

"No way!" Opal shakes her head. "I adore Vanessa. That's all."

"I'm glad. I think... if you said you didn't, that would change things for Simon," Vanessa says.

"But why would I say that?" Opal says.

"If you let your feelings for my sister..." Vanessa pulls her plain bagel from the bag and peels it apart. "She's mean when she's threatened. It's not personal. I promise."

"How am I a threat?" Opal asks.

"Are you kidding?" Vanessa laughs. "You're gorgeous."

"Oh." Opal blushes. "Is that really it?"

"Not all of it. But a lot," Vanessa says.

"That's kind of shallow," Opal says.

"It is," Vanessa says. "I won't defend Lee. She gives into her worst impulses. She's cruel to people who aren't part of her circle. But she's just as vicious *for* her friends."

"You like having someone mean on your side?" Opal asks.

"It sounds awful, but I do." Vanessa takes a long sip of her English Breakfast. "My head of security, Xavier, is the same. He's a lot like Simon. Quiet, thoughtful, patient. But he's extremely capable too."

"Simon isn't?" Opal asks.

"Are you?" Vanessa looks to me. "Capable of hurting someone?"

"If necessary," I say.

Her eyes fix on mine. "If it's not necessary?"

"Hasn't everyone considered that?" I've planned a million different types of revenge against Cole. Everything from destroying his company to taking his life.

I've imagined that a million times.

The visceral justice of my hands around his neck.

I can't tell Vanessa that. She'll never understand. Not with her history.

But I won't lie to her either.

"I've wanted to hurt people before," I say. "People who hurt me. Or my family. But I've never resorted to violence."

"Would you?" she asks.

Yes. "If it was the only option."

Her eyes stay fixed on me. She's thinking, hard, but I have no idea what the fuck it is that's going through her head.

Is she deeming me a monster?

Or declaring me perfectly normal?

We all have fucked-up thoughts.

But most of us don't investigate the risk of revenge.

The cost of ending the man who—

No. I can't go there. Not today. Not with Opal sitting next to me.

"I hope it never comes to that," I say. "But if someone was trying to hurt you or Opal, of course, I'd take action."

"Yeah, but could you actually hurt someone?" Opal asks. "Kill them?"

Without a second thought. "If necessary."

Concern flares in Vanessa's eyes. She pushes it aside. Tears a piece of her bagel.

"Really? You could kill someone with your bare hands?" Opal asks. "Or do you have a gun? You don't have a gun, do you?"

"No," I say.

"What if they had a gun?" she asks.

"Then I'd have to outsmart them," I say.

"Is the security for you?" Opal asks Vanessa. "Are you safe?"

"At the office. Sometimes, abusers come looking for people. We need someone tough. Our whole team is, but Xavier is the best. I trust him with my most delicate situations," she says.

"If you needed a bodyguard?" Opal asks.

"Or if a friend needed one," Vanessa says.

"No! Vanessa! Don't give Simon ideas." Opal looks to me. "See. He's already thinking it. He's going to send me to college with an armed escort. Ugh! We better stop discussing this before he asks for Xavier's number."

"Does it help he's handsome?" Vanessa asks.

Opal sticks her tongue out. "Maybe. If Simon is more worried I'll screw him than need his protection."

"Not commenting," I say.

"Am I going to be this annoying when I'm thirty-two?" Opal shakes her head. "Back to better questions." She holds up her bagel. "Favorite bagel?"

"Plain," Vanessa says.

"Favorite way to eat it? When Simon isn't insisting on a dairy-free life?" Opal asks.

Vanessa looks for something in my eyes. I'm not sure what it is, but she must find it, because she turns to Opal with a smile. "Plain."

"The same as Simon. Ugh." Opal takes a bite. "You're too good together."

"I'm a born and bred New Yorker. Anything else is sacrilege," Vanessa says.

"I am too," Opal says.

"You're special." Vanessa stage whispers, "Simon grew up on Long Island, so he…"

"Overcompensating?" Opal asks.

Vanessa nods. "Does he also claim New York pizza is the best?"

"Simon eating pizza?" Opal laughs. "I'll believe that when I see it."

"Right. The allergy. Sorry," Vanessa says.

"No. There's a ton of dairy-free pizza out there. But even at vegan restaurants, where there's no dairy in the entire place…" Opal shakes her head. "He still won't taste my pizza."

"The brunch place?" Vanessa asks.

"He grills the staff! Every time." Opal shakes her head. "Wait until one of your kids has an allergy. You'll hate it too."

"I'm sure I would," Vanessa says.

Opal squeals *ohmygod does that mean you're in love? Together forever? Having babies?* "You'd have cute babies."

"I'm sure we would," Vanessa says. "But we're still…"

"It's rude to ask other people about their reproductive choices," I say.

Opal bats the air *psh.* "I didn't ask. I offered commentary. And it's family."

"Still," I say.

"Okay, I won't ask Vanessa if she wants kids," Opal says. "But we all know you do. And she knows you do. So if you two are as serious as you look… I think Opal is a really great name for a girl."

Vanessa's eyes meet mine.

This time, I know exactly what they're saying: *Yes.*

I want a future with you.

I see the possibility and I like it.

————

WE LINGER AT THE TABLE FOR A LONG TIME. OPAL AND VANESSA carry the conversation. Mostly Opal asking for every detail of Vanessa's life.

Attending our elite private school. Going to college in Paris. Meeting cute French guys. Spending summers traveling Europe.

The two years she worked at other nonprofits. The MBA training. Starting a company from scratch.

What she does for fun. How she manages to run thirty miles a week when running is truly the worst activity of all time.

She hangs on every one of Vanessa's words.

I listen, but I don't catch everything. Only the feeling of my two favorite people interacting.

Opal wants Vanessa in her life. In our lives.

They talk through a second round of coffee. As we clean up, walk around the park, take in the beautiful, blue day.

The second Opal eyes the subway, she snaps her fingers. "Damn. I'm meeting friends from my art class for lunch," Opal says. "I totally forgot."

"Did you?" Vanessa laughs at the obvious setup.

"Yep. And you two have that gala tonight, right?" Opal asks. "I'll be back around six. If you need help with your dress. Or your makeup."

"You do makeup?" Vanessa asks.

Opal tosses her long hair behind her shoulder. Motions to her lips. "Subtle, huh?"

"It is, actually." Vanessa smiles. "Most girls your age don't have that restraint."

"I do natural. I do punk rock. I do glam. Whatever you desire." She pulls Vanessa into a hug. "I have a thousand palettes. So don't worry about color. Anything you need, I'm there."

"I appreciate that." Vanessa squeezes back.

"I'll text when I'm on my way," Opal says. "Just in case." She releases Vanessa and hugs me goodbye. "Don't fuck it up."

"I'll try," I say.

"Don't try. Do." She pats my shoulder, spins on her heel, skips away.

Vanessa laughs. "She's a Pierce, huh?"

"Demanding and charming?"

"Very."

"Are we near your spot?"

"Nearish."

"Do you want to find it?" I ask.

"Please."

Fuck, that sounds good on her lips.

Chapter Thirty-Three

SIMON

V anessa squeezes my hand as she leads me through the
park.

       We walk a winding path, taking in the bright sky,
the lemon sun, the mix of tourists and locals.

We head north for fifteen blocks. Then she stops at the place
where the path turns.

"It's not as private as the balcony," she says. "There's a real
risk."

"You're nervous?"

She nods.

I pull her body into mine.

She shakes against me. Nervous. And turned on.

I want to give her everything. Everything.

But she's right. There's a real risk here.

More for her. It's always worse for women.

But I know the rules.

And I know—

"Do you trust me?" I ask.

"I do."

"This is still dangerous. But less."

"And you know the police commissioner?"

"Yes, we have secret meetings on the roof."

"You're Batman?"

"I thought you knew."

Her laugh breaks the tension in her shoulders. "How did I miss it?"

"We're all oblivious sometimes."

She turns and looks up at me, affection and desire in her eyes. "Simon, I… I really like you."

She doesn't give me a chance to respond. She rises to her tiptoes and presses her lips to mine.

Then she pulls back and leads me into the throng of trees.

We explore the space until we find a secluded spot. It's not private, but it's out of sight of the paths. We're shrouded by thicker, taller trees.

Vanessa presses her hand to my hip. Pushes me against the wood. "I hate to remove the most perfect article of clothing in existence." She slips her hand under my t-shirt. Runs her fingers over the line of my jeans.

"Then don't." I slide one arm around her. Slip the other between her legs.

She shudders as my fingers brush her thigh.

Higher and higher.

There.

She tugs at my belt as I rub her over her panties. "Simon."

I kiss her hard.

She kisses back with reckless abandon. Exploring my mouth, claiming some part of me, some part I'm desperate to give.

I rub her with slow circles.

Again and again, until she's groaning against my mouth.

Then I pull back. Press my lips to her jaw.

Her collarbone.

The neckline of her dress.

She knots her hand in my hair as I drop to my knees.

I duck under her skirt and roll her panties to her ankles.

She lifts her legs as I peel the fabric from her feet.

I slip her underwear in my pocket, then I wrap my arms around her thighs, and I dive between her legs.

I tease her with a soft brush of my lips.

Then another. Another.

I want to stay here forever. I want to torture her for hours.

But we're in public.

And neither of us can afford to be caught here.

So I tease her one more time, then I flick my tongue against her. I lick her with the steady strokes she needs.

Her hand knots in my hair.

Her hips arch against me.

I rake my nails over her thighs. Not enough to hurt. Only enough she knows I have her.

"Fuck, Simon." She presses her hand to her mouth to stifle a groan.

I take one moment to savor her. I nip at the inside of her thigh. I inhale the scent and sight and sound of her.

Then I give her exactly what she needs.

Fast, steady strokes.

Again and again.

Until she's there, groaning into her palm, rocking against me, coming on my lips.

She gets sweeter, wetter, softer.

Infinitely more irresistible.

I work her through her orgasm, then I pull back, right her dress, rise.

She looks up at me with hazy eyes.

And she kisses me hard and fast.

"Your place." She tugs at my shirt. "Now."

THE WALK TO MY APARTMENT IS SWEET TORTURE.

The doorman, the security guard, the elevator.

I don't make it to the bed.

I barely make it past the door.

I pin Vanessa to the wall.

She pulls my shirt over my head, undoes my belt, pushes my jeans from my hips.

I push her dress to her waist.

When I lift her, she wraps her legs around me.

Then her arms.

I kiss her as I drive into her.

She kisses back with the same mix of need and desire.

And we melt together, there, against the living room wall.

Breathing together, groaning together, moving together.

Until she's there, rubbing herself as she comes on my cock, pulling me over the edge with her.

I hold her there for a moment, soaking in the sound of her groan, the feel of her skin, the sweetness of her body against mine.

The world is ours.

At least for today.

Then I let her down, lead her to the bathroom, clean and dry and dress with her.

In terry cloth robes straight out of a movie.

She smiles as she drapes the fabric over her shoulders.

And when she says, "Spoiled rich boy," she says it like it's her favorite phrase.

Like she's saying, "I love you."

Chapter Thirty-Four

SIMON

My apartment looks different in the afternoon light. Brighter and bolder and a billion times more beautiful.

Already, I want to have Vanessa again.

All day, I want to have Vanessa again.

But I want to be here too. Enjoying a quiet afternoon.

Addressing the things neither of us wants to say.

"Are you hungry?" I ask. It's a normal question, especially given the time and our recent activities, but it feels impossibly loaded.

She nods. "Was Opal right? Are you helpless in the kitchen?"

"Not helpless."

"But not good?"

"Competent."

"But not good?"

My lips curl into a smile. "Not good."

"Do you have anything?" She studies my expression. The expectation on my face. "Anything easy?"

Easy first.

We start first.

Then we talk.

Or is this like discussing birth control?

Is it a bad idea to talk about food while we're cooking?

I don't know.

I know enough about eating disorders to see signs of them. I do live with a teenage girl.

And Opal has her issues with food and anxiety—her allergy causes plenty, even if she won't admit it—but nothing like this.

She has a healthy relationship to control.

She doesn't try to hold on to it for dear life.

Or let go and savor the free fall.

She's not normal in many ways, but she's normal in this one.

"Eggs," I say. "Steak."

Vanessa laughs. "Is it fifty-dollar-a-pound steak?"

"Probably."

She pulls open the fridge. Checks the rows of plant milk, fruit, condiments, prepackaged meals.

She pulls out the eggs. Surveys the other options.

Settles on a stack of tomatoes and a package of dairy-free pesto. "A friend was talking about pesto. She put me in the mood." She turns to me. "Do you normally use something instead of cheese?"

"Avocado."

"How Californian of you." She checks the fruit drawer, comes up empty for avocado but finds a zucchini. "I should have guessed. Simon Pierce only stocks phallic vegetables."

"Fruits."

"Right. Fruits." She holds the long green fruit-vegetable up. "Can I ask you to cut this? Or is it too painful?"

"I can manage."

"Are you sure?"

I nod.

She places it on the counter.

I find the knife and cutting board.

She warms a pan on the stove. "Oil?"

"Cabinet on the right."

She checks our array of flavored olive oils. "Are these good?"

"They're oil."

"Olive oil expires." She smells a canister. Deems it appropriate. "It only takes a few months."

"Opal drowns her salads in oil."

"The salads with the service?"

"Weekend lunch."

"How often do you cook?" She pours Italian herb oil on the pan.

"Once or twice a week."

"The other days?"

"Takeout on Tuesdays and Thursdays. After her class."

"When school starts?" she asks.

"Then we'll change our routine."

"She'll want to hang out with her friends."

"But I'll trap her at Friday night dinners."

"So she arrives at parties too late to get drunk?" Vanessa asks.

"That's a fringe benefit."

"What's the main benefit? C-blocking her?"

"You too?"

She shrugs. "What can I say? I like it."

It's strange hearing her cop one of Liam's lines. Almost wrong—Liam lives to annoy me. But right too.

She wants to be a part of my family.

To be in my life.

It's everything.

I want it all. Now.

But I need to be patient. To give her what she needs. Wait until she's ready.

She motions to the zucchini.

I chop it into thin slices.

Then the tomatoes.

We work quietly for a few minutes.

Vanessa sautés, cracks eggs, adds pesto.

I toast bread.

Heat the kettle.

She finishes. Plates the food. Brings it to the kitchen island. Hands me a fork. "You want to talk about this?"

"If you're ready."

She tastes her eggs. Lets out a soft groan. "I'm not sure I'll ever be ready."

I know how to push. I know how to wait. I know how to get what I want.

But I don't know how to do this.

To support her the way she needs.

So I taste the food, groan over the mix of parsley and pine nuts. "Fuck, this is amazing."

"I know." Vanessa scoops another bite. "I'm a good cook."

"You are."

"I like that you're bad at something."

"Not bad."

"That you aren't great at something." She cracks pepper, tastes again, lets out a soft groan. "It's a rare treat."

"I'm not good at this."

"Eating lunch?"

"Helping without pushing."

She nods and breaks a piece of toast in half.

"I want to support you with this. Tell me how."

Her laugh breaks the tension in her shoulders.

I raise a brow.

"You're just… Simon. Even when you offer help, it's in this take charge way. It used to annoy me, but now… I like it."

"Is that a way to avoid telling me?"

"No." She takes another bite. Chews slowly. "I don't know what to say. I don't think anyone is every normal about food. Not in our world. I wasn't. When I was younger, there wasn't enough."

"And you learned to put other people's need's first?"

She nods. "And this was a way I could feel in control without letting anyone down. Or asking for more. Or taking up more space. It was… it was a fucked-up mess. A spiral of control and slipping and self-loathing that got worse every time until my disorder was in charge. In treatment, my therapist always compared eating disorders to abusive relationships. I understood what she meant. There were girls who wrote to their disorders. Who named them. Talked about them the way people talk about abusers. They wanted to please their disorder, to finally be good enough. Their disorder hurt them again and again and they kept going back for more. But I…" She stabs a tomato. "I hate that thought. That I was like my mother. Or my father. But I was."

"You didn't hurt anyone."

"I hurt myself. I wanted to hurt myself. I hated myself so much, Simon. I wanted to disappear, one ounce at a time. I wanted to prove I was worthy and this was the only way I knew how. It was so many things and… it's not like that now. I'm not self-loathing or obsessed."

"What are you?"

"I don't know. In control. But only enough I can stay in control."

My shoulders tense.

She's not well.

She's hurting herself.

Only a little, maybe, but that's too much.

Everything inside me screams an objection. I want to fight, yell, do whatever it takes to keep her safe.

But that will hurt her. Push her away. Convince her she can't trust me.

I have to wait.

"Most of the time, I'm normal," she says. "I eat three meals a day. I order dinner at restaurants. I drink a few cocktails when I want to celebrate. I run because I love it. I just keep track of everything in my head. And I… I keep track more carefully when I'm under more stress."

"Always?"

"Since my mom got sick."

That was two years ago now.

She's been alone with this for two years.

My heart breaks for her.

And it comes back together, stronger and surer and infinitely more in awe of her.

She finishes her omelet. Tears her slice of bread in half. "I appreciate the concern. I do. I want you to know… I want you to understand. But I'm not there yet. I'm not ready to deal with it."

"Will you?"

"Eventually."

"Are you sure?"

"No. But…" She looks to her mugs. "When it's bad, it's bad. I never want to feel that again. Never."

"Isn't that a risk?"

"I'm careful."

"What does that mean?"

"I only do a little. Enough to cope."

"Vanessa—"

"Simon. I appreciate the concern. I do. But this is mine. Not yours."

I swallow hard.

She tears a slice of bread into tiny pieces. "I'll get help when I'm ready. Until then—"

"What if it gets worse?"

"Then we can talk."

"What would be worse?"

"If I started skipping meals. Or intentionally losing weight. Or restricting certain foods."

"Will you?"

She doesn't answer the question. She turns away. Looks to the floor.

"I'm fucking this up."

She doesn't reply.

"I'm sorry." The words rise in my throat. They're obvious. Impossible to ignore. But this isn't the time. This is the worst possible time. "Tell me what I can do. How I can help."

"You can't. You have to accept that."

I don't know if I can do that.

But I know I can't lose her.

"I don't want to hurt you," I say.

"I know."

"What would hurt you?"

"Pushing too hard. Insisting I eat. Trying to control what's on my plate. I'm not saying you would—"

"Don't apologize. I want to know."

"Okay."

"What else?"

"It's something I do when I feel like my life is out of control. So anything... anything that adds to that."

"What about sex?"

She crosses and uncrosses her legs. "What about it?"

"What do you need there?"

"It's good."

"Good?"

"What we're doing... it's good for me. The focus on my pleasure. You're very generous."

I'm greedy, but I know what she means.

"And the mirrors… It helps to see myself in a different way. To see my body as a vehicle for pleasure, not a thing to critique."

"Is there anything I shouldn't say?"

"Nothing you would say."

This isn't right.

It's still too hard. Too firm. Too demanding.

She needs soft.

I need to be soft.

I move around the table. Offer my hand.

She takes it. Lets me pull her into my arms.

"I won't pretend I'm good at this." I pull her closer. "I care about you. I hate seeing you in pain," I say. "But I want to be what you need here. Not what I think you need."

"You promise?"

"I promise."

She nestles into my chest.

"Can I tell you how much I enjoy your body?"

"Not if it sounds like I'm your fuck toy."

"How gorgeous you are?"

She nods into my chest.

"How much I adore your thighs?"

"Yes."

"That I'll want you no matter how you look?"

"You mean that?"

"I do."

"What if I shave my head?"

"Especially," I say.

Her laugh breaks the tension in her shoulders. "That's your fetish?"

"The truth is out."

"If I shave the eyebrows too?"

"Even hotter."

"I might call your bluff."

"You won't," I say.

"No." She wraps her arms around me. "I won't."

I pull her closer.

"I'm a mess."

"I am too."

"You don't show it."

"I will."

"I… I care about you too." She looks up at me. "Can we not talk now?"

I nod.

She rises to her tiptoes and presses her lips to mine.

She tastes like basil and need.

All of hers pouring into me.

All of mine pouring into her.

I can't explain the way she can. Not yet.

But it's there. It's bright enough to fill the room.

I push her robe off her shoulders.

She does away with mine.

I lift her onto the counter. Drop to my knees to warm her up.

She falls back, falls into this, as I bring my mouth to her cunt.

I'm not patient. I'm greedy and rushed. I lick her through her orgasm. Then another.

Then I rise, wrap my arms around her, bring her body onto mine.

She holds me close as I drive into her.

Again and again.

Until we come together. A sweaty, sticky, groaning mess in the middle of the kitchen.

———

After I clean up, we shower together.

I order lunch. I try not to watch carefully. She doesn't call me on my excessive concern.

We watch an old movie on the couch. Have sweet, slow sex in my bed. Lie there, tangled in each other, until my phone buzzes with Opal's reminder.

"Is it really six?" Vanessa runs her fingers through my hair.

"Almost."

"Can we have another day here?"

"Yes."

She smiles. "I already RSVP'd."

"Cancel."

"Would you?"

"Yes."

"Really?"

"I would."

She traces the line of my jaw. "Opal will be here in fifteen minutes either way."

"We can stay here all night."

"How about ten minutes? Then I put on a robe. And we get dressed and you attend as my date?"

"Deal."

"Do you see everything as a negotiation?"

"Don't you?"

She smiles, guilty. "Some things."

I pull her into my arms.

"Not everything." She melts into my chest.

Chapter Thirty-Five

VANESSA

I drag myself from Simon's bed right as Opal arrives.

She catches me sneaking to the bathroom in my robe.

Goes to talk to Simon.

I'm pretty sure she goes to high-five Simon, but I can't really complain. If it was Lee offering a congratulations?

Fuck, I like him.

I really like him.

I change into the long black dress he bought for me—not quite formal enough but better than last night's gown—and text Celine to check in.

She offers her own congratulations. Insists she's fine. Enjoying the alone time, actually.

What did Tammy say?

I need to enjoy my weekend for once. To take a break from saving the entire world.

I can't do that, exactly. I'm attending a gala tonight. That means asking for money.

But everything else—

I'm okay.

Better than okay.

Amazing.

I thank Celine. I fix my hair. I step into the main room and try not to smile in a way that says *I really love fucking your brother*.

Then I let Opal lead me to her extremely pink room.

I sit at her desk.

And I let an eighteen-year-old girl do my makeup.

I expect a disaster—she's young and she's significantly lighter than I am—but Opal is a Pierce through and through.

She aces it.

And when she leads me to the living room, presenting me to Simon like an artist presenting a painting, she too wishes me good luck and tells me she won't be home until her curfew at midnight.

But, just in case, she tucks her cell phone number into my purse.

In case I need to tell her to clear the space early.

Chapter Thirty-Six

VANESSA

"**M**s. Moyer." Preston, my sister's father-in-law, greets me with a smile. "You look as radiant always."

"Nice to see you, Mr. Charles," I say.

"Call me Preston," he says.

I nod as neutrally as possible. I'm in the middle of a highly decorated restaurant, meeting and greeting potential donors at an event celebrating—

What the hell are we celebrating?

Women in STEM.

If we spent half as much time trying to hire women for STEM jobs or encouraging girls to pursue STEM hobbies as we do celebrating women in STEM, we'd make a lot more progress.

But this organization is willing to spend to look generous. They want to look like they help women.

I need money to help women.

Men too. But mostly women. And most people assume survivors are women.

But I'm not here to contemplate the bigger picture.

Only to look professional and schmooze. I can't awkwardly greet my sister's father-in-law. I need to own our greeting.

"Of course, Preston," I say. "Call me Vanessa."

"And Mr. Pierce." He offers his hand to Simon. "I didn't expect to see you here."

"He's my plus-one," I say.

"A date?" he asks.

"Something like that." I catch Simon's gaze. Try not to swoon over his smile.

How can he project this much warmth?

It's intoxicating

"How is Harrison?" I ask.

"You know more than I do," he says. "He's never been one to share with his father."

"He's private," I say.

Preston nods *of course*. Presses his hand to the table next to us, steadying himself. He's not as strong as he was a year ago, but otherwise, his condition isn't too noticeable.

He's a little pale, sure, but that's easy to explain as a habit of working too hard and getting too little exercise. Especially at his age.

Have Lee and Harrison told Preston about their baby making efforts? Either way, he must know. Lee isn't shy about spreading the news. Or bragging about their attempts.

I don't want to bring up something so prickly, so I say, "I only know he and Lee are staying busy."

"They're newlyweds." He smiles, proud. "I only wish they'd take their honeymoon."

"They will." After he's gone. So much for avoiding uncomfortable topics. "When work calms down."

"Work never calms down," he says. "If you put things off, wait until life is easier, you'll never get to them. There's always something else. Another project. Another emergency. Another relative who needs help."

"Another engagement," Simon says.

Preston smiles. "Are Liam and Briar here?"

"No. I'm Vanessa's date, not the other way around. We weren't invited," he says.

"Really?" Preston looks around the room, scanning for the organizer.

"Who did you piss off to make that happen?" I slip my hand under Simon's suit jacket. Press my palm into the small of his back. "That's what he wants to ask."

"It's personal, not professional." Simon scans the room. Stops at a tall brunette with a sharp bob. "An ex of Liam's."

"Liam has exes?" I ask.

Simon looks to Preston. Hesitates.

"I realize young men have sex," Preston says. "I'm not a fool."

"They were friends with benefits," he says. "That's all I know."

"Are you sure it's that?" Preston asks. "And not the percentage of women in your software department?"

I can't help but laugh. "Way to call him out." I offer my hand.

Preston shakes. "Pierce is below the national average."

"I'll look into it," Simon says.

"Really?" I ask.

"Of course," he says. "It's my responsibility."

The brunette spots us. Shoots Simon an irritated glance.

"Should I ask?" Preston leans in to whisper. "She doesn't seem to like you."

I laugh.

"I don't care if she likes me," Simon says.

"That's something I always appreciated about you," Preston says.

"This is the first I've heard that," Simon says.

Preston smiles sadly. "Neither one of us was prepared for

your father's passing. I suppose sons never are. I was older when I lost my father, but I wasn't ready. How could I be?"

How can anyone be ready?

I was terrified to lose Mom. I still am. She's better now. She's in remission.

But cancer returns.

And even if it doesn't, she's mortal.

One day, I'll lose her.

One day, I'll lose Daddy.

"I'm sorry. You're here to celebrate your love, not listen to an old man talk about grief," Preston says.

"You're not old." I don't add *we're not in love*. I don't feel that. I don't know what I feel.

Something.

Everything.

"Perhaps not, but I hope I'm wise." He clasps his hands. "I hope you realize what you have. With each other. And your families." He looks to me. "Your parents are lovely people."

"They are," I say.

"Are they here tonight?" he asks.

"No. Mom only attends her events these days," I say.

"Smart," he says.

"I'll have to follow her influence one day," I say.

"Or put your skills somewhere else. Do you need to be the person here, asking for money?" he asks.

"You don't waste words," I say.

"No. I suppose dying does that to you," he says. "I wish I had the chance to know you better, Vanessa. I've heard so much. From Simon. And Liam. And Sebastian. When he was here… every time he saw you and Simon together… Simon didn't hear the end of it."

"He was persistent," Simon says.

"It worked," Preston says. "I'm glad it did. I could always

tell. Every time. He's loved you for a long time." He pats Simon's shoulder. "I'm glad you've finally seen it."

Preston drops that conversational bomb, then he turns and heads to the brunette.

Fuck.

I try to find something to say, but I can't. There are too many things in my head.

My mouth is sticky.

My throat is dry.

Simon's gaze is intense.

He moves closer. Close enough to whisper. "I do."

"You do?"

"I love you." His voice is steady. "You don't need to say it back. You don't to say anything." He holds my body against his. "I just wanted to say it."

He presses his lips to mine.

It's there, in his kiss.

I try to find a reply. But I don't have that either.

He loves me.

I…

He…

Fuck.

"Go. Save the world." He releases me.

I nod and move into the fray.

An older man in a navy suit greets me. He recognizes me. Wants the chance to donate in front of a friend.

I nod along with what he says, but I don't hear him.

The neon letters flash in my head again and again.

Simon loves me.

And he's a good luck charm.

Every donation is better than the last.

After two hours, I having funding for the quarter.

And Simon loves me.

I don't know what to say. Or if I'm ready to say it back.

But I want to see him. I want to collapse in his arms.

I want everything.

I duck out of the ballroom and find a quiet space in the lobby. My phone is heavy with messages from donors and work.

And one from Celine.

It's simple. A good luck.

But it's a signal too.

I need to check on her.

And tell Simon I want all his feelings and want to share all of mine.

How can I sum up *I think I feel the same way, but I'm not ready to say it* in a short text.

There isn't anything sufficient, so I keep it simple.

Vanessa: I'm wiped. I'm going to crash at home tonight. Call me tomorrow.

It's not enough, but it's what I have.

I text Celine my code, call a rideshare, step outside.

It's a beautiful night. Warm air. Blue sky. Sidewalks humming with conversation.

Conversation and cigarettes.

I move to a less smoky corner. Slip my cell into my purse. Focus on the Empire State Building.

Purple today. Probably for some NYU event. But it feels like it's for me.

For us.

"I hate to interrupt," a man says. "But I had to say hello."

This is it. My last friendly chat. Then I'm done.

"Vanessa Moyer?" he asks.

It's dark here. I can't make out the details of his face. But I'm not sure they'd help. He's completely average.

A man in his fifties, medium height, medium build, non-descriptor grey hair, equally average suit.

But even with his bland handsomeness, he's familiar.

Why?

"Cole Fitzgerald." He offers his hand. "I've admired your work for a long time."

I shake. "Thank you."

"I'm not nearly as memorable as you." He smiles warmly.

So we have met.

And he knows I can't remember him.

Shit. How do I know him?

"Arts education?" It's the first thing that comes to mind.

He nods. "My wife is involved."

"Is she here tonight?"

"At the bar." He laughs. "She hates mingling."

"I know the feeling."

"She adores you," he says. "Always compliments your gowns."

I can't ask her name. I can't admit I don't remember him or her. So I smile. "It's nice to see you, Cole, but I'm on my way home."

"Walking?"

"A car."

"I'll wait with you."

Firm but polite. That's what Daddy says. But Daddy doesn't run a charity. And he's a rich white man who grew up in this world. The standards for *firm* and *polite* are different. "You should join your wife. I'm sure she misses you."

"I don't think so," he says. "She tires of my tedium." He drops his voice to imitate hers. "'If I have to hear another lecture about Lichtenstein.'"

"You don't like his work?"

"It's pedestrian."

Lichtenstein is far from my favorite artist, but I appreciate his ability to marry fine culture and mass culture. He appeals to art historians and comic book fans alike.

There are plenty of people who don't enjoy pop art. But

there's a certain type of art snob with a strange lack of appreciation for anything new and different.

"My sister loves him," I say. "She runs a gallery."

"Would I know it?"

I name the place.

"One of my favorites," he says. "Beautiful photography."

"I'll pass on the compliment."

"My wife introduced me. She's the one with taste."

"No? The Lichtenstein doesn't disqualify her?"

"Are you an artist? You have a real eye for beauty."

Is that flirting or something else? It's strange. Weighted.

"I try." I look to the street as casually as possible. A smoker. A limo. A cab.

No sign of my Lyft.

The cab driver rolls down his window. "You need a ride, sweetheart?"

Maybe.

"She's waiting for a car," the man says.

The cabbie ignores him. "Why wait? I'm here now."

I pretend to check my phone. "I think my driver canceled. I better go before the place is slammed."

"Of course." He offers his hand again. "It was lovely to see you, Ms. Moyer."

"You too." I take his hand.

He shakes at first. Then he pulls me into an embrace.

It's too tight. It's awkward. It's completely wrong.

And then it's not.

Someone is pulling him away.

Simon.

He tosses Cole against the glass wall. "What the fuck do you think you're doing?"

Cole starts to reply.

But Simon is too fast. He swings his arm.

His fist his Cole's face.

Bam!

I see the letters. The tiny dots and bright colors of a Lichtenstein.

It doesn't seem real.

It's a nightmare.

A strange man.

A violent Simon.

A monster.

I need to go.

I don't ask or answer or wait. I turn to the cabbie. "Uptown." I reach for the door. Slide inside.

Simon releases the guy.

He looks at me. Asks for something with his eyes.

But I can't look back.

I pull the door closed. "Hurry."

The driver speeds onto the street. Uptown.

To my apartment.

The drive passes in a flash.

All of a sudden, I'm saying hello to the doorman, walking past security.

The elevator.

The hall.

My apartment.

Celine sitting on the couch with Seb.

Sebastian.

All at once, it clicks.

That man. He's her husband.

And Seb's father—

That's Bash.

Simon's brother.

Chapter Thirty-Seven

VANESSA

"Vanessa? Are you all right?" Celine rises from her seat on the couch. She studies me with her gentle grey eyes. As if we're friends. As if this situation isn't hopelessly fucked.

"No."

"Is it your friend?"

"Yes."

"What happened?"

"He loves me."

Her brow furrows with confusion. "That's wonderful."

"He hurt someone."

Sebastian.

Bash for short.

Or Seb.

Why didn't I see it?

No one ever called him Sebastian, but I knew it was his name. We all did. We laughed about how he was nothing like the crab in *The Little Mermaid*.

"Have a seat, Vanessa." Celine's voice stays soft and maternal. "I'll fix tea."

No. I need to explain.

No. I can't explain.

But I have to say something. "Your husband. What's his name?"

"Cole."

"Fitzgerald?"

She nods.

"I saw him tonight." I don't know how else to explain. "I need to move you."

"Please, Vanessa."

"No." Firm. I need to be firm. "It's not safe. He saw me leave. He saw me and Simon together. He… Simon pulled him off me."

"Cole tried to hurt you?"

Did he? Was this about her? Or another man trying to cop a feel? "No." The word feels like a lie. A false promise. The kind my mother made. *He's a good man. He just gets angry sometimes. He'll never hurt you.* "I don't know. Either way, we need to move you." I find my cell. Ignore my missed calls from Simon.

I call Xavier.

No feelings. No panic.

Practical steps.

The guard outside is extra careful. Xavier is on his way. With backup. To move us. But this is it—if someone is watching, they'll see us.

If Celine wants to take the nuclear options, it's do or die.

I call Regina. Check the status.

Not perfect. But we can make it happen if absolutely necessary.

It's her choice.

It's not my choice.

It's not about my father or my mother or my sister or my—

Whatever Simon is.

I place my cell on the table. Deep breath. Slow exhale.

But my thoughts aren't straight.

They're a mess.

"Do you want a drink?" I ask.

"Let me."

"I don't want tea."

"Okay." Celine moves into the kitchen, finds the bottle of gin in the fridge, pours two glasses. "I'm sorry."

The gin burns, but I swallow in two gulps. I need the steady. The calm. Anything to ease my nerves.

Control.

I need control.

The way my father did.

The way Simon does.

We're the same.

We're monsters.

"Xavier is on his way," I say. "He'll take you somewhere safe. Regina will be there to brief you on your options. There's a shelter in another city. For security reasons, I don't know. They'll help you get settled."

"Or?" she asks.

"It's your choice," I say. "The option is still there. But there's no going back. You say goodbye to your friends and family until your husband is no longer a threat."

"Vanessa, I'm sorry."

"You were scared. You didn't know where else to go."

"I should have told you," she says.

Maybe. I don't know anymore.

"That is why I came here," she says. "Because I trust you. I just—I wanted to be near him. His life. His family."

"You don't owe me anything."

"Do you believe that?"

No. That's why I need to go. I'm involved. "Stay safe. Keep your son safe. That's all I want."

"Please, let me apologize."

"That's not necessary."

"Please," she says.

I nod.

"I'm sorry I wasn't forthright. Truly. I should have told you what happened to Bash. I should have told you I knew you. But I—"

"You didn't know if you could trust me."

"No. I trust you. I have. But I... I was embarrassed," she says. "To admit it. To admit how desperate I've become."

"You're trying to protect your son."

She nods.

"That's what we both want."

"Thank you." She throws her arms around me. "For everything."

My phone buzzes twice. Xavier's signal.

Then his knock.

Celine releases me. Composes herself. "Thank you."

"Promise you won't go back to him?" I ask.

"I promise."

My shoulders fall with relief. Everything else is a mess. But if she sticks with that—

If she and Seb are safe—

Then it really will be okay.

I open the door.

But it's not Xavier.

It's Simon.

Chapter Thirty-Eight

VANESSA

"Vanessa—" Simon reaches for me. Stops himself. "I need to explain." He looks past me.

Sees her.

Recognitions spreads over his face. "Your guest."

He stares, dumbstruck.

I've never seen it before.

Simon Pierce speechless.

It should send warmth through my body.

Instead, I'm cold all over.

"I'm sorry," he says. "I didn't mean to scare you."

But he did.

And we both know.

"I love you," he says.

It doesn't sound the same.

It doesn't sound like potential and possibility.

It's not beautiful or sweet.

It's a noose.

I see the desperation in his expression.

But it's not a need to prove his love or a need to keep me safe.

It's anger and hate and hurt.

His fist smacking that man's flesh.

A desire to cause harm. To kill.

I can't blame him.

If someone hurt Lee, I'd want to kill them too.

I understand it—intellectually.

But now it's happening.

I close my eyes, and I see my mom huddled in a corner. My biological father swinging his arm.

The cries and bruises and dread.

He's not safe anymore.

Nothing is safe anymore.

Xavier arrives just in time.

He looks at Simon. Opens his mouth to tease me. Stops himself. "Is Mr. Pierce assisting?"

Simon looks to Celine.

She nods.

I shake my head.

Xavier steps inside. Pulls the door closed. "Ms. Moyer, can we speak privately?"

"Two minutes." I lead him into my bedroom.

He presses the door closed. "It's late. We won't make it to the safe house before closing. Mr. Pierce lives in a secure building. The three of you should stay tonight."

"I can't," I say.

"The two of them?"

"If Regina clears it," I say.

"Are you okay?"

"No."

He doesn't probe. "We'll be fast." He nods with understanding then shifts into the take-charge, no-nonsense man I know. "She'll be safe. I promise."

I nod.

"I'll give you a minute." He ducks out of the room. Moves around the main room. Helping Celine pack. I don't know.

I lean against my thick door until Xavier knocks. Two short knocks. His code.

The main room is cleaned of Celine's things. And of her and Seb.

Xavier nods. "Thanks for your hard work, Ms. Moyer." He nods something else to Simon. Then he leaves.

And it's us.

And the eight million fucked-up things between us.

"I do love you," Simon says.

"I know."

"Come over. Please. Stay with us." He offers his hand. "Hold my hand when I say goodbye to my nephew."

"Simon—"

"Please, Vanessa."

"I can't. I'm sorry. I… I can't do this."

"Are you sure?"

"Yes. I'm sorry."

His heart breaks in front of me.

He reaches for me one more time.

Again, he stops himself.

This time, he turns, and he leaves.

And I'm alone.

And nowhere is safe.

Chapter Thirty-Nine

SIMON

When I was first investigating my brother's death, I learned about Celine's pregnancy.

I didn't know if the child was Bash's or her husband's, but I knew I couldn't act until he was safe.

How could I put an innocent in harm's way?

Even if he shares his DNA with a monster.

Now that I'm here across from him?

I don't have to ask to know.

They have the same blue eyes.

The drive is fast. Xavier is good. He secures the apartment. Helps us inside.

Thankfully, Opal is at Briar and Liam's place. Secure.

Xavier assures me Vanessa isn't in physical danger.

He doesn't add *don't get the wrong idea. She's not okay. You hurt her, asshole.* But it's in his stare.

He does another pass on the apartment, then he goes to check the building.

Leaves me alone with my nephew and the woman who stole my brother's heart.

I never understood how Bash could be so stupid, so reckless.

Now, I do.

I'd do anything for Vanessa.

No matter the danger.

If there was some man who might hurt me for loving her—

I'd never let that stand in my way.

Bash didn't have a chance. Not with Cole willing to play dirty.

"I didn't expect to meet again this way." Celine settles on the couch with her son in her lap. He's asleep. Peaceful. Beautiful.

"Me either." I try to remember to host her. "Do you want something to drink?"

"No. Thank you."

"Dinner?"

"I ate at Vanessa's."

"Your son?"

"Seb."

Fuck. She named him after Bash. "He'd love that."

"I know," she says.

I met Celine briefly a few times, but I didn't know her. Only what Bash said.

She's exactly as he described her.

Gentle.

Beautiful.

Luminous.

Scared.

She's still scared, now.

He respected her fear. He worried about her.

But he didn't understand the depth of the danger.

He believed he could save her with love.

I tried to convince him otherwise. But not because I thought this would happen. Because I thought she would stay with her husband and he'd be miserable and heartbroken.

I didn't understand either.

"Did he know?" If he were here; if he knew he had a son—

He'd never take that back.

"No," she says. "It was early. I didn't realize until a few weeks after…"

Fuck.

"At first, I believed it was an accident," she says. "And Cole believed Seb was his. Then he didn't and I left. Your brother gave me Vanessa's name. He trusted her."

He did?

He knew it was that dangerous.

He knew Cole might hurt her.

Hurt him.

"She's a good woman," Celine says.

"She is."

"You two are together?"

"We were."

"What happened?" she asks.

"I scared her."

Celine nods with understanding. For Vanessa? For me? I don't know.

She keeps talking, but I don't hear her.

My ears ring.

Bash's son is in my house.

His son.

And Vanessa is gone.

Maybe forever.

I don't stop and sink into my feelings.

I take action.

But right now?

It's nearly impossible to keep my thoughts here, in the apartment.

I help Celine set up in the spare room. I talk to Xavier about keeping the place secure.

I think about calling Vanessa for hours.

Celine and Seb are leaving tomorrow. They're going to another city. I'm never going to see them again.

Unless—

Unless I do what Cole did.

There are two choices here.

Both are horrible.

Which can I survive?

Chapter Forty

SIMON

W hen I first discovered the truth, I was sure of my path.

I investigated my options.

I assessed the risks.

I considered the alternatives.

Only one course of action made sense—Justice.

The end of Cole's life.

Exactly what he did to Bash.

But that isn't justice.

It's revenge.

That's why Vanessa is afraid. Because she sees this side of me.

Because she knows these are the thoughts in my head.

She sees me as a monster.

How can I argue?

The vision of Cole's death still sends relief through my limbs.

I want to end him.

I want to hurt him.

I want to savor his pain.

My thoughts are awful.

But they're only thoughts. There's still a chance for me.

If I take action—

Then I'll truly be a monster.

As bad as he is.

As despicable as he is.

And Vanessa will never love a monster.

Who would?

All night, I toss and turn.

I sleep in fits. Dreams of princes who slay dragons. Visions of a future without Vanessa. Without the warmth of anyone with a hint of principle.

Memories of Bash.

The brightness in his eyes. The passion in his voice. The joy in his smile.

He wouldn't approve.

Opal wouldn't approve.

Liam either.

Even Adam—

He knows what I know. He took his own path to revenge. Tortured himself over deceiving a woman he paid handsomely.

My family is many things.

But we aren't monsters.

The sky lightens.

I rise. Clean. Find Celine on the couch with a mug of tea, her son in a bassinet in front of her.

"He's asleep," she whispers. "For now."

"I didn't hear him."

"He's quiet. He screamed as an infant. I didn't rest for a month. But since I… he sleeps soundly now. Most nights." She looks to him. "He'll be up soon. Sooner, if we don't whisper."

"I can leave."

"No." She stands and motions to the kitchen island. "As long as you don't grind beans."

What can I possibly say to her?

How could you let this happen to my brother?

How could I let this happen to the two of you?

I'm sorry I failed him.

I don't say anything about Bash or his son or the danger lurking outside the apartment. I offer to fix another mug of tea.

She accepts.

We move to the kitchen island.

I suggest breakfast.

Celine asks for nothing.

Accepts every offer with gratitude.

Except for the low hum of the air conditioner and the hiss of the kettle, the space is silent.

I toast bread, fry eggs, find jam, knives, plates.

Celine sits on a stool, sips English Breakfast mixed with coconut milk.

She's graceful.

Even more than Bash described.

"This is strange," she says. "For me too."

I spread marmalade on my toast, take a bite, try to taste the orange zest. For a second, the flavor is bright. Vivid. Then it's gone. The world is grey again.

"He talked about you a lot." She takes a dainty sip. "He hated that you didn't approve. He looked up to you."

"I know."

"Because you were competent and smart. And because you were principled."

No one's ever called me that.

"He wanted you to deem his actions moral. He wanted you to see things his way, to see love was more important than anything. I told him most people don't approve of adultery, but he…"

"He didn't let anything stand in the way of love."

"He didn't."

"It wasn't about your status as a married woman," I say.

"You approved?"

"No. But I worried too. Worried you'd break his heart." I escaped most of my father's old-fashioned views but not that one. Marriage is sacred. "He believed you'd leave. I knew better."

"I told him I wouldn't."

"He didn't listen."

She smiles. "He was headstrong."

"A Pierce curse."

"He convinced me." She breaks her toast in half. "I didn't think it would happen, but he did. He brought color to my life, one shade at a time. Then one day, I woke up and everything was bright, and I believed I deserved love. I made plans. I was ready."

"That was when—"

"A few weeks later."

"Did Cole know?"

"I didn't tell him," she says. "But he sees everything."

He put the pieces together. The changes in her behavior. The arrangements she made. The glow of love.

It surrounded both of them.

It was as bright as anything Bash did.

"It wasn't the first time I thought about leaving," she says. "Or took steps. But it was the first time I had a reason." She rubs her wrist. "An outside reason. Then…" Then Bash died.

Adam was in critical condition.

The rest of us didn't know how to survive.

"Grief consumed me," she says. "I lost my nerve. Lost my drive. I believed it was an accident. Even with the timing. Even after I realized Cole was suspicious. Even after I realized I had to leave for Seb…"

"When did you see it?"

"A friend confessed," she says. "She'd seen me with Bash.

Mentioned it on accident. Cole is charming when he wants to be. She didn't know… she didn't realize…"

A friend, trying to do the right thing, tell a man about his wife's affair.

"He was suspicious," she says. "Whenever I met someone. No, when I was happy. He assumed it was that. Long before it was. Then… maybe he already knew. Maybe he always knew. I'm not sure."

"I hired an investigator."

"What did you find?"

"Nothing legal. Noting I can use against him. But enough I know."

"I don't have anything there." She stares at her mug. "I'm sorry."

"He hurt you?"

"Yes."

"I'm sorry." I would have said something different a few days ago. Something stupid. Now?

I understand.

Love is a tangled mess.

"I wish I did," she says. "I wish this went differently. I wish I could go back to that day. Go to a different hotel. Beg my friend not to say anything. But I…"

"You'd never erase your son."

"No. Of course not."

"He wouldn't want that."

"I know," she says. "I loved him."

I doubted that.

I didn't believe it.

I thought she was a bored housewife, looking for an escape.

But she did love him. It's everywhere. It fills the room.

"I didn't believe him," I say. "When he told me. I'm sorry."

"You didn't know me."

"But I knew him. And the way he talked about you... I should have believed him."

"What did he say?"

"Things I shouldn't repeat."

She smiles. "He had a way, didn't he?"

"He did."

"He was the only person who still used the term 'making love.'"

"Actually bringing it into the universe?" I quote him.

"More with every kiss, every breath, every groan," she finishes the quote.

The silence falls.

We miss him.

We can't do anything to bring him back.

"I've been lost a long time," she says. "But I've grieved, I've put myself back together. You... you haven't done that, have you?"

"No," I admit.

"Bash talked about you. How smart and strong and sure you were. Even now, I can see it. You're tough. Practical. Logical."

"We were different."

"Very." She smiles. "He would have stopped and felt it. Maybe too much. But you... you can't run from pain, Simon. It will catch up with you. I wish I could do something to make that easier. Make it better. But I can't. And Bash... he wouldn't want you to carry this burden forever."

"He wouldn't want me miserable."

"But you have to feel it. If you ever want to move forward."

She sounds like him.

The man who embraces every feeling, ugly or beautiful.

Who sings love songs on long walks.

Who savors life.

But she isn't Bash.

Bash is gone forever.

My baby brother.

I failed to protect him.

I can't fail to protect his son too.

I have to make it right.

The way he would want.

It will destroy me either way.

But this—

I thought I owed him something else, making an effort to love, to find love, to at least fuck Vanessa.

And I did.

But this—

This is what he meant.

Choosing love.

Choosing life.

No matter the cost.

Chapter Forty-One

SIMON

Celine and I finish breakfast without small talk. There's nothing to say.

Nothing to make this right or bring him back or erase the truth.

After I finish, she asks if I want to meet Seb properly.

I sit on the couch.

She smiles as he kicks at the air, scoops him into her arms, holds him to her chest.

This beautiful, graceful woman my brother loved.

This beautiful, graceful woman my brother wanted to marry.

And she's here, in my apartment, with their child, the picture of maternal affection.

Willing to do anything for their son.

I understand. Intellectually.

But when she shifts him into my arms, when I hold him, feel his tiny hand around my finger, watch his eyes move across the room—

Bash's eyes—

Bash's curiosity—

Bash's love of life and everything in it—
I understand on every fucking level.
This is what makes sense.
What we have to do.
Xavier knocks.
This is it.
"Ready, Celine?" he asks.
She nods. And she waits patiently.
I hold him for a long time. Until my arms are numb.
But even then, I'm not ready to say goodbye.
I slide my nephew into his mother's arms.
I squeeze his tiny hand one more time.
Then I send them away.
The last piece of my brother.
Gone.
Lost to me forever.
But safe.
Alive.

Chapter Forty-Two

VANESSA

My mom notes my puffy eyes, hugs me, asks if I'm okay.

When I say no, she gives me space.

I sit in my bedroom, the one I claimed when we moved into Daddy's massive apartment, and lie on my bed.

Still a twin.

Still covered in red sheets.

Still cozy and warm.

My only safe space, for a long time.

And it's still safe, practically speaking.

But the rest?

I don't know.

I lie in bed, leafing through my copy of *The Bell Jar*, wondering why it took so long for anyone to realize I had a problem.

And I still do.

The same.

And different.

The day passes. Darkness falls. I find a lighter book. One of Lee's castoffs. A melodramatic teen drama.

Filled with problematic shit.

And a beautiful, brief escape.

Only for a few minutes at a time. The problematic shit pulls me out of the fantasy. But those few minutes—

I need them.

Eventually, Lee knocks on my door.

She doesn't wait, of course. She slips inside. Climbs into bed with me.

"What happened?" she asks.

I don't know where to start, so I wrap my arms around her.

"Are you okay?"

"Better with you here." And I know she's okay. I know she's alive and vibrant and with someone who will never, ever hurt her.

I'll never have to say goodbye to her son or daughter because Harrison is after her.

I'll never have to lose her that way.

A million bad things might happen, but not that.

"Do you want to talk about it?" she asks.

I shake my head.

"Do you want to talk about the new position me and Harrison tried?"

I nod.

"It's that bad?"

"It is."

"Simon?"

"Everything."

"His dick is too big?"

My laugh breaks up the tension in my shoulders. "Of course."

"And he's a minute man."

I shake my head.

"No technique?"

I shake my head.

362

"No ability to be gentle with your heart?"

"Can we not talk?"

"Of course, Vee. Whatever you need. I love you."

"I love you, too."

It's easy with her.

It's not easy with anyone else, but it's easy with her.

I'm lucky. My sister is always here for me. She's always ready to protect me.

She's always ready to help me put myself back together.

I've never given her a chance.

I've never let myself show weakness.

This time, I do.

This time, I fall apart.

———

Lee and I stay up all night.

In the morning, she calls in sick. And then calls in sick for me.

She fixes breakfast poorly, makes tea, streams a comedy known for its obsession with doing the right thing.

We don't talk about Simon or work or the fucked-up state of my life.

Only what we want to eat for lunch—definitely not more of her cooking—and where we want to get tea.

She convinces me to go to a fancy spot in midtown.

It's a beautiful day. Bright but not hot. Vibrant and alive.

And, there, in the air-conditioned cafe, sipping Earl Grey and nibbling on scones, I tell her about my parents.

What I saw.

What I remember.

What she's always known but never heard from me.

She hugs me tightly. So tightly, I think she'll never let go. All maternal softness and gentle love.

Then she snaps back to the Lee I know. "You need to talk to someone. A professional. Deal with this before you go back to the office."

"I know."

"What if this isn't healthy for you? This work?"

"I can't abandon my job."

"You can't save the world if you're drowning."

"Lee—"

"I'll make the appointment." She pulls out her cell, makes a few calls, bam.

I have a session with a therapist who specializes in survivors.

A referral from the therapist who works with us.

A long time coming.

Chapter Forty-Three

SIMON

For a week, I bury myself in work. I push aside the questions that rise to the surface.

I ignore Celine's advice to stop and feel.

I accept Lee's request to give Vanessa time.

Friday, I wake up, shower, dress, eat breakfast, prepare.

But I don't go to work.

I go to our childhood home.

For the entire three-hour drive, I stare out the windshield, listening to Bash's favorite record on repeat.

One of Dad's new wave titles.

Romantic and sexual and energetic.

Everything he was.

I arrive late afternoon.

I step into the big, empty house. Take in the size and feel of the space.

The massive foyer, the winding stairs, the living room, the ballroom behind it.

The backyard where I ran laps with Adam.

The pool where Liam took his *friends*.

The waves crashing into the cliff.

Every place haunted by memories of Bash.

Teaching him to waltz in the ballroom. Arguing about installing a television in the entertainment room. Debating the merits of fucking in the library.

He didn't read.

For all his romantic impulses, the man never picked up a book.

Trish greets me in the kitchen. The space where Bash snuck bourbon into his coffee. Convinced Trish to teach him how to cook. Covered the counters in messes he promised to clean.

None of us learned to keep a house.

We always had someone there, paid to do it for us.

At boarding school, we were expected to keep our space neat, but that was all.

I learned to care for myself in college.

Liam and Adam too.

But Bash?

Somehow, he always knew. He took it upon himself. He wanted to care for the people he loved.

Emotionally.

And practically.

The way I would. That's what he always said. *I know you can sear a steak, Simon. But can you sear your heart?*

I'd tell him his metaphor made no sense.

He'd find another.

He'd find a million ways to tell me I needed to open my heart.

He had his flaws. Plenty of them.

But he was more vibrant and bright and alive than anyone.

More in love with love.

Usually, I curse the concept for what it did to him.

Today, I understand.

Today, I stop and feel it.

A little at first. Between sips of coffee and bites of crumb cake—Trish insists. When I take my eyes off my shoes to watch waves crash into the cliffside.

When the light in the ballroom catches the chandelier and I hear his laugh in my ears, as vividly as ever.

Trish fixes a fancy meal. Agrees to my arrangements for Opal. My messages for my brothers.

After dinner, I sit on the lawn outside, watching the sun sink into the ocean, letting memories of Bash overwhelm me.

After two hours in the dark, I go to his room.

Even though he rarely used it—he and Liam went to an all-boys boarding school with much stricter weekend leave policies than the school Vanessa and I attended—

Even though he hasn't lived here for years—

The room is Bash.

All lush fabrics and vibrant colors.

As headstrong and romantic as Bash.

He's gone.

He's gone, forever, and he's never coming back.

It hits me again.

Again.

Not the massive waves that threatened to grind me to sand, the ones I felt after the news.

Or the small ones I tried to dam.

Something in between.

Something I can't block anymore.

I lie on his bed, and I put on his favorite album, and I let it wash over me.

A little at a time.

Then all at once.

Chapter Forty-Four

SIMON

For days, I play Bash's old CDs, watch his DVDs in the home theater, flip through his barely touched collection of books.

For a romantic, he wasn't much of a reader.

Only poetry. Because it was short and sweet and as intense as he was.

I find the poetry book I gave him as a graduation present.

I read every single line.

The sweet sonnets. The odes to love. The erotic.

The pages are worn, dog-eared, covered in scribbles.

Not notes on the poems themselves.

His own lines.

Roses are red

Violets are blue

I prefer slant rhymes

And going down on you

Silly and sexual and loving all the same.

I close my eyes, but that doesn't stem the tears or the memories.

The first time he confessed he was in love.

The night he laid outside, in the stars, heartbroken because a woman left him.

The morning he told me he was sleeping with a married woman.

I know you'll never approve, Simon, but I need you to understand.

I love her.

Not the way I've loved anyone else.

More.

So much I can taste it.

The birthday party he spent with two concerns.

Meeting Celine after.

And convincing me to fuck Vanessa.

Keep staring, Simon. I need another twenty. I already have Adam's cash. He bet you'd look for thirty seconds. He believes in your restraint. Liam? Not so much. Said a lot I shouldn't repeat.

I know, I know.

You stare because she's gorgeous.

Because she's beautiful.

Because she's sexy, and you want her long legs wrapped around your waist.

And probably some fucked-up politically incorrect shit I won't ask you to face.

But that's all bullshit.

Not the assessment.

Vanessa is all kinds of gorgeous. And she's smart and powerful.

What's sexier than a smart woman?

And, yes, you're staring because you want to see her dress on your floor.

But you're staring because you want to see her wake up in your bed too.

Because you want her and you need her and you love her.

I teased him about it. Told him he was drunk. Drunk on champagne, not love.

He was wrong—I didn't love Vanessa yet.

But he was right too—I wanted her in every way and that scared me.

And I didn't resist her because she hated me.

Or because she frustrated me by besting me again and again.

Then, I was young and immature.

Now, I appreciate the challenge. The way she made me better.

She still does.

In a million ways.

And the one way Bash did.

I wouldn't be here if he hadn't asked for this promise.

I wouldn't be here if she hadn't torn me open.

Now that we've agreed not to tell lies, let's make a deal. It's my birthday. You owe me. I don't care that I'm twenty-five and old enough to not expect presents.

I learned this from you, Simon.

Playing all the cards I have.

And I know you.

Duty-bound until the end.

So how about it?

Promise me you'll try. Give Vanessa one night.

One time.

A date, a fuck, a long conversation.

Whatever you want to call it, as long as you go in with your heart open.

Carpe diem.

You might die tomorrow.

Do you really want to die never having kissed Vanessa Moyer?

I know I don't want to go out knowing my oldest brother is forever miserable and alone.

So promise.

And if I die tomorrow, I'll die happy.

He didn't die the next day.

It was a few weeks later.

Adam fell apart.

I had to stay strong. To take care of Opal, to keep the company running, to ensure Adam and Liam's survival.

For a long time, I told myself I had no choice but to move forward.

For a long time, it was true.

But it's not. Not anymore.

Adam is well. Liam is in love. Opal is an adult.

And I'm far behind.

Still stuck in this space between darkness and hope.

I know what Bash would want.

But I can't honor that.

Not yet.

Not until I know what I need.

Chapter Forty-Five

SIMON

After a week, I stop sleeping in Bash's room. I spend the nights in my bed. Spend the days looking over his things, moving around the house, taking long walks around the grounds.

I see a little clearer every day, but I stay in a haze.

I'm shocked when Liam arrives.

It's a Friday afternoon. A warm, sunny day.

He barges into the house, yells, "Lucy, I'm home," and runs —actually runs—up the stairs.

He doesn't knock.

He pulls my door open, jumps into my room, and shakes his head *this is a sad state*. "Vanessa is downstairs."

Fuck.

"Take a shower. Put on a clean suit. Make yourself presentable," he says.

Opal's footsteps pound the hall. "Why did you run?"

"Early bird gets the worm."

"What's the worm?" Opal asks.

"I won. That's what matters."

She pushes past him to step into the doorframe. "Jeans, Simon. Wear the jeans."

"Simon doesn't own jeans."

"That's why I brought some," she says. "And the Taylor Swift t-shirt."

Liam looks at her like she's crazy. "We want her to think he's functional, not losing his mind."

"Trust me," she says.

He shakes his head. "The suit."

I float through my shower. I barely look at my clothes.

Vanessa is here.

Vanessa came to see me.

Am I ready?

Is she?

I don't know. But we're both here, and I have a million things to say to her.

It must be the same for her.

I step into the hallway.

Opal and Liam stop to stare.

They look from me to each other, not sure who won the argument.

"I swear, Simon, you're a rich guy cliché." Opal shakes her head. "Are those boat shoes?"

"They're definitely boat shoes," Liam says.

"Simon, I take it back. Wear the suit. Woo her a little," she says.

"Don't throw a win," Liam says to her.

"I won?"

"This is closer to yours than mine."

"No, it's not! It's executive on the weekend! Mine is fun older brother."

"I'm a fun older brother," Liam says.

"And you wear boat shoes!" She shakes her head *this is ridiculous* and storms down the hall.

He goes after her.

They're having their own debate.

And I'm here.

About to talk to Vanessa.

I see her as soon as I step onto the hallway balcony.

She's standing in the foyer in a wine sundress and wedge sandals. Patient. Curious. Radiant. "Your family says you're a mess."

"I am."

"I have been. But I… I'm doing better."

"You look beautiful."

"You look like someone else. Are those boat shoes?"

"They are."

"Do you have the cigar and whiskey too?" she asks.

"The whiskey."

"The yacht?"

"Not yet."

She smiles, but there's a sadness to it.

This is a mess.

And neither of us knows how to clean it up.

"Damn, I brought my bikini for nothing," she says.

"The pool's heated."

"I'll jump if you jump," she says.

I move down the stairs. Step onto the hardwood floor.

She looks different this close.

Still strong and regal.

But soft too.

Tired.

The way I am.

The way I constantly ignore.

"Let's sit outside," I say.

She nods and moves through the ballroom, out the French doors, into the massive backyard. "It looks different than it did at the rehearsal dinner. Bigger. Emptier."

"It is."

She runs her fingers over the expensive patio furniture. Looks between the wicker chair and the wicker loveseat. Chooses the loveseat.

I sit next to her.

"Liam is worried," she says. "He asked me to come and talk to you. I told him it won't help, but he was persistent."

"He's good at that."

"Was he right?"

Yes. Her presence is a balm. Hearing her voice, seeing her smile, knowing she's okay—it's exactly what I need. "It's good to see you."

"You too." She smiles softly.

For a second, everything between us is easy. Simple. The painful, beautiful desire for love and connection.

Then she looks to the table, and I don't have a clue what she wants or what our futures hold.

"Everything got to be a mess, didn't it?" she asks.

"It wasn't what I expected."

"Me either... I've been on leave. I needed time to sort through things after that... no, I needed it before. I've needed it for a long time."

"Your job?"

"It's not good for me. Not the way I'm doing it now. I'm not sure if I need to redraw boundaries or find something else, but, for once, I'm actually considering it."

"Are you okay?"

"With leaving?"

I nod.

"No. But I'm getting there."

"Thank you for helping her," I say. "Both of them."

"You're welcome." She looks to the ocean. "I'm sorry you lost them."

"They're still alive."

She nods.

"That's what matters."

"It's not easy," she says. "To put that ahead of everything."

"You do this every weekend?"

"No. I schmooze every weekend. I don't interact with survivors very often." She lets out a soft laugh. "But even this... I'm close to it. Thinking about it all the time. And since I haven't processed what happened with my mom... I guess I have to stop and do that before I can decide."

"That's brave."

"Quitting?"

"Taking care of yourself."

"You're not doing too bad yourself. Spending two weeks locked in the mansion."

"I have nothing on Adam."

She smiles. "Do you think it's easier for him? Having the scars outside?"

"He has them inside too."

"He's stronger than us, facing it."

"No one is stronger than you."

She looks me in the eyes. "You really see me that way?"

"Always."

"There's strength in vulnerability. And you're—" She reaches out, brushes my hair from my eyes. "You're rocking the unkempt look. And the rest too."

"I'm trying."

"It's scary."

"Terrifying," I say.

She rests her head on my shoulder. "I didn't come here with a plan. I just wanted to see you."

"Let's start over," I suggest.

"How?"

"Try this the normal way."

"I'm not familiar with this concept of normal."

"We date."

"Dating? That either."

"I call and invite you to dinner."

"A call? That's normal?"

"As normal as I get."

She smiles *true*.

"I call, pick you up—"

"I'm thirty-one and we live in Manhattan. You don't need to pick me up."

"I'm calling," I say.

"Fine, but we'll meet at the restaurant."

"We dine, drink, talk."

"Fuck on the balcony?"

"Not until the third date."

"What about the good night kiss?"

"If the moment strikes."

"And good night fuck?"

"Fourth date."

"The balcony was the third date."

"Special balcony exception. I'm not easy."

She laughs. "I have to make it through four dates without mounting you?"

"You do."

"Can each course count as a date?"

"Dinner and dessert, but not appetizers."

"What about a movie?"

"Only if it's a serious movie."

"What qualifies as serious?" she asks.

"Black-and-white photography."

"Subtitles?"

"Either," I say.

"In that case, how about a double-feature, then dinner?"

I laugh. "Impatient."

"Very."

"I like that about you."

"I know." She runs her fingers over my chin. "How much time do you need?"

"Two weeks."

"Two weeks is good."

"Then we start over." I offer my hand.

She takes it. Then she leans in and presses her lips to mine.

An approval kiss.

Not a normal way of accepting an offer.

Not a traditional makeup or apology.

The two of us, leaning to soften, trust, compromise.

It's a mess.

But it's perfect.

Chapter Forty-Six

VANESSA

Warm air hits me as I step out of the elevator.

The soft murmur of conversation.

The orange glow of sunset.

This is it. Friday night. Rooftop restaurant.

My reunion with Simon.

Has it really been two weeks since I sat next to him?

We've texted here and there. Small updates and words of encouragement.

Mostly, I've been busy. I hate to use the cliché, but it's true. I've been working on myself.

In the last two weeks, I've resumed therapy, confessed my utter lack of togetherness to my family, and arranged a six-month sabbatical from work.

As of today, I'm officially on leave.

For the first time in my adult life, I'm not trying to build a business or change the world.

I'm focusing that energy on myself.

Am I ready to touch Simon? I want to drag him to my bedroom. I want to spend the weekend fucking his brains out.

But my heart can't handle it.

I have to go slow this time.

With my next step, I see him.

Simon is standing at the bar in a dark grey suit, tall and broad and strong. He turns to me and flashes me a panty-melting smile.

Then he does something even more irresistible—

He blushes.

My heart thuds with every step. My stomach flutters. My body buzzes.

He watches me approach. Offers his hand. "Aviation?"

I run my fingers over his palm. "That depends."

"Oh?"

"Does a drink count as a date?"

"If we finish at the bar."

"Is that why you're early?" I ask.

His smile widens. "Is that why you're early?"

No. I'm early because I'm terrified. But I don't say that. Instead, I rise to my tiptoes and press my lips to his.

He tastes good, like whiskey and Simon.

Need floods my body. The intense, physical craving. And something else, something deeper.

A desire for his heart and soul.

He pulls back with a sigh. "I missed you."

"I missed you too."

"You look gorgeous."

"Thank you."

He runs his thumb along the straps of my eggplant dress. "New?"

I nod. "And this?" I tap his silk tie. "You stole my color."

"Borrowed."

"Did you ask?"

"Do you like it?"

My lips curl into a smile. "It suits you."

"Does it?"

"Very father of an NYU student."

He laughs. "Older brother."

"Very older brother of an NYU student."

He touches his forehead to mine.

My body hums. With warmth and need and affection and that indescribable feeling of safety.

He's safe.

I trust him again. Have the ability to trust him again.

I'm not past my fucked-up thoughts, but I'm making progress.

The bartender interrupts. He looks at us funny when I order an Aviation, but he fixes the drink without comment.

My gaze goes to Simon.

We stay like that for a long moment. Quiet. Still. Absorbing the feel of reunion.

It's only been two weeks.

It feels like two hours, and it feels like a million years.

"You look good," I say. "Handsome, yes. But also… good."

"I am."

"You promise?"

"On the way to healing." He curls his hand around my neck. "You?"

"On the way."

He pulls me into a slow, deep kiss.

Again, my body buzzes. My head swims. When we break, I gasp for air.

Then I find it.

Find my footing.

My place.

My ability to marry lust and love. And maybe even a little loathing.

The bartender drops off my drink. "On your tab?"

"Close it out," Simon says.

"Almost to our second date," I say.

"Counting the minutes?"

"Yes. But… waiting is good."

"Waiting is good." He raises his glass. "Only."

"Only?" I raise my glass.

"I need to win you over with my personality."

"You do."

"That's a challenge."

"It is. But you're up for it."

Epilogue

SIMON

It hits me the second I open the door. Oranges and honey.

The scent of Vanessa.

The sight of her coat on the rack.

The sound of her gasp.

She's here, on the couch, watching TV with Opal. Finished with work early. These days, she finishes work early or very late.

She's still on leave, focusing on a new job with a sister organization, mentoring young women.

Mostly teenagers. A few college students. All completely and totally enamored with Vanessa.

She claims otherwise. She claims I exaggerate. Or, at least, see through a prism of love.

She's right. I don't see her objectively. I see beauty and joy in every step.

I'm as bad as Bash ever was.

I'm the one professing the beauty of the Sting song *Every Little Thing She Does is Magic*.

To myself.

I never subject anyone else to my romantic impulses.

I've grown. I haven't turned into a different person. I'm still pragmatic and ruthless and capable.

But I'm capable of opening my heart and loving too.

"Oh my god. Is she seriously—" Opal gasps. "Again?"

"It's her go-to move," Vanessa says.

Opal squeals as the character on TV propositions a man at a bar. *The Americans.* I didn't think Vanessa would convince Opal to watch any show she adored, but she knew exactly how to sell it.

Sex.

The cold war era spies solve every problem with sex.

The way Vanessa and I did when we started.

We're better at talking now. But neither one of us is great at full disclosure or softening or leaning on someone else.

We try. We work at it. We get better every day.

And we do understand each other when we're dressed.

But when we're naked?

We make even more sense there.

We read each other even better there.

Vanessa is still every bit the exhibitionist. She still prefers gentle to rough. But she's more open to new adventures.

And I—

Well, I still struggle with my worst impulses. There are days I dream about vengeance, but I stay true to my word. I stay patient.

My P.I. is watching him, but this time it's not to hurt him. It's to keep Seb safe.

He's not well, but with his resources it could be years before nature takes its course. Years before Adam or Liam had the chance to meet their nephew.

But he will. And they will. And I'll do whatever it takes to keep my family safe.

Adam, Liam, Opal, Seb, Celine.

And Vanessa.

Everyone I love.

Fuck, I love her.

It overwhelms me every time I see her.

Even the sight of her coat on the rack makes me warm all over. The signs of her here, in my space, in my life, in my heart.

"Simon, close the door," Opal calls. "We're trying to watch." Her attention returns to the TV. "Oh my god."

"I know," Vanessa says.

"He's never going to let me watch it alone now!" Opal says. "You did this on purpose, didn't you?"

"How else can I make sure you only marathon with me?" Vanessa says.

Opal pretends to pout, but it only lasts a second. She savors her TV sessions with Vanessa. All her time with Vanessa.

She still lives and dies for Briar—

Not to mention her actual boyfriend—

What a fucking mess—

But as with her choices in TV, clothes, and hair, I know better than to offer input.

As much as I hate it, Opal is an adult. A college student with the ability to run her own life. And I respect that.

Most of the time.

"Okay, okay, but I'm getting a real vibe here." Opal nods to me. "An *I will hear some weird shit no matter how loudly you play that music vibe.* I have to study anyway, so…"

"Where are you going to study?" I ask.

"Simon!" She shoots me a death glare. *I will not be the c-blocker here. Don't make me one.*

"Are you going to the library?"

"I'm not taking your car to the library." She shakes her head as she pauses the show. "People will think I'm out of touch!" She rises, stretches her arms over her head, lets out a yawn.

"Besides, the new coffee shop has the best vegan cheese cake. And it's open until ten, so…"

"We'll be quiet after ten," Vanessa says.

"Heard that one before." Opal shakes her head with mock outrage. "You kids need to learn to contain yourself." She grabs her backpack, steps into her shoes, offers me a goodbye hug. "See you then."

"Good night, Opal," Vanessa calls. "If I'm not here when you get back."

Opal shoots her a *get real* look.

Vanessa blushes. I can tell now. I don't see the color in her cheeks—that's nearly impossible—but I see the change in her eyes, the curve of her lips.

Opal laughs as she skips out the door.

The thing closes with a thud.

We're alone.

We haven't been completely alone in days.

It's ridiculous how badly I need her.

But I do.

I need every fucking drop of her.

"Is it already seven?" she asks.

I nod.

"Should we eat?"

"Do you need to eat?" I keep it gentle. It's always my instinct to be firm, strong, commanding, but that's not what she needs. She needs softness and understanding.

I'm not good at it yet, but I'm learning.

I want to be better.

That's how I feel with her. The same way I did when we were fourteen.

Without trying, she inspires me to be better.

With her wit and intelligence and effort and passion.

And seeing this beautiful, capable, poised woman want me?

It's everything.

But it's not because she's beautiful or capable or poised.

It's because she's Vanessa. It's some indescribable quality she has.

Because nearly everything she does feels like magic.

Bash is still in my head, but it's not the way he was. Not a voice haunting me. A memory that inspires me to try harder.

And the question I have planned for tonight—

That terrifies me.

What if she says no?

What if she says yes?

What if I fuck everything up?

Everything is good right now. She's working through her issue with her parents. With the concept of marriage. With her inability to put herself first.

She's working a job that doesn't take too much from her.

And I'm dealing with my grief. The waves still come, but they're smaller, easier to ride.

We're happy.

And, here I am, about to ask for more.

I don't want to fuck this up, but I can't help myself. I'm greedy when it comes to her.

"Where are you going?" she copies my phrase. "Good or bad?"

"Good." Scary. But good.

"I can wait to eat if you can."

I nod.

She rises from the couch and moves toward me with steady steps. She's slow, patient, regal.

Impossibly sexy in her short wrap dress.

Impossibly sexy in everything.

I wait for her to approach.

Wait for her to bring her lips to mine.

She consumes me with her kiss. Asks for all of me. Offers all of her.

Then she takes my hand, leads me into the bedroom.

I'm not patient today. I need her too badly.

I need to feel her body against mine.

Vanessa breaks our kiss with a sigh. She looks me in the eyes and undoes the knot holding her wrap dress together.

Slowly, she pushes the fabric from one shoulder. Then the other.

She's standing in our bedroom in only a purple silk bra and panty set.

She's perfection.

She always is.

I take a step toward her.

She shakes her head. "Wait." Vanessa unhooks her bra and does away with her panties.

Then she sits on the bed, spreads her legs, brings her fingers to her clit.

She draws circles on her tender flesh.

Slow at first.

Then faster, harder.

It's the sweetest fucking torture, watching her push herself closer and closer, watching her fingers curl into the sheets, watching her lips part with a groan.

Her eyes close.

Her breath hitches.

Her entire body tenses and relaxes as she comes.

Vanessa's groans fill the room.

She falls onto the bed, a puddle of need and satisfaction.

For one perfect moment, we both linger there, in the beautiful place where she has everything she needs.

Then she pushes herself up, and motions *come here*. When I do, she hooks her fingers into my belt and pulls me onto the bed.

She undresses me slowly, taking her time with every article, with every brush of her fingers on my skin.

My lips find hers.

I kiss her softly.

Then harder.

She rolls onto her back, pulls my body over hers, wraps her legs around my waist.

I fill her one inch at a time.

Then we move together, Vanessa's hips arching as I meet her, pulling me farther and faster.

Again and again.

Until it's almost too much to take.

I flip her over so she's on top of me, so I can watch her take me again and again. "Touch yourself, sweetness."

She presses one hand to my chest. Brings the other to her clit.

For a moment, her eyes meet mine. She holds my gaze as she rubs herself.

Then her eyes close.

She gives in to the sensation, working herself to orgasm as she grinds against me.

Then she's there, coming on my cock, the most beautiful thing I've seen.

Her pulsing pulls me over the edge.

I work through my orgasm, then I collapse with her, a sweaty, sticky, satisfied mess.

We lie there together for a long time.

Then we untangle and there's no more waiting. No distractions. No buildup.

This is it.

Vanessa invites me to shower with her.

I tell her to start without me.

Then I find the tiny box in my coat. Set it on top of the rumbled sheets.

But that's not quite it.

I move her dress. My tie. The shoes.

There.

Perfect.

"Simon." Vanessa steps into the doorframe. "Are you coming?"

I turn to her.

She studies me for a moment. A long moment. That gorgeous, perfect lingering *I love to drink the sight of your body* gaze.

Then she looks to the bed.

Sees the ring box next to my tie.

"Is that…" She takes a step into the room.

I pick up the ring box, and I meet her in the middle of the room. "I know it's early. If you need time, I can wait."

She nods.

"But I'm ready. I know what I want. I want to spend the rest of my life with you." I drop to one knee. Open the ring box. "Vanessa Moyer, will you marry me?"

Her eyes go to the ring. "You're asking when we're naked?"

"When else?"

She nods. "Okay."

"Okay?"

"Yes. I'll marry you."

"Tonight? We can fly to Vegas."

"Simon!"

"We can."

"You'd never get married without your family there."

"We can bring them."

"In your private jet?"

"Pierce's private yet."

"You're ridiculous."

"You love that I'm ridiculous."

"I do. I love you." She offers her hand. "I want to. I want to marry you… just not tomorrow."

"The day after?"

"I don't know. It might take me awhile."

"I can wait."

"For how long?"

"As long as you need. That's what I want, sweetness." I slide the ring onto her finger. "I want to be the person you need."

Want More?

Get another taste of Simon and Vanessa in an extended epilogue.

New to the Pierce Family? Check out *Broken Beast* for Adam and Danielle's story. Turn the page for a sample.

Tempting Teacher, Max and Opal's story, is available to pre-order. Keep reading for a preview.

All caught up on the Pierce Family? Get your fix with *Dirty Deal*, a super steamy billionaire Cinderella story.

Broken Beast - Excerpt

ADAM

Get Broken Beast Now

"I'm sorry, Mr. Pierce. I dug into every pocket of this asshole's life. And there's nothing I can use. Not officially."

"Unofficially?"

"He has a vulnerability. A woman." He shows off an image on his cell.

A woman holding a sheer sheet to her chest.

Not one of Neil's grainy, long angle photos.

The work of an artist.

Black and white.

Soft lighting.

Beautiful composition.

He scrolls to the next.

The same woman, standing at the window, in the glow of the morning sun.

Her hair swept over her shoulder.

Her head falling to one side.

Her bare back on display.

"She's hot, huh?" He chuckles, pleased with himself. "And even better from the front."

My stomach churns. I'm overcome with the urge to protect her. It's not like me.

After what happened with Bash, I gave up on protecting anyone.

"She goes by Beauty," he continues. "Broken Beauty, technically. There's plenty available publicly, but I can dig if you want more." He raises a brow. "You like her, huh?"

"She's talented."

"I'll say." He chuckles. "She must have a hundred self-portraits on her site. More on social media. She's got the followers to match too. A few hundred thousand on Instagram. Two, three times that on her site."

I pull up her website.

There it is, a picture of her standing in front of a mirror, bathed in soft white light.

The image is well-composed.

The lighting is perfect.

And she's gorgeous.

An unfamiliar sensation overtakes me—desire.

I want her.

I haven't wanted anyone in months, but I want her so badly I can taste it.

"How does she know Fitzgerald?" Is he a fan? Or is there more?

"He's obsessed with her. Shows up at the gallery where she works once a week to buy a new piece. Just to talk to her. Doesn't let on that he's seen her naked."

Mostly naked, but what's the difference?

"He hasn't crossed the line, but it's only a matter of time. I can put eyes on him. Set up a honey trap. Who knows? Maybe she's game to participate for the right price."

"No." It's not enough to put a dent in his marriage, career, image. I need to do better. "I have another idea."

A divorce will destroy his finances.

But a marriage?

That will destroy *him*.

Get Broken Beast Now

Tempting Teacher - Excerpt

OPAL

Pre-order Tempting Teacher Now
(Coming May 12th, 2022)

The hotel bar is the perfect place for an illicit tryst.
Adult.
Anonymous.
Upscale.

This isn't a college party. Not even a college party at my famously fraternity free university.

It's close to a high school party, really, given my background. Prep school, rich kids, thirty-million dollar apartments overlooking the park.

The setting is right. But the sounds are all different. Soft jazz and quiet conversation, not hip-hop and truth or dare.

Which is more accurate?

Truth. Are you here to meet a stranger for a one-night-stand?

Dare. I date you to find Max and kiss him.

I take a deep breath and push an exhale through my nose. I don't fit into this world, not completely, but I understand it. My brothers thrive here. They've taught me how to blend into the demure, tasteful space of the rich and powerful.

And, hey, I have a fake ID and a lie about my age. Max will believe I'm twenty-one. Probably. Hopefully.

I run my fingers over my leather clutch as I scan the space. A couple in a corner booth. Two women in suits, talking business. A working girl at the bar.

And, there, in the other corner, a man in a suit and a hot pink tie.

Max.

The sliver of silk pulls me towards him. It's all I know about him, physically anyway. He's in a hot pink tie. I'm in hot pink shoes.

We match in the best possible way.

I take steady steps towards him. Slowly, he comes into focus.

Broad shoulders, dark hair, dark eyes, light skin.

The hot pink tie against his stark white shirt.

He's…

Perfect.

Not at all as I imagined him and exactly as I imagined him.

Handsome and powerful and intense.

His eyes stop on mine. They study me carefully, taking in every detail.

The intensity should unnerve me, but it doesn't. I want all his attention. I want him staring like I'm his favorite panting.

That's the other thing we have in common.

Art. And a mutual desire for him to tie me to his bed.

I stare back into his eyes. Nod a hello. Let my lips curl into a smile.

He doesn't smile back. Instead, he holds up his hand and motions *come here*.

On anyone else, the gesture would annoy me.

On Max?

Fuck. I'm already in over my head and we haven't even said hello.

With every step, my heartbeat picks up. My temperature rises. By the time I arrive at his table, I'm on fire.

He stands. "Opal?"

"Did the shoes give it away?"

His eyes flit to my feet. "They suit you."

"Thank you." My stomach flutters. "The tie suits you." Really. He has the high contrast complexion to pull off the whole bright pink on white on black thing. He looks bold and sexy and masculine all at once. I love that he's wearing pink. I love that he's secure enough to sit in a fancy hotel in a hot pink tie. I love that he's teasing me.

I already like him.

We've agreed to one night and I already like him.

Fuck.

"Max." He offers his hand.

"Opal."

"Your coat."

I let him take it. "Thank you."

His fingers brush the back of my neck. He traces a slow line across the wool then he shifts the coat off my shoulders and folds it on the booth. "Sit. Here."

I nearly drop onto the leather bench.

He sits next to me, at the curve of the bench, so he's perpendicular, so he can touch me and look me in the eyes at once. "Comfortable?"

"Yes. Thanks."

"Do you drink?"

"A little."

"What do you like?"

What can I order to sound elegant and mature? Without trying too hard? I don't know wine. Or cocktails. Or anything besides expensive whiskey and cheap vodka. The two alcohol choices of the prep school crowd. The booze from Dad's study or whatever they can convince someone outside the liquor store to buy for twenty bucks.

"It's not a trick question."

Is it that obvious I'm nervous. "Spicy."

"Only spicy?"

"Sweet too, but mostly spicy."

"Fitting." He smiles.

My heart skips a beat. His smile is gorgeous. Perfect. Addicting.

Max hails the waitress. Orders two cocktails, something called tropical heat, and asks for privacy.

"Of course, Mr.— Max." The waitress spins on her heels and leaves.

"Do you come here often?" My cheeks flush. "Sorry, that's a cliche, isn't it?"

"Don't apologize for feeling nervous." He looks me in the eyes.

We're not supposed to share personal details. That's one of our rules. But we can handle a little small talk. "Do you like it here?"

"I do."

"What do you like about it?" I ask.

"The company."

My blush deepens.

"Have you been here?"

"I've been to this type of place. My brother attends a lot of fancy events in hotel ballrooms. I come with him sometimes."

"Do you like them?"

"I like dressing up and sipping craft cocktails. But hotels always look like hotels, no matter how hard they try to make them look nice. And there's something sad about them."

"The transparently corporate attempt at decor?" He motions to an abstract painting on the wall.

Shades of grey in the shape of a martini glass. It's completely competent and utterly uninteresting. "I hate it, too."

"What would you put here?" he asks.

"What would you?"

"To fit the mood?"

"If that's what you want to accomplish."

"We're in an expensive hotel," I say. "It should feel that way."

He nods in agreement.

"But it should be specific too. So travelers remember they're in New York."

"The best of the MoMa?"

"Maybe. I do like pop art. But I don't think it fits here. I'd do something simpler. Photography maybe. Black and white panoramas."

"The skyline?"

I nod. "Too obvious?"

"Obvious isn't bad."

"Maybe the MoMa then. Prints of the most famous paintings from New York museums."

"To assert your cultural superiority?"

"New York is the greatest city in the world."

"Have you been to that many?"

No, but I am a born and bred New Yorker. "Enough."

"Were you born here?"

"How did you know?"

"I can always tell."

"You're not a New Yorker?"

"No, I but I've come to appreciate the charms of the city. And its citizens."

Fuck. I must be as pink as my shoes.

"You have the best art in the US."

"I know."

"Should I compliment the coffee now?"

"Who needs coffee when you have art?"

"What's your favorite painting?"

"In the city?"

"Drowning Girl. Lichtenstein."

"The MoMA."

"I go almost every weekend."

"Alone?"

"Usually."

"You're self-reliant."

Because of the painting? Or because I go on my own. "I am."

"Do you trust me?"

"As much as I could trust anyone in this situation."

"Not that much?"

I swallow hard. "A little."

"Smart." His gaze shifts to the waitress.

She steps into our space with a smile and sets two drinks on the table. Something bright pink, in a martini glass with a chili sugar rim. "Enjoy."

"Thank you," Max says.

She leaves with another smile. Is it friendly or interested? No, it doesn't matter. She's doing her job. I'm here for one night with him. And he's being polite.

I may be nuevo riche (sort of), but I'm never an asshole to servers. Even when they're assholes to me.

"Try it." He pushes one glass to me. Picks up the other. "If it isn't to your liking, I'll order something else."

I bring the drink to my lips and take a sip. The kick of pepper, the sweet, fruity flavor of pineapple, and a depth from the cranberry and orange liquer. "Perfect."

He swallows. Coughs. "Spicy."

"You think?"

"You don't?"

"A little."

"Are you one of those people?"

"Which people?"

"With an obscene tolerance for spice?"

"So I hear."

"Does that mean you enjoy pain?"

"I haven't tried it." Not really. "Not with someone I trust."

"Do you trust me enough?"

"Yes."

"Are you sure?"

"No."

He smiles. "I appreciate the honesty."

"You won't change your mind?"

"No. I want you to stay honest. I like your sincerity."

My cheeks flame. It's hot in here. It's way too hot in here. I take another sip, but the drink does nothing to cool my temperature or calm my nerves.

Still, it feels rich.

Rich and complex, with the perfect mix of heat and sweetness.

Like Max.

"It's brave," he says. "Admitting vulnerability. Admitting inexperience."

"Thank you."

"Okay."

"You remember the safe-word?"

"Cranberry."

"I'm not planning any scenes. Not for a first time. Unless that's what you're looking for."

"A scene?"

"A role play scenario."

"Do you do them?"

"Sometimes. It depends on my mood. My partner."

"Do you want to do one with me?"

"No," he says. "I want to be who we are. Two strangers, meeting at a bar, for one night of adventure."

It sounds sexier on his lips.

Or maybe it's the reality. We're not trading texts about times and preferences. We're here. I'm not wondering if he's short or tall, thin or muscular, handsome or less handsome—

He's here and he's just right. Even though he's not the tallest or the broadest or the most typically handsome.

I prefer the intensity of his features.

The perfect height—in my heels we're eye to eye.

The lean muscles.

He's just… right.

"Does that work for you?" he asks.

"Yes."

"Is there anything else you haven't mention? An injury or a medical condition?"

"I'm allergic to dairy."

He finishes his drink. "Is there anything I've missed. Anything you want me to know?"

One night. No last names. No details. All dirty promises. "Nothing comes to mind."

He stands and offers his hand. "Then I'm ready whenever you are."

Pre-order Tempting Teacher Now
(Coming May 12th, 2022)

Author's Note

When I first met Simon, in *Broken Beast*, I knew he needed someone as capable, confident, and successful as he was. Not a young woman in need of a certain kind of education or financial assistance. Someone who lived in his world, who navigated his world as well as he did.

Someone his age, with his kind of money and power.

Alpha vs alpha, so to speak.

As soon as I met Vanessa, I fell in love with her wit and elegance. She's the perfect match for Simon. As guarded and protective as he is. And as in need of softness as he is. And I knew Vanessa was the heroine I'd been waiting for —

A heroine who was an actual, factual adult (with her own apartment and business) who still struggled with her teenage eating disorder.

Because these things don't disappear.

I'm older and wiser than I was at seventeen, but I still love the same music, and need to disappear into writing, and struggle with relationships, and fall into depressive phases.

I didn't grow out of my brain chemistry. I learned new skills and I learned how to better deal with my brain chemistry, but I didn't magically escape my desire to stay in control.

Vanessa is smart, confident, capable and struggling. That is the real experience most people have with mental health. They don't grow out of it.

They try harder, they do better, they learn new tools, and they deal with it, every day, for the rest of their lives. It gets easier. It gets better. But sometimes it gets worse. Sometimes, people relapse, even if they try hard and do well.

That's the reality of addiction for most people. It's a lifelong struggle. And I want to capture something real in my books, so people like me, people who struggle, who love others who struggle, see their experiences reflected in the text.

No matter how old you are, it's okay to struggle. It's okay to need help. It's okay to not be okay.

I wrote about a lot in this book. I hope I did everything justice. And I hope you found something true and real and compelling. And, of course, I hope you fell in love with Simon and Vanessa as much as I did.

I hope to see you for Opal's book.

Love,
Crystal

Acknowledgments

My first thanks goes to my husband, for his support when I'm lost in bookland and for generally being the sun in my sky.

The second goes to my father, for insisting I go to the best film school in the country, everything else be damned. I wouldn't love movies, writing, or storytelling half as much if not for all our afternoon trips to the bookstore and weekends at the movies. You've always been supportive of my goals, and that means the world to me.

A big shout out to all my beta readers. And also to my ARC readers for helping spread the word to everyone else in the world.

To all my writer friends who talk me down from the ledge, hold my hand, and tell me when my ideas are terrible and when they're brilliant, thank you.

Thanks so much to my editor Marla, and to Hang Le for the cover design.

As always, my biggest thanks goes to my readers. Thank you for picking up *Ruthless Rival*. I hope you'll be back for *Tempting Teacher*, Max and Opal's story.

Printed in Great Britain
by Amazon